P9-ASJ-739

Man Corn Murders

Man Corn Murders

Lou Allin

FIVE STAR
A part of Gale, Cengage Learning

Detroit • New York • San Francisco • New Haven, Conn • Waterville, Maine • London

Five Star Publishing, a part of Gale, Cengage Learning.

Set in 11 pt. Plantin.

Printed on permanent paper.

LIBRARY OF CONGRESS CATALOGING-IN-PUBLICATION DATA

Allin, Lou, 1945–
Man corn murders / by Lou Allin. — 1st ed.
p. cm.
ISBN-13: 978-1-59414-750-0 (hardcover : alk. paper)
ISBN-10: 1-59414-750-7 (hardcover : alk. paper)
1. Grand Staircase-Escalante National Monument (Utah)—Fiction. 2. Wilderness areas—Utah—Fiction. I. Title.
PR9199.4.A46M36 2009
813′.6—dc22 2009001220

First Edition. First Printing: May 2009.
Published in 2009 in conjunction with Tekno Books and Ed Gorman.

Printed in the United States of America
1 2 3 4 5 6 7 13 12 11 10 09

Dedicated to those who celebrate the magic
of the Four Corners: Edward Abbey, Ellen Meloy,
Ann Zwinger and the legendary Tony Hillerman,
whose every book is not only a sacrament
but a damn good read.

"It's the roughest country you or anybody else ever seen; it's nothing in the world but rocks and holes, hills and hollows. The mountains are just one solid rock as smooth as an apple."

—Elizabeth Morris Decker,
Hole-in-the-Rock Expedition, 1879–80

PROLOGUE

She shivered in the eternal cold, the scratchy burlap bags chafing without comfort. The sensation of freezing in a Michigan snowbank without the merciful dispatch of a few hours. But she was a thousand miles from home. Heat had been Utah's first amoral lesson, yet better to wither in the desert, stunned into quick unconsciousness, the sun scorching out life's heartlight like a thread of tungsten in a brilliant bulb.

How long had she been here, three days, four, a week since the last drop in the water bottles and final crumb of the Power Bars? On her watch, Mickey waved his silly, tireless arms. At first she had tried to keep track, sung, counted, babbled fairy tales, movie plots, observing the daily benediction of a shaft of silver under the heavy door, the barrier that had bruised her aching shoulders. When she still had a voice, she screamed at the dulled sounds of distant airplanes. Were they still looking for her? Then, too thirsty and bone-weary to care, she had floated into unconsciousness.

She sneezed again at the dust, her chest tight with pain, hands still aching from having traced with bleeding fingers the outlines of the shadowy prison. Fifteen by fifteen at foot count, squared rock, a packed dirt floor. A crude bunk bed with a straw mattress sat at one side, her hiking boots tucked underneath. Wire-spool tables and rough shelving leaned against slick walls. Empty bottles and cardboard boxes, a tacked-up wall calendar. Bottle tops with brittle cork and empty cigarette packages faint with tobacco. A place where laboring men slept, not lingered, her museum of heightened senses, a personal jail, soon a mausoleum.

Now she was too weak to leave the bunk, her tongue swollen and her lips cracking against every shallow breath, and she prayed for blessed release back into a warm, wet womb, her own barren into eternity. The tears had surrendered days ago, resummon them though she would to bathe sore eyes. She blinked a final time as cotton closed her ears and the pain fled, leaving her fresh and strong, moving her young muscles with the spirit of a freed colt. Down a long, shimmering road to greet her came Mom and Dad, trotting beside them Nipper the Parson Russell terrier with his eager bark. The light shard appeared faithfully as it always had and always would, its stagecraft approved by a small striped lizard scuttling in search of a tasty bug.

Chapter One

The blacktop stretched into the distance, shimmering waves of heat rising like streamers. The land moved its bony thighs, a desert of yucca and sage punctuated by outcrops of Navajo sandstone with crumbling talus. Terry Hart white-knuckled the wheel of the truck, peering at a long, thin stick on the road. There was no way to avoid it, but they'd pass over without harm.

Judith stared ahead, then into the side mirror as they went by. "My God. It's moving! You ran over a rattler."

Terry pulled over as they watched the diamondback's death agonies, whipping and slashing. "Should we go back to . . ."

Her aunt gripped her arm. "Count the rattles? Put it out of its misery? Its spinal cord snapped, but the reflexes are there. Do you know how many people are bitten by 'dead' snakes?"

Thank God they were nearly in Escalante. Moments later Terry saw the signs for the Broken Bow RV Park. She pulled in, noticed that most of the good sites were taken, and aimed for the rear.

"Stop! For God's sake!" Aunt Judith thrust a chubby leg onto an invisible pedal and clutched the dashboard like a lifesaver ring.

Terry braked, skewing the GMC Sierra 2500 4 × 4 and splashing a cup of cold coffee out of its holder onto her lap. A yelp bruised her ear. She glanced behind the seat into the affronted butterscotch eyes of a small light-brown dog with a white-tipped tail, and then forced herself to count to eleven. Judith's nerves were as taut as hers. They'd driven that morning from distant Flagstaff, a long haul at fifty miles per hour across the massive Glen Canyon Dam into Utah, up to Hatch and then east again. Only the lucky crow could fly in a straight line in this tortuous country. "What's the matter?"

Her passenger pointed a shaky finger at a stenciled sign above the gate, where her niece had headed to make a generous turn in the backlit. "Clearance nine feet. What's the RV?"

Terry paled as she pounded the wheel, her heart tattooing in her chest. "We would have sliced the top like opening a can of Spam. I'll have to reverse. Pass the Valium."

With a wince at her bursitis as she eased out, Judith cast a tutored eye on their predicament, and then began flagging directions for a 747. Terry wiped nervous sweat from her face and followed the frantic hand signals. With such careless aplomb the salesman in the Parma Town RV Center had demonstrated the twenty-one foot Fleetwood fifth wheel. "Child's play," he had bragged, tooling in and out of slots like driving a kiddie car at Cedar Point. She never could calculate the angles at which the beastly trailer unfolded like mirror writing. Slowly, perfectly, then suddenly angling at a perilous ninety degrees that banged their plastic totes piled in the box against the front housing.

This was their third week out from Ohio. They'd lumbered west from suburban Cleveland through rolling farmlands of Indiana and Illinois, the lush green kudzu topiary of Missouri, under the golden arch at St. Louis, delayed through Amarillo while Judith traced billboards to a restaurant with a seventy-two-ounce steak free if you could eat it all in an hour. Then they had dallied in New Mexico touring Bandelier, the first of many Four Corners ruins in the well-thumbed guidebook, photographed the petroglyphs near Albuquerque, and headed west toward Grants and into Arizona, inspecting the jaw-dropping Sunset Crater volcano and the haunting outlier ruins of Wukoki.

At last, they manuevered with difficulty into the only open space. "Luckily there's no grass to destroy," Terry said, hopping from the chrome step bar into a punishing July heat she was learning to expect and uprighting a plastic garbage can the bumper had overturned. "Red rock and desert sage." Her gaze appraised a few spindly cottonwoods recently planted. In an optimistic lifetime they might offer shade. How different from the leafy streets of Lakewood, flanked by stately rows of noble maples and oaks older than the Civil War.

Tut wiggled between the front seats and bounded out, receiving a hiss from Judith. "He did it again. Vomited into the cup holder. So sneaky. I never heard him." She reached for a plastic bag and plucked a paper towel from a handy roll.

After registering at the office, disengaging the truck, and hooking up to water, electricity, and sewer with the experience of a pro, Terry cranked down the awning and unfolded the lawn chairs. From a plastic carryall, Judith retrieved the cheap portable grill. Beef was choice out west, even if prices were eye-popping.

"After that Flagstaff supermarket, I'll never complain about groceries at Fisher Foods again. Fruits and vegetables cost the very earth, even next door to California. $1.39 for an avocado laid by a hen. How do they pay the grocery bills?" Judith asked, bringing frosty Coronas to the picnic table and dropping heavily into a chair.

Terry fingered her short auburn hair, welcoming the rising wind. "Where can they spend their money out here? No symphony, opera, theater. It's probably a day's drive to the nearest mall. Lower heating bills, though."

"The simple, uncomplicated life of the Old West, nineteenth-century once the dirt is washed off." At fifty-eight, Judith Davis was newly retired from pounding world history into hormone-charged teenage brains.

Two large black-and-white birds jousted with each other over a crust of bread left at a nearby site. "Comical," Terry said.

"Magpies, I think. Their territory is west of the Mississippi." She was exploring new hobbies as her leisure time expanded.

Serving up half an hour later, they forked into juicy ribeyes, rice pilaf and salad on the side. "Tomorrow we'll look up your old friend, Deborah. What was the name of the place?"

"Sunset Years. A retirement ranch. God knows this dry climate is a damn sight better than ours. I feel perkier already." Judith flexed her wrist, then coaxed a small muscle from her flabby arm. "Maybe I'll even cut out my Voltaren. Bad for the gut. Try that gluco-whatever I read about on the Internet."

Terry smiled to herself, admiring the sensational parfait of reds, golds and blues lighting up Big Sky country. Her mother's younger sister, Aunt Judith was a borderline hypochondriac, but she'd raised Terry after Norm and Nancy Hart had died in a Lake Shore car crash caused by a bored teenager tossing a cement block from an overpass. On her eleventh birthday, returning from Euclid Beach, she'd been in the back seat of the Aries. The broken glass from the windshield had left wicked scars above her knees, a reason she avoided bathing suits and short shorts. Moving across Belle Avenue to Judith's house when her own was sold, Terry had continued in the same schools, and gone like Judith to Ohio State, receiving her degree in journalism. Then she'd slipped into a comfortable but uninspiring job writing small-town copy for the suburban *Lakewood Sun-Post.* Ten years ago. Nothing ever changed but the stoplights.

"I'll ask the park owner about directions," Terry said, taking the dishes into the trailer. The blasting air conditioner kept it blissfully cool, justifying thirty-five dollars a night. She had bought a guide to free camping at Bureau of Land Management sites, but had second thoughts about the lack of electricity. What seemed a frugal idea in her cozy living room now seemed primitive, not to mention highly risky far from the safety of crowds. Suppose an armed militiaman was roaming the area?

"Dove Randolph's place? About ten miles," Gail Stewart, tall and beefy in pink overalls, said at the office. Apparently he accommodated a dozen old folks in converted bunkhouses. With approval, she added that they were frequently ferried in for church and civic outings. "Take Route Twelve east and turn at Sagebrush Creek Road. And don't haul no trailer to Hell's Backbone or the Hogback toward Boulder. We hadda send a tow for the last guy blew his tranny near Calf Creek Campground."

Terry sucked in her breath. Calf Creek had been on their list of campsites. "Hell's Backbone? Hogback?" she said to herself. The West had such picturesque and dangerous names. Where had she finally moved last year to her own apartment? Rocky River. Now there was a name for romantic conjuring.

Out of touristy politeness, she let herself be ushered through the makeshift museum, a few framed shots of early Escalante, but only postcards, slides, and a jar of fake arrowheads. Instead of the heavy turquoise and silver bracelet Terry coveted, a display rack held flimsy earrings made in Japan with pseudo-native symbols and parakeet feathers. Collecting a handful of tempting brochures, Terry mentioned the Anasazi.

Grinning with undisguised pride, Gail motioned her outside to a squared-off earthen mound. "It's a pithouse," she explained. "My son's school project." Together they descended a lashed-together pine log ladder into a deep, round hole. Overhead, a series of crude beams from a center post had been daubed with mud and smoothed. "Rained in like hell before Chad figured to leave an open layer of twigs to siphon off the water. Rebuilt the whole shebang three times. Gotta give him credit for injinuity."

Perhaps Clinton's finest legacy, Escalante-Grand Staircase National Monument was opening up, a boon for the economy but leaving environmentalists and developers dueling about rich oil and coal deposits leased before the legislation. This remote and forbidding territory of over 1.7 million acres had been among the last officially mapped, a beautiful raw-boned woman both deadly and tempting. "Depends on how you figure it, closest settlement or closest shack, the Kaiparowits Plateau's the most isolated territory in the continental U.S. Do any exploring, you be careful, hear? One fool was lost for seven days. Didn't have the sense to carry a topo map," Gail added, her serious hazel eyes sending a warning.

Terry returned for a long-awaited shower, gyrating in the tiny nook, drying herself with one foot on the toilet lid like a contortionist and mopping up spray escaping the thin curtain. The trailer was a marvel of efficiency, chock-full of appliances, drawers and storage bins, but the brochure that claimed it could sleep six had outfitted the Munchkin crew. Her aunt was ensconced with her books in the queen suite. "Up with Mother, Tut," Judith called, and the dog leaped into place, tucking nose under tail. Terry chose a Spiritlands CD: drums, chants, flutes, and exotic bird calls. Then she yanked the sofa at the rear into a quasi-bed and began consulting *Ancient Ruins of the Southwest,* noticing her aunt's tickoffs and jottings.

"You circled Anasazi State Park at Boulder, but Gail at the office said that the grades are pretty wicked," she called. "Good thing we're making camp here and not hauling the trailer."

Judith got up to pour glasses of bottled water, setting one on the breakfast table next to Terry. They had learned to avoid the chemical taste of treated park water, next to which Cleveland's taps dripped Perrier. "Can't get dehydrated," she said as she popped ten vitamins and supplements into her mouth. "Evaporation sneaks up on you."

Terry watched the routine. "Is your will updated? I'm no expert with the Heimlich maneuver. You're going to choke someday."

A crunch followed, then a gulp. "Cher almost did. Now I bite the big guys in half."

Chapter Two

"Not that useless Indians cap. Wear a decent hat, will you? The heat is brutal." Judith tossed her niece a large Wal-Mart straw model with a dyed blue feather.

Terry shuddered at the fancy headgear. "I feel like I'm in the Easter Parade."

The perilous Hogback that snaked its way down into Calf Creek and back up was their first real introduction to diving into the depths of the earth. Until well into the Thirties, a mule had transported the mail between Escalante and Boulder. Terry held her breath as her eardrums popped. Judith gazed deliciously out the window, one foot from a fatal drop-off.

"Doesn't Utah believe in guardrails?" Terry asked, nearly stalling as they fell in behind a thirty-foot rig reduced to a mere crawl. At last the panting beast pulled off at a rare opening to let traffic pass.

"There but for the sake of an extra tranny cooler go we," she observed with a satisfied smirk. "The GMC dealership was right about special equipment for hauling."

When they arrived at the Visitor Center in Anasazi State Park, Judith began entering data into a small notebook, her careful, cursive handwriting filling pages quickly. Terry learned about the natives' early life in pithouses, then above ground in simple adobe dwellings. Over centuries, the pithouses metamorphosed into kivas: holy places or social meeting chambers? Reconstructions counted one for every ten rooms, but the number included tiny storage nooks. In the last period before their mysterious disappearance in the thirteenth century, the era that gave them the romantic, magical label of cliff-dwellers, they left the fertile valleys for picturesque alcoves under foreboding bluffs like those at Mesa Verde, often with water sparsely available below. Primitive aesthetics or a sudden need for defense as they fought for diminishing resources in a period of severe drought? As she stood transfixed at a rainbow parrot-feather cloak pristine after seven hundred years, she marveled at their art. Mexican trade routes were well established, as witness the telltale copper bells from Cobre Canyon. Anthropologists theorized that the Anasazi had migrated as far south as the huge Casa Grandes site in Chihuahua, Mexico, where they blended with the population.

In her shorts pocket she fingered, with disturbing mixtures of pride and guilt, a shard of pale gray pottery, its parallel black lines and decorative dots a visual link to the last millennium. South of Grant's, far along the crusty, shoe-shredding El Malpais lava beds, past La Ventana Natural Arch, into unmarked grazing fields, the guidebook had led them to the remote Dittert site. Explored briefly in the Sixties, then covered up, the scattered brickwork and unprepossessing mounds were surrounded by livestock ambling down to drink at the same small stream utilized by the Anasazi. Had it been wrong to snatch treasure from an errant hoof?

Judith hailed her in the gift shop, brandishing an oversized hardback book. "Here's a shocking theory about cannibalism. *Man Corn* by Christy Turner. Certainly challenges the stereotypes about peaceful tribes living in their lovely cliffhouses. No one wants to answer my questions." As she raised one bushy eyebrow, a park ranger looked the other way. A native woman hurried off as if shunning lepers, but Judith stuck out her pointed chin. "Sixty-five dollars. Steep. But we'd never find it at home."

Terry leafed through the pictures, appalled at the forensic evidence. Pot-polished stew bones. Cut marks on ribs. Blackened skulls indicating a primitive barbecue. What a contrast to the pastel shell necklaces, the checkered black patterns on the two-handled cups and delicate bowls in the display cabinets. "If the Hopis, Zunis, and Navajos claim to be distant relatives in charge of the lands now, this is very bad publicity."

Judith gave her a tutorial nudge. "Not the Navajos. They're Athabascan. Migrated a few hundred years ago from Canada according to linguistic evidence. But the Hopi translated Anasazi to mean 'ancient enemy.' Hardly a compliment."

"DNA might settle the controversy. Why hasn't anyone thought of that?" asked Terry.

Judith put a finger to her lips, then tucked the book under her arm as she headed for the cash. "Maybe they have. Politics, dear. Don't ask. Don't tell."

They worked up an appetite touring the adjacent Coombs Village site, which thrived until a devastating fire in 1275. Leafing through the book, Judith noted that Turner had considered bone evidence from one excavation there, but dismissed it. "Honest enough. I respect a conservative scientist."

Following the cashier's recommendations to the Kiva Coffeehouse, perched on the approach to the Hogback with a glorious view, they sat later in coolness and considered the hand-lettered menu. "Authentic Mexican food at last. Forget that Taco Bell mush," Terry said, salivating at the prospects. "Even blue corn enchiladas. Very exotic."

A peppery salsa with corn chips served as appetizer, setting the stage for the fire to come. Judith's posole was a tasty stew with succulent chunks of pork and soft hominy swimming in green chile. Terry opted for the chile rellenos, and they arrived plump in a crisp batter. Five glasses of ice water called for a sixth.

"So tell me about Deborah. Is she shy like you?" Terry asked, tongue-in-cheek, monitoring her aunt's face.

Judith maintained a deadpan expression. "Much more outgoing. She taught American history. The Civil War was her territory. Loved the theory that Lincoln's assassination had been a cabinet plot. She headed up the department at Lakewood High when I signed on, broke me in gently. She's been in Utah for ten years. Retired early and took partial pension." Judith tapped her chest. "Heart trouble."

"Did she have family out here?"

"God no. Old maids both of us, like that card game you hated. A sister, I think, died long ago in childbirth."

"You'll have a great visit." She thought for a moment. "If she's able to get around, let's take her out for a scenic drive and bring her back to the RV for dinner."

"Better stock up. Had the buffet every Thursday evening at Menopause Manor, the old Miller's on Detroit Avenue. Deborah always ate like a horse," Judith replied, drizzling the last puffy sopapilla with dark honey before devouring it in orgasmic delight.

With no major newspapers for sale, Terry bought a local rag as she waited in the truck for Judith to comb the drugstore for Vitamin B 75's. Page two caught her attention. "No sign of missing girl lost in desert May 30th." Melanie Briggs, a Michigan State anthropology student on a summer school dig, had been driving a Jeep when she'd failed to return to the field camp in Dixie National Forest. All her belongings were left behind. Melanie had been well acclimated to the region and often forged out alone. Didn't everyone carry cell phones out here, Terry wondered?

When her aunt climbed in, Terry passed over the paper, pointing at the story. “It’s scary. That could happen to us.”

Judith snorted in contempt. “It’s sad about the girl, but we’re no teenagers. Forewarned is forearmed.”

Chapter Three

Terry awoke to the whine of the water pump under her bed. Her aunt switched off the roaring air conditioner and plopped a glass of calcium-fortified orange juice and a cup of strong coffee onto the table, navigating backward with aplomb. Pulling herself to a sitting position, Terry grabbed a corduroy backrest. The juice slipped down with a satisfying bite. "Where to this morning? Deborah's?"

"That can wait another day until we get oriented. I'm too excited about what I've been reading." Judith edged into the kitchen nook, adjusted her new bifocals, a hard-fought surrender, and found her place in a copy of *Hole in the Rock,* chronicling the 1879–80 Mormon mission that had sent two hundred and fifty men, women and children on an ill-scouted fool's errand to forge a shortcut southeast to the San Juan area they would call Bluff City. Taking eighty wagons and hundreds of cattle, they carved a road into the wildest country imaginable.

"Then at the end, for God's sake, straight down that cliff eighteen hundred feet to the mighty Colorado, blasting a path with dynamite. The blind horses went first. Some eye disease had hit that summer. Other beasts, scared out of their heads, had to be whipped. I want to stand on that historic spot." Rising from her seat, her spare tire bumping the table, she assumed the pose of patriarch Brigham Young overlooking the Promised Land.

Terry shifted on the bed, a slight crease on her brow and her heart rate suddenly spiking. What dangerous wilderness did her aunt expect them to explore, even with the 4 × 4? Asphalt roads and freeways were bad enough, but off-track travel raised alarming prospects. "Well, as long as we don't run into any tr—"

Judith's spoon clattered against her mug as her voice shifted into lecture mode. "Trouble is not your middle name, Terry. When we went to Orlando last summer, you told me we needed an inflatable travel companion. Thought you were twitting me on my weight until I saw that dummy installed in the back, wearing your Indians cap. Stuck in the mire of the stuffy *Lakewood Sun-Post*. Weddings and funerals. And that insufferable bore Jeff with spreadsheets for brains." At the stricken look on her niece's face, she stopped and reached out a hand. "Oh, my big mouth. It sounded so intriguing. You choose the route, dear. It's your truck."

If that wasn't blackmail. Terry answered Judith's double-edged apology with an ironic smile, especially about Jeff, the tax accountant with dandruff. Losing her parents had made her retreat into a cautious shell. She envied her aunt's bravado, her willingness to cash in CIDs to purchase the trailer. "Die the day before you go broke, and you'll die happy," Judith often said. Terry had bought the truck. Her parents had been so well insured that the cost barely made a dent in the burgeoning mutual funds. And maybe Judith was right. Who would inherit Terry's pots of gold?

She finished the bacon and eggs Judith presented as necessary fortification against a long day's activity. After Tut licked the plates, she led him to the poo-poo park where she dutifully scooped up, armed with a plastic bag, glowering at a Lhasa Apso owner who decided that Tootsie Roll deposits gave him a dispensation. Wishing she had the courage to make a biting remark, she swallowed back her contempt.

At the RV, Judith was showering, so Terry made lunch with a mind to the heat. Butter instead of mayo. Monterey Jack cheese instead of meat. Sweet-sour jerky and two apples. A daypack with three water bottles from the freezer.

"We'd better tell Gail where we're going . . . just a precaution," Terry said as they clamped the screen door to the outside door, then locked it. "Not long ago, a hiker was lost for sev—"

"First the girl. Now this. Relax, will you? Fifty-seven miles is like driving to Akron." Her aunt offered a withering glance as she considered the rising sun, heading for half-broil. "Let's go before that sun scrambles us into omelets."

On the edge of town, cutting off from Highway 12, its sign bearing a beehive, Utah symbol of humble industry, Hole-in-the-Rock Road began its red dust journey without spectacle, wide and flat at first, bearing evidence of a grader. Every few miles, a plain wooden marker with a stylized covered wagon marked the original, rutted trail nearby. In the distance, the Kaiparowits Plateau reared up on the right, its monstrous Cretaceous-age shale benches an austere contrast to the dark orange petrified late-Jurassic dunes that awaited them down the road according to the Monument guide. "Strange name, Kaiparowits. Sounds like a Brooklyn deli," Terry observed, stopping to read the map, even though the road looked like a straight shot to the Colorado.

"Ends in *s*, not *z*. It's Paiute. Mountain home of the people. Anyway, enjoy Escalante while you can," Judith said, pointing to a cholla cactus bursting into riotous pink and yellow clusters. "Soon enough, the ubiquitous golden arches will spoil this beauty. You'll be able to say that you 'saw it when.' "

The arid plains seemed ill-suited to livestock, but with the Land-of-Many-Uses ethic, ranchers grazed the area. A coal black steer blocked their passage, stark against the red brick background, stubbornly observing the interlopers. The lean, muscular animal seemed ill-inclined to budge, and Terry imagined sharp, white horns gouging the Sierra's pristine pewter paint. With a grunt, Judith reached across to the wheel and gave him a honk, galvanizing the animal into an irritated trot. "For heaven's sake take the initiative. We can't wait all day," she said, folding her arms, one foot tapping the carpet.

The first stop past Ten Mile Spring was Devil's Garden. They drove in a few hundred yards and parked beside the lone vehicle, a battered Ford Explorer with a missing rear window in the cap and a bumper sticker from the University of Michigan, Ohio State's favorite rival. Terry grabbed the daypack, and they wove their way toward a maze of eroded rock, bizarre goblin shapes eight feet high with dull crimson striped bodies and gray flattened caprock heads, nodding like malevolent, bonneted mushrooms. Tut began lifting his paws in accusing supplication.

"Should have left him in the truck with the air on," Terry said, grateful for the sheltering hat. "I can't believe these temperatures. Flagstaff was Alaska."

"Out in the Burning Hills area, underground coal fires actually heat the ground. Dante's Inferno come to life."

On a spacious ledge beneath an overhang of rock, they sat and sipped coolness from thawing water bottles. The surrealistic landscape was peopled by more fantastic shapes. "Hoodoos," Judith said, as Terry got up to snap a few photos with her Minolta. "Entrada sandstone. Erosion leaves harder material on top. The wind sculpts the rest."

"What's this interest in geology?" Terry asked, surprised at yet another side to her aunt.

"History is history. I nearly changed my major, falling in love with the aptly named Dr. Laroque, one of OSU's icons. He must have been nearly sixty, but what a charmer with that leonine mane of silver hair. Did you have any classes in Orton Hall, a quaint place built from stones from every state? Ate my lunch sitting on a bench near an Egyptian mummy in the glass case. Who knows how or even when it arrived?"

"My Catholic roommate Molly thought it was a sacrilege to display a human body so casually. I wonder if it's still there."

Suddenly a man stepped from around a pillar, and Tut gave a timid bark. They nodded a hello, and he approached, leaning his tall frame into the shade as he petted the dog. "Spectacular, aren't they?" he said, removing a holstered water bottle and taking a drink, then wiping his mouth with his hand. "If the Mormons had been more superstitious, maybe they'd have run back to Salt Lake City."

Terry laughed. "And we wouldn't be admiring these forms. No one but a true believer would have built a road through this hellish landscape."

"Ah, but beautiful under its own principles. Landscape writes the rules, a character in search of an author. I took a Spanish lit course once, and something from Ortega y Gasset stuck with me. 'Tell me the landscape in which you live, and I will tell you who you are.' " Discovering that they were from the East, he cautioned them about the route ahead.

"Pretty rough the last few miles. What are you driving?"

Terry bristled at the thinly disguised paternalism. *We don't give a damn for the whole state of Michigan. We're from O-hi-o.* "Four-wheel-drive truck. We'll be fine."

"I'm on a dig nearby in Dixie National Forest." He introduced himself as Nick Bradshaw from the University of Michigan anthropology department, supervising ten students working on a small village, so far only indeterminate piles in an open field. He suspected that over the next few years they'd find and stabilize at least twenty separate rooms. "Dig and sift. Learn what we can and backfill."

Judith blinked. "Backfill? You cover it up again? That seems like a wasted effort."

"Even so, you have to maintain those remains. And it costs a fortune for modest places like Aztec and Salmon over in Cortez, Colorado. The government's not going to build a park around penny ante ruins."

"We prefer smaller, undeveloped spots like the Dittert site near Grants. We had it all to ourselves and I . . ." Terry cleared her throat and peered at the tiny trail of mouse feet leading toward a hole under a manzanita bush. "Are there more of those gems in the Four Corners?"

"Too many to count. With land at a premium, developers have moved in. Indian Camp Ranch near Crow Canyon in Colorado is selling lots. Guaranteed one ruin per buyer, from five eras already identified. But you need to hire an expert to excavate, and you can't sell any relics, merely 'harbor' them."

"Sounds like legalized archaeological piracy," Judith said with a sniff. "Next thing they'll be putting up condos on the Custer battlefield, not that he was any hero, mind you. Arrogant braggart."

"On the other end of the scale, cliff houses like Mesa Verde are glamour spots, but to me, they're pure Disneyland. Born too late. I wish I'd been with Wetherill in 1888. He might have been a pot hunter, but without his efforts, Mesa Verde would be a pile of dust. It's a race against time, odds against us. Even the last extensive discoveries in Grand Gulch have been accessible until recently to idiots driving quads." He waved his hand. "You never know. In some tiny arm of these thousand miles of canyons, an unbroken bowl, a miniature corncob, a tattered yucca sandal. That's what I hope to touch." With a dreamy look in his eyes, he cupped his hand in reverence.

His thick, curly brown hair was cut short around the neck, framing a pleasant, square face as he removed his tan Stetson and swiped his forehead on a denim shirtsleeve. No shorts for him in the heat, but loose cotton pants. His work boots were more sensible for slickrock walking than Terry's Birkenstocks or Judith's white Mephistos.

"Take care now," he cautioned as they stood to leave. "This country is a killer. One of our students went off alone six weeks ago and never came back."

"We read about that tragedy. Didn't she tell anyone where she was heading?" Terry asked.

"Melanie was a solitary girl, liked communing with the desert, exploring alone, despite my warnings. She had a habit of forgetting to jot her destination on the sign-out sheet. The Jeep she took didn't turn up, so she probably drove into a remote location and ran into trouble. Without shelter and water, after a day or two of this heat, death is a forgone conclusion."

"There isn't the chance that she was abducted, I suppose," Terry said. Wide-open spaces seemed safer than dark city alleys, but with fewer witnesses.

"One in a million. You're not going to find a serial killer behind every rock. The simplest solution is usually right. She took a risk and lost."

"No cell phone?" Terry asked.

"They don't work out here. Do you really miss those ugly towers?" He spread his arms with a laugh.

Nick took his leave to follow a small trail to the west while they returned to the parking lot. "A lovely man. And no ring," Judith said as they got into the truck.

"Stop matchmaking." Why had she noticed the color of his eyes? Sea-green with amber sparkles. She fumbled with the CD collection, chose "Elvira Madigan," and slipped it into the player. "You said the Mormons drove cattle, so where did they get the water?"

"Those cowboys did the damnedest job. Scouted ahead for the seeps. Ten Mile Spring. Twenty Mile Spring. Poor souls dug for their lives. Six weeks turned to six months. 'Spring' isn't what it sounds like. Even the rivers are tiny creeks. Luckily they had beef on the hoof. Bet they got pretty stringy."

"Not tender like man corn," Terry added with an ironic chuckle. What would the sweat-soaked pioneers have made of this mobile living room? Suddenly she felt like the world's crassest consumer.

Gradually the road turned to washboard, and the only choices were to creep or fly, dislodging their skeletons or risking a flip. Terry chose a speed in between, an unhappy compromise, and continued to receive sharp looks from Judith. The next stop was Willow Tank, a simple cabin with empty livestock corrals. Inspecting the area, they watched a small pipe dripping liquid gold into a tin trough.

Dust so coated the truck that Judith pulled out a Windex bottle and paper towels to clear the windshield, standing precariously inside and leaning around the open door. As they forged into the never-ending plains, broken by treacherous *z*-shaped arroyos, Terry noted that they hadn't passed one vehicle. Suppose they broke down? Since entering broiling Texas, they'd kept several gallon jugs of water in the box as a safety precaution, but they couldn't hike far lugging that load. Terry bit her lip. She should have overridden Judith's objections about leaving word with Gail.

Dance Hall Rock rose from the flats like a proud Sumerian temple, offering a spacious, level surface sheltered by a sandstone bandshell. Terry took several shots, though without perspective the scene would lose its majestic effect. Toting lunch, they trudged a hundred yards in the blazing noonday sun, huffing like spavined carthorses as they climbed into the monument's embrace. Terry sat down, sick with worry, the unexpected cool of the rock only feeding her anxiety. "I'll bet it's 110 degrees. This was a big, big mistake. What if—"

"Stop whining. You know my motto: All experience is valuable. We didn't come this far to cruise roadside tourist traps and go back to the RV to watch sitcoms at night."

"That's not what I meant, and you know it."

Judith poured water into a circular depression in the stone, and Tut lifted his lips in appreciation, the uncanny expression non–dog owners would interpret as aggression. As he slurped, she opened a sandwich bag, thumbed the contents with approval, and passed another to Terry. Munching an apple, Judith summoned images of staid pioneers cavorting with fiddles and concertinas on a cool fall evening. Mormons weren't celibate Shakers. Polygamy had been difficult for authorities to stamp out, even with the national government receiving that crucial promise as a condition of statehood. Finally, she insisted that Terry take her picture dancing a polka, while she sang, "Who Stole the Kishka?" at the top of her lungs. "Frankie Yankovic. Cleveland's Elvis. God love him."

On the way back to the truck, Terry peered cautiously as they edged past an ominous rock shelf. "Don't bother looking for rattlers at this time of day. They're as hot as we are. Gone to ground like sensible creatures," Judith said.

The air conditioner greeted them with a blast of heavenly ether. As Terry navigated the countless switchbacks slithering through the precipitous gorges, the land melting at the lip, she appreciated what impossible engineering the settlers might have faced without these bulldozed crossing places. How great their faith must have been. Overhead screeched the circle of a dark desert bird. A raven, or a buzzard ordering lunch?

The road deteriorated as Nick had predicted. Washboard had been murderous, but now they had to stop every five minutes to manage the angular terrain without damaging the truck. Terry gripped the wheel until her fingers ached. She felt a brief resistance and heard a scraping sound. What was vulnerable in the underbelly? Brake lines? Shocks? An axle? Narrow corridors resembled dry stream beds. Time and again she got out in frustration to muscle aside fallen boulders while Judith urged the truck forward inch by inch across the fractured slickrock, her lined face purposeful, intense, smiling through. One chrome steptube was dented. Terry was floored by heat and fear, her shirt sticking to her back, her neck sunburned. Iron bands of pain clamped her head. Suddenly she realized that the reassuring wooden wagon markers had disappeared. Had she taken the wrong fork at the last two junctures? Which way led back? They didn't have a compass. Could they follow their own tire tracks? Even so, there was no place to turn around.

As they rounded a corner, an impassable stretch challenged like an ancient, roaring god. Terry swore under her breath and pounded the dash. "That's it. The Fat Lady just sang. If we broke down, we'd never get out walking."

Judith flapped the map in her face. "Hole-in-the-Rock's only a mile or two. We can't turn back now! You're being ridiculous."

Folding her arms like the stubborn, defiant child who'd refused piano lessons and pouted for a trumpet, Terry took deep breaths to quell her shaking voice. If Judith didn't know their capacities, someone had to break the news. "I'll hear about this until hell freezes over, but frankly I don't care. Somebody has to make a sane decision."

The inglorious retreat was a silent death march as Judith seethed. In contemplation of a shower, a meal, and a good book, preferably about a polar expedition, Terry felt her heart rate ease as her guilt rose. After miles of total quiet, she sought a way to placate her feisty companion, stopping to point out a magnificent layered sandstone formation along the Straight Cliffs.

"Doesn't that look like Jeff's head?" No response. Then she consulted the Monument map in a last-ditch effort to salvage what had started as a lovely day. It was only three o'clock. Egypt summoned images of intriguing temples, but was located another ten miles on a secondary road. According to the sidebar cautions, Peek-a-Boo Gulch late in the day would make a brutal hike. She needed something tame but memorable. A fresh start.

Then she peered at the small print beside an innocent green dot. "Batty Pass Caves. That sounds interesting. How about it?" And only a short distance from the road, she thought with returning confidence. "We're near Twenty Mile Spring, too." Two pickups had flown by in clouds of dust, tossing beer cans with aplomb.

Her aunt shrugged frosty acknowledgment, her hands folded on her lap like a Mother Superior. At the turn, the side road was level, heading toward the Kaiparowits Plateau. After ten minutes, Terry began to regret her rare bravado. Every mile in meant another out. What a stupid and dangerous impulse. Her stomach lurched at the idea of another failure. She gulped and looked over at Judith, whose face wore an emerging smile. Diminishing to a cowpath, the track split and resplit, leading into scrubby pastures dotted with sage.

On barely defined tracks beckoning onward and upward, they entered the foothills, switchbacking every fifty feet. As Terry swallowed a lump the size of Long Island, in a merciful finality, a rock-strewn parking spot stopped their passage, decorated with the skeleton of a rusty black sedan embedded in the detritus, pocked with buckshot, its glass a shattery green mosaic. When they got out, Tut didn't lift his head, snoring in the cool.

"Al Capone's getaway car?" Judith said, unable to resist a mystery. "Judge Crater's last stand?"

Terry walked around with uncertainty, her eyes following an impassable rutted track snaking to the heights of the bench, lurching like a drunken sailor through fallen boulders and washouts at forty-five-degree inclines. Another potential disaster, but safe now, she thought with relief. Then as she turned, she noticed her aunt staring at three large wooden doors cut into the small hill behind them.

"These aren't caves. Clearly they've been blasted out. An old mine site?" Judith asked.

Like the entrance to a fortress, the first door opened with a creak. They froze, hands raised to protect their faces, but no bats flew out. Inside was an abandoned workshop, dust motes roiling in the sun. Rolled maps, crumbling at the touch, sat on crude tables. Cobwebbed jars of nuts and bolts, newspapers from the Fifties full of Ike's smiley mug and Mamie's wicked perm. After inspecting a Chesterfield package with a nostalgic sigh, Judith picked up an *Argosy* and groaned at the politically incorrect female on the cover. Then she held up a *Mad* magazine with a freckled face. "I always thought Alfred E. Neuman looked like Howdy Doody. Do you suppose it would be all right to take it? It's not an artifact."

"Weird. Look at that." In the center of the room was an overturned, half-completed wooden boat, an incongruous work of art. "Where would they launch it? Lake Powell was a pipe dream when this project started. A sense of humor must have kept them sane in this desolation," Terry said, starting to laugh.

"Isn't it lovely and cool in here? I could almost lie down and take a nap if there was a bed."

"Dusty, though. Think of your allergies."

"What, me worry?" One corner of her mouth rose at her joke about Alfred E. "I left Cleveland's postnasal drip behind."

Outside they inspected the next door, bearing the same heavy wooden bar that dropped into a U-shaped metal phalange. "What's in here?" Terry wondered.

Chapter Four

The distant warbly croak of a raven accentuated the perfect stillness. Something else, though. Not rotten, but hardly the dry-boned atmosphere of the other room. Judith began sneezing, searching her pockets in vain for tissues. "Another nonevent. Meet you at the truck."

Terry stepped forward into the shadows with a queasy feeling of invading personal space, moving from the workroom to a bedroom. This must have been where the men slept: a bunkbed, rough shelves bolted to the walls, a torn straw hat, coat hooks, barrel tables. That a modern backpack sat on the floor didn't quite register. She shook her shoulders in nervous relief, then called, "Come here, Judith. You can rest in this nice rock motel and . . ." Suddenly her eyes found the bottom bunk in shadow. A pile of rags? Clothes? A head? Why would they need a dummy like Dubya? She moved closer, then lacked breath to scream. An old woman . . . or a girl, what was left of her. The skin looked mummified.

Swallowing against the urge to vomit, bitter bile flooding the back of her throat, she retreated with shaky knees to the truck, bracing herself on the door handle. Judith was blowing her nose as Terry stumbled an explanation. "You found what?"

Together they returned to the cave doorway. Judith put one foot over the threshold, but Terry grabbed her arm, gesturing to her own scuffmarks on the dirt floor. "We don't want to leave more traces. The police will need to see what happened."

Judith's raptor eyes surveyed the scene, pupils widening. "Anyone can add two and two. It's obvious the poor soul's been trapped here. Things have been knocked down, old dust disturbed. Those paper wrappers, the water bottles." She focused on the body, unafraid to confront death, a faithful attender of funerals while Terry sent a personal note and avoided what she considered a barbaric custom. "My Lord. Those shredded fingers. She must have been trying to get out."

"Let's go."

Judith knelt stiffly, pointing at a shiny object in a corner beside the door. "A bracelet. It must have broken off with her efforts." She shuddered as she rose, then straightened her shoulders like a self-chastened soldier.

"That girl in the paper. What was her name? Melanie . . ." Terry's voice wavered and a touch of panic gripped her chest.

"Briggs." Judith steepled her nimble fingers and tapped them in thought, computing a mental audit. "Where's that Jeep Nick mentioned? She couldn't have walked here, locked herself in and died."

Terry leaned against the door, starting to shake. The pathetic evidence of the last supper of Naya and Power Bars moved her to tears. An excruciating death. How long had Melanie been missing? Six weeks? Surely she couldn't have survived half that long. How she must have tried to stay alive, hoping that someone would come to the rescue, knowing she wouldn't see the sun again. "Let's get back to town," she said, putting an arm around her aunt for her own comfort.

"Shouldn't one of us stay to—" Judith asked, her fuzzy brows contracting.

"To what? This isn't a wake, and it's not as if thunderous hordes of tourists will be arriving on a bus."

Terry felt uneasy at her first crime scene. Bonne Bell Cosmetics was Lakewood's signature, not murder, though one prominent case had put the area on the map. In 1954, young osteopath Sam Sheppard in nearby Bay Village had been convicted of murdering his pregnant wife, Marilyn. Dr. Sam spent ten years in the Columbus penitentiary before his conviction was overturned and he was retried and successfully defended by F. Lee Bailey, ending his life as a professional wrestler fighting a drug addiction. After nearly fifty years, DNA evidence had cleared his name and identified a handyman as the killer. As an odd addenda, that handyman murdered a Lakewood widow in 1999 and was convicted, dying in jail.

Back at Broken Bow, Gail was waving a Bouncer Class A with California plates into a site. Four bikes nestled like puppies on the rear carrier. "Police?" she said in bafflement at their question, lowering her voice. "Haven't had anything stolen, have you? My park's a safe place. Sheriff Reggie Chisholm's office is down on Main. Across from the Zion Bank. What happened?"

"We found . . . something at the Batty Caves. I don't think we should say anything more now," Judith replied with a bland smile, leaving the woman with an O of surprise on her cherubic mouth.

The small Victorian house resembled Dorothy's without the Kansas wheat field. A mailbox painted like a police cruiser sat at the curb. A white picket fence surrounded the yard, and the gingerbread trim on the house was freshly painted. Left to its own devices, spindly grass made an easy-care lawn, but someone had been watering the lush orange tiger lilies by the brick path. "Sheriff," a makeshift sign on the door read, to which was added in crabbed pencil lettering, "Come in. Don't waste time knocking. I'm half-deaf anyway."

Inside was a room with a battered rolltop desk, a swivel chair with a worn leather seat and two wooden pressback chairs that drew Judith's interest. A corkboard of posters introduced

America's Most Wanted. On a rickety table, the world's filthiest coffee pot harbored a deadly inch of blackened brew. A pot-bellied stove sat in a corner. Down a short hall the outlines of a kitchen appeared, accounting for a smell of bacon grease probably embedded in the walls. "Where's the jail?" Terry wondered aloud.

A flush sounded. Then a man about sixty entered from a side door, wiping his hands on a towel. With a belly like a twenty-pound sack of rice, he wore brown work pants and a tan twill shirt with a silver star pinned crookedly on the pocket. "We got a room with boarded windows and a cheap-o lock. Haven't needed anything more. High school kids get up to pranks on grad night. Sicker than hell on our 3.2 catpi . . ." He cleared his throat as Judith's teacherly eyebrows arched on automatic pilot.

They introduced themselves and told him about the sad discovery in twenty-five words or fewer, as Judith would say. He sat down with a thud, his plum-red face fading into pink. From a squeaky desk drawer he hooked a quart of Jack Daniel's and two glasses. "Shock," he explained, waving an invitation declined. The bottle gurgled several healthy draughts past his Adam's apple. He squeezed his bees-winged eyes shut for a moment, then passed a shaky hand across a balding head with a friar's grey fringe. While they stood like schoolgirls at a spelling bee, he flipped open a notebook.

"Jesus. Jesus. Gotta be Melanie Briggs." He gave them a hard stare. "You didn't move the body or mess with nothing, did you?"

Terry winced, unable to imagine closer contact with the corpse. "Of course not."

"What you say about the remains makes sense. Protected from scavengers and weather, bodies dry up out in the desert. Grandpappy found some 'a them ancient peoples sealed in their cliff houses. Hair, teeth, skin, everything shipshape after seven hundred years."

He seemed to mellow under the influence of the liquor, or maybe he was relieved that the disappearance had been resolved. Stereotypical, bumbling small-town lawman or a *Heat of the Night* rerun?

"Now tell me again what here caves you're talking about, and for Lord's sake sit down, ladies. Where's my manners?" he said in avuncular fashion, licking the tip of a stubby pencil and opening a creased map. "After I take your deposition, better stick around for a few days in case we have further questions."

Back at the trailer, the ubiquitous frozen chicken Terry again had forgotten to resuscitate would have to bide. As the mournful hoots of a Great Horned owl keened a haunting death knell, they sipped beers in the darkening twilight, preoccupied about horrors worse than any Hollywood script. From form more than appetite, Terry went to the pay phone by the laundry and ordered pizza delivery.

When the young man arrived with a charge of twenty dollars, she handed over the money and a tip without complaint. Judith had cobbled together a spinach salad, which they ate without gusto.

"I've forgotten all about Deborah," Judith said soon after, leaving her meal half-finished. "Bodies have a way of putting things into perspective." She gazed into the pooling darkness.

Along a sandy patch across from their trailer, four o'clock flowers had opened their fragile pink petals to emit a musky fragrance. A few hawkmoths began to scent them out, fluttering in the still night air.

Chapter Five

Though usually her aunt was perking at six, out west she and the dawn were tardy students. A pale peach glimmer flickered in the eastern hills as Terry decided not to tune in the radio, especially after their gruesome discovery. Judith deserved a few more minutes of sleep. She'd moaned more than once during the night. Her arthritis kicking up after stress? Terry picked up a copy of *Wetherill* and read for half an hour. When she finally rose to make coffee, Judith woke with the noise.

"What a nightmare!" her aunt said, stroking Tut, who was treading the covers in search of cerebral rabbits. "It was about that poor girl, or you, or me. I don't know. So confusing."

"So describe it. Free therapy. I can say 'yesssss' and 'go on' without a medical diploma."

Judith wiped sweat from her brow, forcing a smile. "Remember that ride at Euclid Beach with the little boats and the dark, ominous tunnel? Hours passed, and we didn't come out. Round and round, besieged by goblin men."

"Flashback to Devil's Garden. Very Freudian."

"He's been discredited, Terry. Post-Victorian sensibilities."

"I couldn't get the sight of Melanie out of my mind either. Maybe we'll find out more in the next few days. The autopsy should be thorough in such a high-profile case."

"If we'd gone to visit Deborah yesterday, or if you hadn't turned back on Hole-in-the-Rock, none of this would have happened." She leveled her eagle gaze at her niece. "We were meant to find her."

"Let's go to Sunset Years. What else can go wrong?"

They followed Gail's directions to Randolph's ranch. Judith had been worried about Deborah for months. Usually the woman wrote faithfully at holidays, but an Easter card had gone unanswered and another letter in May. Deborah had grown increasingly hard of hearing, so phone calls hadn't been an option for years.

Rows of barbed wire fence marched their posts toward the entrance to Sunset Years, a faded rainbow logo by the gate with a "Horseback Rides" sign tacked on. In the sandy soil, narrow-leaved yucca jousted with six-foot spiked white blooms. A dozen bony cattle roamed the sparse grazing land along with a companionable flock of sheep. One grizzled ram turned a lazy eye in their direction, shaking its massive black head against the flies. They drove over the clanky metal guard. A slim deterrent, Terry thought, but perhaps cattle didn't like to risk their hooves slipping through the grate. The ranch was a half-mile in, near an arroyo defined by lofty cottonwood trees announcing a water course. Judith spied a small orchard with what looked like apricot trees.

A rustic ranch house in weathered board had a huge wraparound porch with a dozen rocking chairs and a padded swing designed to catch the evening breeze. The barn, outbuildings and bunkhouses seemed sturdy, likely unchanged for decades. Terry parked near a horse-watering tank. Beside the house, a wheelchair ramp had been constructed. The adjoining corral swirled with dust clouds as a young man trained a frisky colt running circles around him on a lead, shaking its head at the constraint. "Come for a ride? Hot this afternoon, but if you can take it, the horses can," he called.

"Maybe another time. We're looking for Deborah Winters," Judith replied.

He tipped back his broad-brimmed felt hat with a boyish grin revealing buckteeth. "Better go inside and see Dove. Don't worry about knocking."

They opened the screen door into a large room, at one end an assortment of tattered easy chairs and sofas grouped companionably around a fieldstone fireplace with a swivel television in the corner. Magazines and boxed games of Monopoly and Clue were piled on a table along with a checkerboard and chess set. A long trestle table with a dozen wooden chairs was set with heavy blue plates, a vintage nickel Coke bottle of scarlet penstamen providing cheer.

From a doorway came a thumping, accompanied by music, a vocal group in close harmony. With a laugh, Judith nudged Terry. "The Andrews Sisters. 'Don't sit under the apple tree with anyone else but me.' Mother sang us to sleep with that tune."

Seeing no one, they walked tentatively into the kitchen. A native girl with long, shiny black hair held by a beaded band was chopping meat on a butcher's block. Industrial-sized cans of fruit, vegetables, catsup, and baked beans lined the shelves. Cooking was homestyle basic in the West, Terry thought, noting boxes of canned milk and bags of flour. No quick trips to town for incidentals.

His back to them, a silver-haired man stood at a huge stove, stirring a blackened cast iron pot as a spicy fragrance filled the air. A green enamel fridge was decorated with a collection of magnets. Looking up, the girl stopped her cleaver in midair and turned down the sound on a small boom box. "Dove," she called.

The man turned toward them, setting down the spoon and turning off the burner. He wore patched jeans and a chambray shirt tucked over a concave belly on a lanky frame. The heels of worn leather boots creaked as he walked over in a cowboy roll.

"Howdy, folks," he said with a curious smile, his voice hoarse and labored.

Judith shook his hand. "Judith Johnson. And my niece, Terry Hart. We were passing through Escalante and hoped to visit Deborah Winters."

He coughed into a handkerchief, excusing himself. "Would you ladies like to go into the living room? Be more comfortable. Carol can bring some coffee."

Judith declined, but with Western civility, he ushered her out of the kitchen and into a soft easy chair with a footstool. Terry followed, bemused at her aunt docilely accepting direction from a man, albeit an attractive one, aging pleasantly as the boards on the house, an indefinable strength to his years.

Judith pressed her hand against her chest as she stared at him, her eyes creased with worry. "Deborah *is* here, isn't she? I've been writing to . . . don't tell me—"

"Shucks, no, Ma'am. Deb went north to Washington to live with her nephew." He scratched his head in calculation. "Back in April. It was sudden, all right. But the feisty old gal always made snap decisions. Got plumb fed up with the summer heat, I guess. And with her dicky heart, she didn't get around like she wanted. We're out in the boondocks. In Seattle, she could take the bus, go downtown whenever she wanted. Don't have a vehicle here, you're outta luck. And truth to tell, the medical care's not that close."

"That's strange. I'm sure she hated big cities," Judith said, her eyes narrowing in a gimlet question. "That's why she left Cleveland."

"Got her number," he offered, searching for a piece of paper on a telephone stand. He scrawled quickly and handed her the information.

"Like to stay for lunch?" he offered. "Least I can do for Deborah's friends who came so far." Seniors began to totter in, one in army fatigues streaking forward in a wheelchair, bashing a sideboard and hastening others out of his path.

"Careful there, Ralph. You're not racing at the Indy Five Hundred," Dove said with a chuckle, settling the man at a table and flicking open a napkin to tuck under his chin. People chatted in small groups, and a spritely imp in a lavender tracksuit turned on the television and thumped the top until it settled on a fuzzy news program. A thin woman trailing an oxygen tank sat beside Ralph and patted his hand.

"Got yourself a couple of cute girlfriends, Dovie?" asked a chubby fellow with a shiny bald head. Ancient twins in gingham dresses tittered, scalps pink beneath their sparse hair. A tiny hump-backed lady with frizzy strawberry red hair asked over and over in a loud, insistent voice as she waved a notebook, "And who was there?" No one answered. Oddly enough, she wore a tailored business suit, misbuttoned though it was.

"Do stay and talk. Just for a minute, dear?" asked a bundle of denim, one chubby batwinged arm bearing a massive turquoise and silver bracelet. Her thick white hair was bound in two braids, circling her head Heidi style. "Visitors are scarce as rain. Especially young ones." She pressed Terry's shoulder and pointed to a seat by the gigantic fieldstone fireplace, guarded from above by the massive head of a black bear.

Dove cleared his throat and swallowed, his Adam's apple jiggling the corded neck. "Got to get back to the kitchen, ladies. Nice meeting you." Judith asked if she could use the bathroom, and was directed down a hallway.

Terry settled onto a comfortable but threadbare sofa, noticing the dotted Swiss curtains and a burnished pine board floor with a fresh coat of wax. "What a lovely bracelet," she said.

The woman rotated it, the silver glinting in the sun shaft through the window. "There are many kinds of turquoise. This is Lone Mountain from Nevada. The purer colors are more valuable, but I fancy the matrix." The stones were dark blue with black veins.

"It's gorgeous. I'm on the lookout for one," Terry said.

"Word to the wise, my dear. My late husband sold jewelry in Phoenix. Even experts misappraise twenty percent of the time. Dyes alter the colors. Shoe polish darkens white veins. Some pieces are mere plastic resin. I recommend visiting the Turquoise Museum in Albuquerque."

"Thanks for the advice. I had no idea." She looked around with approval. "Do you like it here?"

"I should say," the woman who had identified herself as Cora Jones answered. "Came out from Lalaland, that's LA, my lungs were a squeaky accordion. Now I'm off every day for a mile constitutional. Well before ten, of course, these merciless summer months. And the price of retirement homes back there like to knock your blessed socks off. Damn bloodsuckers. Pardon my French. I don't know how Dove keeps the charges so reasonable."

Smoothing her salt and pepper pageboy haircut, Judith joined Terry on the sofa, entering the conversation like a hot knife through butter. "So Deborah's gone to the rainy country."

"I was so sorry to see her leave." Cora pointed mournfully at decks of cards on the mantle. "Played a fine fourth at bridge. Took piles of pennies off us. Now we have to make do with Thelma." She cocked her thumb at the redhead in the business suit, who sat in a corner perusing an upside-down *Modern Maturity* magazine, peering at them from time to time.

Terry gave Cora a quizzical glance. "Bridge?"

"She's sharp enough some days. You know how that old plankton gums up brains. Sad, though. Our girl Thelma used to write the society page for the *Denver Post.*"

Carol brought in a platter of sandwiches while Dove carried a steaming porcelain cabbage tureen. Judith and Terry exchanged knowing nods and headed for the door as people wandered to the table, scooted out chairs, and clattered cutlery.

As they walked down the front steps, a low whistle caught their attention. A thin, wiry arm beckoned from the side porch, hair like a stoplight. "I know something you don't know," Thelma said in singsong fashion, head turned to one side from her bowed position. Her fuchsia lips, a toddler's coloring efforts, pursed in amusement.

Terry cast a sidewise glance at her aunt. "Oh? What's that?"

A giggle shook the crooked shoulders. "Can't tell. Can't. The Fourth Estate is a sacred profession. One is honor-bound to protect privileged sources."

"I understand. Journalism is my job, too," Terry said with forced indulgence skirting condescension. Geriatric psychology was not her forte.

"Really? Then it's all right. I knew they'd send someone. Don't show him your press card. It wouldn't be safe." She dropped into a whisper hard to hear over the yee-haws of the cowboy in the corral and the blaring of the TV inside. "She's gone west."

"You mean Deborah? That's what we heard."

"Debbie's gone west, she has. The old way. Do they call that a metaphor or a simile?"

The irritated ring of a triangle from the porch made them all jump. Carol furrowed her brow, then went back inside.

"Dear comrades, I can't talk now." Thelma scuttled off like a neon turtle.

Terry asked, "What do you make of that?"

Her aunt tsked, then tapped her temple in a universal gesture of dementia. "Yet I wonder. Could Deborah be here? In some reduced state where she doesn't want to see us?"

Terry nudged her arm. "You're being rather dramatic. Why would he give us the phone number?"

Judith stared at the ranch house, narrowing her hooded eyes like a venerable eagle, running her mind through its paces. "Something's fishy. Instead of looking in a book, he had that information memorized."

"Not only fishy, but plain rotten. Do you smell something? And I'm being literal."

Judith sniffed and looked around. "Now that you mention it, I thought I nosed a whiff of . . . surely they have indoor plumbing and not an outhouse."

Terry sighed and checked her watch, feeling her appetite vanish. Her turn for dinner. Too late to thaw the chicken. "Dove seems like a decent man. It can't be easy running a place like this. He probably doesn't break even. If you're worried, why not go back and talk to Thelma again?"

Judith waved her hand in dismissal. "Ga ga girl. We'll try the Seattle number. Experiment with that phone card you bought."

But the number was busy until they went to bed at eleven.

Chapter Six

"Deborah hated the damp, mind you, loathed that mildewy Cleveland weather. Soggy crackers one day after opening a Ritz cracker box. One Christmas I bought her an electric brisker. There is no eternal way she would prance off to rainy Seattle." Easing from the bed in striped pajamas, down the three carpeted stairs, she resembled a well-nourished convict. "I need a carrot juice fix. My antioxidants are in the basement."

"Call that nephew again. He has to answer sometime. If she's not there, ask plenty of questions." She felt strange, tutoring her aunt in reporter mode instead of the opposite.

Shaking her head, Judith made sure the blinds were closed, then tossed her pajamas on the bed, rummaged through the closet and selected tartan shorts and a loose white shirt. She took a can from the fridge and poured a tall glass of pulpy juice, swallowing in satisfaction. Her hand found Dove's slip of paper on the table and she grabbed it along with the phone card. "Back in a mo."

The radio weather report projected a perfect day again, cerulean sky and blistering temperatures. Did people notice a climate only when changeable? Didn't it ever rain? Terry made toast with a flat tin apparatus on the burner, then slathered her pieces with Cheese-Whiz and peanut butter. Can't get too much calcium, or could you? After an unnecessary hysterectomy for ovarian cancer, a result of visiting too many alarmist websites, Judith was alert to possible osteoporosis. Terry could hear her voice: "Hated milk all my life. And if you don't fancy a cracked pelvis at sixty, at least eat some yogurt or normal cheese, not that toxic sludge."

Terry considered the label, the stuff of creepy science fiction. Modified milk ingredients, but in parentheses after "cheese" came pepsin, microbial enzymes, and calcium chloride. Terry reminded her aunt that health cookbook author Adele Davis had checked out well before her threescore and ten, blaming her fate on junk food devoured in her benighted teens. *Prevention* magazine guru Rodale hadn't fared much better, nodding off discreetly into death during a television interview.

When Judith returned with a perturbed look, Terry remembered the time difference and winced. "It's six. Bet you got them out of bed."

Hauling out the All-Bran and vanilla soy milk, Judith joined Terry at the breakfast table, giving a sharp glance at the Cheese Whiz jar. Spooning into her cereal, she gave a "brack" at the taste. "I smell a fraud. I should have been from Missouri, the Show Me State." She related her conversation with a Mark Randell. "Once Deborah showed me her family's genealogy chart. There was no Randell. I have a memory for details." She paused, adding honey to her coffee. "Sounds awfully similar to Randolph, a quick alias to fit the towel monograms."

"Are you sure you're not jumping to conclusions? How did this man sound?"

"Sleepy. What would you expect? But on guard with a quick story, one we can't check." Judith picked a coffee ground from her lip and deposited it on the edge of her plate. "Deborah wasn't there. Gone touring California with some Jeannie person. They're hitting every Spanish mission down the coast, one each fifty miles, the traditional horseback ride."

"Maybe she'll write when she gets back." Terry frowned. "Or maybe not. This trip does sound convenient."

Her aunt browsed through the brochures on the table, then chuckled as she pointed to an advertisement for horseback riding. "Good excuse for another call at Sunset Years."

Terry did desultory shopping at Escalante's only grocery, a tiny store stocking the basics at premium prices. Hard to begrudge their minimal profit with the high costs of transport. After selecting a spongy green pepper, a wizened onion, and wedge of jack cheese, along with a bag of tortillas at the due date, she was pleased to find fresh milk and cream from Weber's, a Utah dairy.

Expecting a speedy exit, instead she took second place at the counter behind a tall, wiry woman in her late thirties buying a Paul Bunyon load: frozen chickens, a fifty-pound bag of potatoes, a case of canned tomatoes, jumbo jars of peanut butter, along with a dozen loaves of bread. Five boys crowded around, pushing products toward her.

"Aggie, how about Count Chocula? Cook's oatmeal tastes like glue."

"Tang is cheaper than frozen orange juice."

A carrot head with a cowlick fingered the candy bar rack, but Aggie's cool eyes tethered them on invisible leashes. Terry admired her subtle defenses against childish nagging, a force that could wear down Mount Rainier. "Hey, *Troy!* Can we get the video? Like history. Like it's Saturday tonight," called the smallest, about ten, as he snatched a cassette from a display.

"Like all day long, Sean. Maybe if those potatoes get peeled by four sharp . . ." Her light brown hair pulled back by a sweatband, Aggie corralled them like heifers, arming them with red licorice whips and allowing the video to pass muster as she signed for the totals. Odd that the boys seemed so close in years.

"Quite a family," Terry said to the clerk after they left.

"Naw," he replied. "Second Chance Ranch. A place for

problem kids. Parents send them here from all over the U.S. My day they marched off to military school."

"Neat. Does it work?"

"Seems to. Strict but fair. Have to earn privileges. Can't even call home the first few weeks. Now and then you get a bad one, though. End of May, five older boys went on an overnight in the desert. One left the tent at midnight, and lit out for God knows where. Caught him late the next day, hitching a ride over by Collet Top. Hungry as a bear. Didn't take enough food for more than one meal."

"Sounds like he was lucky. The desert's a dangerous place," she said, remembering Melanie.

Terry grabbed a local paper from the pile, then left the store, intrigued about the ranch's concept. How would street kids from New York City or Chicago adjust to this Spartan life? Maybe boot camp treatment shocked them back on track. What a concept for a human-interest story. Would Aggie cooperate, or would privacy concerns muzzle the organization?

After returning and sorting the groceries while Judith showered, Terry opened the weekly. Instead of world news, a naive expectation, she was greeted by the smiling face of a blonde girl, a studio photo, perhaps for a yearbook. Melanie Briggs. She stared at the lovely image as she had turned from the grim reality. Though the black-and-white format gave no hint at eye color, her long silvery blonde hair called for blue. Merry and confident, they reflected the admiration of the camera. A slight bump on the nose added an interest absent in perfection, and her soft eyebrows were natural. A brief biography listed some of her college activities, including being a Wolverines cheerleader as well as the secretary of Pi Beta Phi, and belonging to the Anthropology Club. Then Terry came to the part that twitched her interest. Forensic investigators had decided that the bar had accidentally fallen into place when the door was closed or blew shut. Her backpack contained her wallet, with thirty dollars in cash and a Visa card. One fact couldn't be explained. No one interviewed at the dig could imagine why she had gone to the Batty Caves, a small industrial dumpsite with no fascination for relic hunters.

"So they aren't pursuing any leads?" Judith asked, toweling her short gray hair during Terry's summary.

"Seems not." She squeezed her eyes to recall that foreboding moment. "I didn't examine the door. Could it have happened like that? A freak accident?"

"Should have told someone where she was going, I suppose you'd say, Ms. Cautious."

Terry firmed up her lips against a reply. Then she checked her watch. "The morning's nearly gone. Let's have lunch and go out exploring, but about that horseback riding, let's not jump the gun. Plenty to do around our base camp. Kodachrome's not far. And Capital Reef could make a day trip."

They heard a drone overhead and reached for the same pamphlet: Bird's Eye View of Red Rock Country. Soar Down the Canyons Like an Eagle. Special Family Rates.

An hour later, a few miles out of town they pulled into Robbins Aviation, which ran heli-tours and plane rides. One green army surplus helicopter sat on a circular pad. Along the tarmac were parked two older Cessnas. At the counter, a perky apple-cheeked girl described the options. Hearing the prices, Terry gulped at the imagined swipe of cards in meltdown and motioned her head toward the door.

"We'll take the half-hour-plus for a hundred twenty dollars apiece." Judith gripped her arm and flashed a smile to melt iron. "Might as well go whole hog. What good is money going to do us in Cleveland? Do you want to cruise over the garbage in Lake Erie? I counted dead fish on our yearly grade school excursion to the Cuyahoga, the only river to catch fire. The

Flats may have fancy bars and restaurants now, but you didn't stroll there at night in my day."

In comfortable chairs, they waited, leafing through aviation magazines on the side table. Finally, the girl came out from behind the desk. "You're on the next flight, ladies. Meet your pilot, the owner himself. Christopher Robbins," she announced as a man entered through a rear door.

"Please call me Chris. No relation to Winnie the Pooh." Chris's age bridged the twenty-five-year gap between the women, a brush of gray at the temples and the smooth, browned skin of a Westerner. He wore black chinos, a maroon cotton shirt with pearl studs, and a tailored leather vest trimmed with snakeskin to match his gleaming boots.

Along with a portly, bulbous-eyed man from Connecticut who sold insurance and sweated Rorschach patterns onto a pale orange polyester leisure suit, they found themselves in a four-passenger Cessna, peering over the flashing landscape. While they flew, Chris chatted about state history and the environmental issues before and after the park legislation.

"I'm glad to see the land protected," he said. "By the Seventies, uranium was a dead issue, but there was a push to develop the oil deposits during the fuel crisis. Five 4,200-gallon tanker trucks in and out per day. When I took over this outfit ten years ago, they did aerial surveys for resource companies. Big money, but I couldn't stomach it. Can you believe that they were planning to build a three-hundred-megawatt coal-fired power plant down there?" He pointed toward a shallow red basin, majestic in its solitude, a giant's dry whirlpool of concentric circles of burgundy and yellow. Within minutes they had crested the Kaiparowits Plateau and were soaring down the Colorado toward Bryce Canyon.

"We avoid tracking the park road," he told them with pride. "Spoils the effect for the tourist ants. Winter's the prime time.

Picture these colors dappled with pure white snow. Photographers go wild. Summer you're better off in the air. The scenic drive loads up lockstep from the Visitor Center to Yovimpa Point."

"Just like the Grand Canyon," Judith said. "My friend Nadine paid twenty dollars admission there and couldn't find a parking space. Never saw anything but the next car ahead."

Chris nodded. "Tourists are my bread and butter, but I respect sensible limitations. The Grand Canyon is a prime example. Eight hundred thousand people per year fly over the place. That means a visitor below sees or hears a flight every seventeen seconds."

"Now I'm feeling guilty about being up here. But it's breathtaking," Terry said.

"God bless America!" the salesman cried as they rushed past delicate, tracery towers of Entrada sandstone, along sliced-off fins and eroded buttes with petticoats of talus.

"Why do they call it Escalante? What does the Spanish mean?" Terry asked, her grade nine lessons with Señor Benevides a distant memory.

"If I head out a few miles, I can give you a better idea. Escalante means staircase, but it's also the name of an eighteenth-century padre converting the Puebloans." Chris accelerated abruptly in a sharp ellipse.

The tiered vistas defined themselves, confessing antediluvian secrets under his patient tutelage. "Think of it like an eroded layer cake. The chocolate cliffs at the bottom, then the vermilion, the white, the gray. Zion Canyon's way over there, then the pink cliffs of Bryce. I'll turn around to give you the idea. Hang on, now."

Encouraged by the whoops of Terry and the salesman, Chris put his plane through its paces. Then she noticed her aunt clutching the sides of the seat and breathing so hard that the veins of her neck stood out. Altitude problems? Silent, Judith waved off Terry's inquiring eyes and the pointed offer of a nest of plastic bags from under the seat.

Finally, they landed as smoothly as a graceful seagull flicking its wings across a beach. When Judith staggered getting out, Chris took her arm and led her to a chair inside, signaling the clerk for a drink of water from the cooler. "Miss Johnson, I feel downright responsible, being such a show-off. Can I take you ladies to dinner to make up for my thoughtlessness?"

Her face ashen, Judith sipped slowly, looking away in embarrassment. She wiped her glasses shakily as Terry touched her shoulder. "That's very kind, Mr. Robbins."

"Chris, please. We're not formal out here."

Judith managed a smile at last. "I'm sure my niece would love to go. I'll be fine. Inner ear adjustments. Or maybe these wretched bifocals. Food is the last thing on my mind. A night's rest is the best medicine."

Later at the RV, with Judith dozing in bed, Terry opened the door to Chris's knock and came outside. She'd chosen a casual pair of cream Capri pants with a cobalt blue silk shirt. Chris had changed to charcoal slacks and a red Polo shirt. "They make a great steak at the Cowboy Blues," he said as they entered a shiny black Lincoln Navigator. He gave the Sierra an amused once-over. "See we're rivals in trucks."

"Anything but a Ford. 'Fix or repair daily,' my dad used to say," she said with a shy nicker.

"This is my baby, silly as it sounds. Nobody drives it but me. First new vehicle I ever bought. Went all the way to Phoenix on a special order."

Chris's choice of restaurant was as enticing as his conversation, exploring everything from history to politics to the upcoming All-Star game. From the arrival of juicy steaks, onion rings hot and spicy, baked potatoes moist within papery crisp jackets to the second bottle of California Iron Creek cabernet, Terry never peeked at her watch.

"Why import from France when the best is next door?" he said. "Just don't drink any Utah stuff, no matter how good the tourist propaganda makes it sound. Foxy grapes."

"Exactly like Ohio's Point Pelee. Some states should be enjoined against making wine," she said with a smile. She hadn't been so relaxed with a man in years. Jeff nearly put her to sleep, but that wasn't the same.

When she returned, still savoring the warm caramel crème brûlée, Terry saw her aunt reading and noticed an empty can of Bush's Vegetarian baked beans by the stove. "Feeling better?"

Judith pursed her lips in mischief. "Naive girl. And I hope you had a good time with that handsome man. Makes Jeff look like a scared mouse. Anyway, we're all set. Errol Flynn in *Dawn Patrol* tomorrow. Can't subject horses to heat. And we won't be bothered with tedious guides. I told them we were good riders."

"Aunt Judith, I've never—"

"Leave it to me. I can read a horse's mind at fifty paces. At sixteen I guided riders on my own. My first summer job in the Valley."

CHAPTER SEVEN

In the Sunset Years corral, Terry's scuffed Nikes and Judith's pristine Mephistos made perilous riding gear. Terry stood in greenhorn embarrassment, rubbing sleep from her eyes as the sky lightened. Craig, the teenager who had been training the colt, gave their feet a cool eye and folded his arms. "City folks. Dove has a pile of castoffs ought to fit." He led them to a storage room at the end of the bunkhouse.

Brushing cobwebs aside, with the smell of old sweat and oiled leather in their noses, they sorted through a selection of battered and dusty boots. As they hobbled out, legs bowing from the rounded heels, they noticed Thelma leaning from a window, finger to her lips. "Joining her fantasy might be our best strategy," Judith said quietly.

Dressed in a smocked nightgown, Thelma peered at Craig disappearing into the barn. Then she beckoned them over. "You're back, of course. Did you speak with my publisher? I won't return without a twenty-five percent raise. Pardon my disheveled appearance. I barely put my face on." Her Brillo-pad red hair was tied into pigtails, black-penciled eyebrows perpetually surprised.

They turned at the sudden clatter of sounds from the kitchen at the main house. Thelma gave a tiny peep, then whispered in a fractured soprano as she bent over the sill. "Second trail right. The Poodle. That's the spot." Then she smeared on grape lipstick, blotted it with a tissue, and crept from the window with the exaggerated motions of a hesitating cartoon character.

"Anne of Green Gables on her death bed," Terry said. "What do you suppose she meant?"

Her aunt paused, hands on hips. "Steady on. Demented or not, she's given us clear directions. The Poodle concept seems promising. Reading the signs is a lesson in life. Too bad we can't ask the boy, but that would blow our cover."

Chuckling, Terry mouthed the last three words while they walked to the corral. Judith had said that she had spent her allowance going to the Homestead or Grenada Theater every Saturday from the age of five. Films noir were her favorites, especially Robert Mitchum in *Farewell, My Lovely* and *Cape Fear.* That dimpled chin had melted her heart despite the bad boy's reputation with marijuana.

"Ready, gals?" Craig asked, leading a bay and a chestnut with white feet. "Got two frisky cow ponies, Nufflo and Prince. Y'all said that you rode, right?"

"Born in the saddle before you were a plasmic idea, young man," Judith said with a toss of her head.

Terry stared apprehensively at the beasts, their broad tails swatting flies, Prince snatching an errant purple thistle near the fence. If modest size meant anything, they were safe enough. She watched her aunt seize the reins confidently and huff her bulk into the huge Western saddle like the Hindenburg rising over New Jersey. Attempting a close imitation, she froze in midair, Nufflo shifting nervously. Then a fast hand from Craig pushed her rump up into the seat. She blushed. "Uh, thanks, I guess."

He explained that if they followed the main trail and kept their eyes on Canaan Peak in the distance, eventually they would reach a creek, a shady stopping place near the skeleton of a chuckwagon. They had arranged for a four-hour ride, allowing a return before the sun becomes ruthless.

Judith led the way, urging her heels upon Prince, who capered like a circus pony in response. "Be assertive, Terry," she called. "Yours seems calm, but they smell fear."

"That's not all we'll smell if he tries anything funny. I'm praying as fast as I can." She centered the backpack containing the water and thumped her boots gently along Nufflo's flank. At his spurt into a trot, she tightened her legs and lost a stirrup, flailing for purchase. "Whoa!"

The trail followed an old cattle path with ancient droppings amid patches of rubber rabbitbrush. Clumps of feathery, white-flowered beargrass waved dense panicles almost to the tops of their heads. Though it was barely eight, Terry felt the incipient heat as the desert yawned. A twittering yellow bird broke the silence, and Nufflo shied at the scuttling of a blue-collared lizard making a timely breakfast dash. She grabbed the saddle horn in panic, glad that Judith was absorbed in pointing out a circling red-tailed hawk.

The sun bared its teeth on another clear and brilliant day, complemented by a Navajo blanket dome of royal blue, apricot, burgundy and taupe, as the slow, rhythmic clops of the horses set a restful metronome. Terry's fears had fled for the moment. Cowboying was a free and joyous life, but with water a scarce commodity, she doubted whether the perfect climate made a trade-off. Beauty in the face of death by dehydration seemed an irony. The con trail of an air force jet blazed a foamy track, a reminder that the Southwest was the home of military bases using the vastness for maneuvers.

Circling back and cantering while waving her hat in her hand, Judith called brightly, "Didn't I tell you that Nufflo was a good fellow? Not one single problem."

"He's stuck in first gear, and I'm ecstatic." Then Prince lifted his tail and relieved himself without changing pace. "Nufflo, don't step in . . ."

When a right fork appeared, they paused, shielding their eyes into the distance. The trail looked untraveled, delicate Indian rice grasses high between the tracks, so they dismounted to rest in the shade of a huge wind-sculpted rock. Terry scanned the landscape with a small pair of binoculars. The natural sea blue of the bushy sage and the smooth, pale green branches of the Mormon tea plant let their eyes rest from the pitiless sun.

"Second right, Thelma said." She took out a water bottle and slurped frugally with an eye to their needs. "No sign of a Poodle so far."

"Perhaps the poor soul dreamed about it. We can still enjoy a pleasant ride." Judith reached for a drink.

Terry traced her finger around the strange conical hole of the elephant ant, a trap for insects unable to mount the grainy sand, dropping unwittingly into a waiting, hidden mouth. "As Melanie learned, there are snares everywhere," she observed with a serious expression as a tiny beetle became an appetizer. "The smoothest paths are often the most dangerous."

"You sound like the Old Philosopher in that song from my childhood," her aunt replied, wiping her broad forehead with her sleeve. "What a Nervous Nellie. Where did you get that trait? Certainly not from your family. Your parents spent a night in jail for blocking the road during a peace march in Washington, D.C., the year before you were born."

Half an hour later, Terry found herself lulled into a stupor by the regularity of the pace and the rising heat. A few outcroppings of sandstone appeared, highlighted by the luminous orange Indian paintbrushes nestled among the pale blue of the tiny, adaptable flax plant. The chuckwagon frame Craig had mentioned appeared at a creek, but without inspecting it, they rode on.

Finally, they reached a second turnoff, the ground roughened by traffic, though the sandy soil revealed no clear tracks. Terry checked her watch. "This looks promising, but it's 9:30. We should turn back soon."

Judith sighed. "Another ten minutes. Let's give Thelma the benefit of the doubt. A fine line divides insanity from genius."

Shortly after, a small arroyo forced a detour. They followed the rim of the dry bed until a fallen bank allowed access. Judging by the wavy surface of the sand, water had coursed down, then vanished, sucked by thirsty ground. Climbing out of the wash, they admired the wild cotton that thrived near moisture, white cup-shaped flowers that resembled their namesakes from a distance. The trail followed a curve between two heaps of rocks, an untidy ogre's building blocks. Crowning the assembly stood a ten-foot-high bruised peach sandstone formation, with some imagination an Easter Island head with a long nose and puffy ears. "The Poodle!" they yelled in unison, giving each other distant high-fives.

Still and noble, it seemed to guard a plot the size of a garage. At scattered intervals, rocks outlined three smaller spaces, sticks crossed with yucca twine at one end, a flat bed of tiny round pebbles inside. The natural hardiness of the matty goldenweed's tiny sunflowers and the aptly-named wee white petals of the durable popcorn plant twinned a tribute more lasting and tasteful than cut blossoms or sad, plastic imitations. Thrifty drinkers, they thrived on the summer moisture and husbanded their strength over the dry winters.

After reining the horses together as a precaution, they walked up for a closer inspection. In a climate where time preserved for centuries, the scene could have been a frontier graveyard. Yet as far as the eye could see, no building remains appeared, no chimney, no broken fences or adobe bricks. Had some small party fallen prey to a massacre and found early graves? Judith had mentioned more than one small bloodbath in Escalante's settlement.

Terry knelt at one rectangle, her eyes cruising the ground, reading the features like page proofs. "It's hard to tell, but this looks recent. The soil has been disturbed."

Judith gave a sharp intake of breath. "Do you think Deborah is . . . buried here? And for God's sake, why would Dove lie about it?" she asked, her face contorted with pain.

For a moment they didn't notice the still form lying on the farthest mound. Then Terry caught the flick of an ear. "A dog!"

A small terrier resting its shaggy head on the white pebbles opened one eye and whimpered. Judith knelt to stroke the fur. "What's the poor little thing doing out here? Reminds me of Greyfriar's Bobby, the faithful Scottie keeping vigil at his master's grave."

Terry felt its skin, healthy muscle around the ribs. "It doesn't seem abandoned or dehydrated." The dog licked feebly at the water she poured into her cupped hand and struggled to its feet. "We'd better take it back to the ranch."

Judith scrutinized the beast as Terry lifted it like a limp toy and tucked it easily into her backpack. "An uncut male. Always a bad idea." At Terry's amused look, she added with a wry grin, "Makes them wander."

When they returned, Craig clapped his hands. "Porky! Where you been, loverboy? Another girlfriend?" The dog squirmed free from the pack, leaped to the ground, and ran to his arms, wagging a stumpy tail. He explained that Porky often disappeared for days. "Need to get him fixed maybe, Dove says. There's a bitch in heat at the next ranch."

In the storeroom, with sighs of relief they abandoned their hot boots. On the porch, Dove rocked in a wicker chair, whittling what looked like a whistle as fragments littered the floor like woodpecker leavings. He started to speak, then drank from a can of Coke and cleared his throat. "Good ride? Recommend us, we'd be obliged. Need all the trade I can get."

Passing him a hundred dollars and waving off the change, they asked about the gravesite. "Got all the way to the old Mormon place, did you?" he said without a false pare, smoothed the piece with a finger and gave a tentative toot. His crinkled eyes appraised them without blinking. "1890, my Grandpap said. Drank from a bad waterhole somewheres on the way to Escalante. Two kids and the mother died. The father married a local widow and went on to California. We keep the graves clean, remove the tumbleweeds, tidy up the rocks. Our folks like to pitch in and feel useful."

"He thinks as fast as his knife," said Judith at the truck. "What should we do?"

"We need more information. Making a fuss about this after finding Melanie would make us look like asses," Terry said.

Her aunt blew out a contemptuous snort. "Asses are the foundation of civilization. They put one foot in front of the other and don't ask why. We don't have time to haul the trailer to Seattle to follow up on Deborah. Vacation's over in three weeks, not counting travel time back to our boring, uncomplicated life."

Chapter Eight

While Judith grabbed an afternoon nap to "restore the vital juices," Terry explored on foot, following a self-guided map from the Escalante Chamber of Commerce. In 1875 a company of men from nearby Panguitch had named the place "Potato Valley," indicating typical Mormon optimism or crediting the wild tubers in the area. Staking out the town in a broad Zion plat format six blocks by six, they sectioned off generous acre lots on draws. Fruits, vegetables, black walnuts, and even mulberry trees for silkworms flourished in the mild climate. Beyond the limits, each family received a twenty-acre plot, and cattle were driven out to graze on communal pastures. By 1910, the majority of the log homes and adobe dwellings had been replaced by square, practical homes using material from the local brickworks. With thick walls on sandstone or volcanic rock foundations, they resisted heat in summer and held warmth in winter. An irrigation system brought plenteous water from the Escalante River to the flourishing oasis.

Terry strolled for an hour, admiring the sturdy houses, details attracting her keen journalist's eye, a stone granary, the charming iridescence of stained-glass windows and transoms, and massive fieldstone chimneys. Even a few original barns remained. As she studied one three-story homestead, she noted that seventeen children had been raised there, key to a population-based economy, a bountiful union ensuring a prosperous life. One small cabin bore a For Sale sign. What would it be like to live here? Would an outsider be welcome or never quite fit in? Her final stop was the old movie theater, circa 1938, the front inset with petrified wood. On the roof, courtesy to early aviators, the town name was painted. For a moment she wished she had taken notes. Would the *Lakewood Sun-Post* be interested in a travel article? Freelancing for magazines would be a creative alternative to her soul-shriveling social assignments and earn a partial tax write-off of the trip.

Wilting in the torpor like the lone sunflower brave enough to emerge from a crack along the sidewalk, she entered the Promised Land Café. Chatting customers were dusty and sweaty, their Western gear well worn, hats unremoved as they ate. She collected a jumbo iced tea from a serve-yourself bar and slipped into a booth. At a nearby table, a heavy-chested Hopi man in jeans and scuffed boots, his handsome square face darkened by the scowl of angry brows, was talking to a woman with a young child in a stroller, chubby brown wrist circled by a delicate turquoise bracelet. It slept oblivious to the noise, a spit bubble decorating the tiny bowed mouth. The woman, her smooth, tan brow creasing under stress, looked around between sips of chocolate milk. "Tocho, please," she said, giving an embarrassed glance at Terry.

Ever the reporter, Terry pricked up her ears and over-sugared her tea. Tocho spoke more quietly but with growly passion. "So what if I was suspended for two months. It was worth it. That son of a bitch stole that shard from the Old Ones. I recognized the lightning pattern. Probably took it from the ruins at Colt Mesa. Thieving bastard. Maybe he'd like me grabbing souvenirs from his parents' graves back in Noo Yawk City . . . or wherever the hell he crawled from."

The woman tightened her full, expressive lips, shadowed eyes blinking as he pounded the table and rattled the napkin holder. "I don't care if I owe my job to tourists. Maybe I shouldn't have sold out," he said. Suddenly Terry noticed the unnatural pink of his right hand, its frozen attitude. A prosthesis?

"But you frightened that girl. Taught her a lesson even if nobody noticed." Her tones grew accusing. "I did what you said about the gas, too. Now she's dead. That Man Cor—"

His voice hissed like a prodded rattler. "Don't use those stupid words. Who wants whites digging up our heritage? If she was careless enough to tramp into the desert without a guide, she got what she deserved. Nature doesn't play favorites."

"I know you were away when—"

"Could you just leave it, Kaya? Don't we have enough problems?" Terry's glass clinked, and he glared pointedly in her direction. "Let's get back to the station. Chuvio found a couple of hours of shitwork for me. We need to pay the damn electric bill, or haven't you noticed?" Rising to well over six feet, he tossed a balled-up napkin onto his unfinished plate and wheeled away the stroller. Kaya stood slowly, balancing a huge belly, then trundled after him with her head bowed. The screen door snapped behind them as a scratchy version of "Stand By Your Man" crackled from the radio on a shelf behind the counter.

"Are you going to get a T-shirt with 'I Survived Hole-in-the-Rock'?" a familiar voice asked.

Terry looked up and grinned at Nick. "Only if it features a chicken. I bailed out a few miles from the Colorado. That country was brutal. My aunt was so disappointed that she gave me the silent treatment." She explained how that decision had led to a trip to the caves.

He sidled into the booth, placed a ginger ale on the table, and removed his hat. His eyes looked tired, fatigued by the relentless sun or something more punishing. "The sheriff told me that you found Melanie. Those caves wouldn't have been my guess."

"You mentioned that she liked exploring. Could she have

made a discovery? It looked like an old mine site, odd place to visit."

"Like digging at the local gas station. Word around here is that a couple of eccentric guys blasted it out in the Fifties and lived there like hermits, rock hunting for petrified wood and jasper to polish for crafts. I can see teenagers getting up to mischief there, but not our students." His face reflected confusion and sorrow, perhaps some guilt in his role as leader.

"How did she get there? We didn't see the Jeep you mentioned."

He sighed, brushed one finger across his sweating lip, and gulped at his drink. "It was found in a ravine behind the next set of hills. A broken axle, out of commission at one humungous washout."

"So that's what happened." Terry reviewed the scene, flashbacks to her parents' fatal collision chilling her. "She leaves the vehicle, then retraces her route, taking refuge from the sun in the cool cave. Maybe hoping to reach the main road after dark and wait for a lift at first light. Closes the door against the heat. Then . . ." She pantomimed the falling bar. "Starvation."

"Dehydration, the coroner said. You can live weeks without nourishment but not without water. Those bottles didn't last long." He paused, tapping his temple. "They found a faded bruise right here. If the spill knocked her out, regaining consciousness, she might have been disoriented."

"It's a theory. I guess they can make the pieces fit."

Nick rocked back in his chair, supporting himself with long legs. "Her parents flew out from Lansing to Salt Lake and then rented a car to get here. I wouldn't go through that again for a million bucks. The mother never stopped crying. Thought the old man might have a heart attack. Melanie was their only child."

"Aren't the park authorities liable for the accident?"

"I was hoping for compensation from the government for her

parents. A token gesture, of course, but you can imagine the logistics. Break your leg climbing in the Monument, who's to blame?"

Terry shrugged, finishing the tea and pressing the cold glass against her forehead. The lethargic overhead fans made more noise than breeze, fighting a losing battle against the heat from the counter grill. They sat in silence for a moment. Then she remembered Tocho's bitter words. "Do you know the couple with the stroller who just left? That chip on his shoulder's bigger than Dallas. I felt sorry for the woman."

"Tocho Nuvamsa. A ranger at Boulder. Met him when the gang went to the Coombs site. Kaya's his wife. She clerks at the Shell station."

Terry leaned forward. "There could be something more. I overheard him mention Melanie, though not by name. I think he suspected I was listening. He took great offense to that Man Corn theory of hers."

"Don't I know. She was obsessed with the idea. It's an expensive book for a student, but she could quote every chapter. Talked it up all over town. The other students at the dig rolled their eyes every time she opened her mouth."

"Cannibalism is a cool topic in the lab or in fiction like *Hannibal.* Not over a coffee with descendants. What's your opinion of the concept?"

"Turner's opponents claim that he skewed the evidence, included marginal sites to plump up the figures. Yet we can't deny cut marks on bones, pot polishing. Whether for ritual consumption, tribal revenge, or social punishment, who can say? Even the threat of a witch is a powerful tool. Less than one hundred years ago, a panic took over an entire pueblo and several people were killed."

Terry narrowed her eyes and traced crosses on the table. She'd been privy to a loaded conversation, and she needed to repeat it before the details faded. "Kaya said that he'd scared Melanie." She paused, combining Tocho's temper with his formidable physique. "Could he have gone as far as—"

Nick waved his hand in dismissal. "Apparently they had some strong words at the museum. Melanie could be snide and self-righteous about her convictions. The kids saw the whole thing from a distance. To be on the safe side, I asked around about him. Met his high school math teacher at a church supper. Nuvamsa climbed out of a poverty trailer park to go off to the Gulf War. He lost the hand in a grenade accident helping a buddy. When he returned, he and his brother built his family a house. He's respected among his people, no matter how much steam he blows. He wouldn't jeopardize his career."

"From his tone, I'm not sure he values it anymore. Was he suspended from his ranger job because of Melanie?"

"Apparently not long after, a tourist came in wearing a pottery shard with a hole drilled in it. And that pushed him over."

She crunched the melting ice cubes, felt the shard scorch a hole in her pocket. Judith knew nothing about it, a rare secret Terry had guarded. "Tacky."

"He called the man out. Rude or gutsy, depending on your perspective. The guy was a hotshot corporate lawyer, didn't take kindly to being lectured . . . by one of a darker hue, if you get my drift."

"What's the big deal about a shard? Aren't they all over the place?" She assumed a wide-eyed naive expression.

He reached for an ashtray. Removing the lone butt with a fork, he cleaned the glass with a napkin, turning it in his hand in mock inspection, fingering the smooth scallop at each side. "What is this artifact? A holy relic? Ceremonial receptacle?" he asked in mischief. "If everyone took the clues home, or even moved them, we'd never know the bad habits of this extinct Marlboro tribe."

In the face of his earnestness, as much to excuse her actions as to marshall a defense, Terry played Devil's advocate, walking her fingers across the table toward the butt. "Suppose I saw a fragment smack in the path of a grazing steer. One minute a piece of history, the next ground into dust."

The corners of his eyes crinkled into a reluctant smile. "True enough. But if we want to unscramble the mysteries of where these people came from, why they left, where they went, we'll need every scrap of evidence. Suppose the piece you took . . ." Her face flushed, and he paused. "Speaking hypothetically, of course. Suppose that item forged a missing link? And like a cold beer on a July scorcher, people rarely stop at one. Conscience diminishes with each deed. A fine line divides curators from pot hunters. The jury's still out on Wetherill, despite his honors at Mesa Verde and Chaco."

She counterattacked with Judith's grade twelve world history lessons. "What would remain of the Elgin Marbles if they hadn't been removed from the Grecian temples? At least they're safe in the British Museum."

"Whoa! If the fine doesn't convince you, and it could be stiff," he cautioned, "starting at two hundred seventy-five dollars and ending at five years in jail and a hundred thousand dollars, maybe you'll respond to superstition. It's bad luck to take anything from a site."

"Bad luck. Now you're reduced to a scare technique." Terry's pulse rose in the heat of the exchange. Dueling with Nick summoned a new energy, an unfamiliar but compelling challenge. "Another myth designed to frighten tourists. The kivas may be only rec rooms in apartment complexes. The corrugated pottery is ordinary cookware. What's sacrilegious about collecting the equivalent of a broken McDonald's plastic Coke cup? Can you steal from a modern landfill?"

"Spoken like a true looter." He finished his drink, then leveled his penetrating green eyes at her, glinting with gold flecks. "The Four Corners Area has been the scene of serious thefts. Not shards, but big time pillaging."

"Surely not until recently. What about access?"

"Things were quiet until technology entered the picture. A hundred years ago, you're talking horses, picks, shovels, and buckets of sweat. Then later, before protective laws were a dream, dozers and front-end loaders began plowing into the remains of ancient settlements. God knows what the ham-handed vandals destroyed. Luckily the Edge of the Cedars Park at Bluff has a stellar collection donated by a few wealthy benefactors."

Terry snapped her fingers as her voice picked up speed. "Donated! My point exactly. I saw a stunning parrot feather cape at the Boulder museum. So fragile. If not cherished, it would be ashes now."

He sat forward and spread his hands. "Conceded. But many treasures remain on private land, well-kept family secrets. Black-and-white jugs on the mantel." He gestured out the window to the distant hills. "What remote sites remain we can't even guess. In this country, shifting sand or erosion can conceal or reveal quickly."

"So despite the laws, there's still money to be made from contraband relics?"

"You bet. Only last year a gang was caught red-handed hauling four pickup loads out of an undiscovered cave. Pristine cups, jars, bowls, arrows, bows, and even human burials. The authorities got a lucky tip on that one."

"A personal mummy. Very gruesome. Who would pay for that?" The image of Melanie on the bunk returned to her unbidden.

"Very popular with European or Far Eastern millionaires." His strong hands steepled, the nails trimmed and clean despite his heavy work. "Here's the escalating scale. A prime jug selling for a thousand in the wilderness brings ten times that in Albuquerque, forty in New York City, and ninety in Europe. Prices have shot into the hundreds of thousands for a large Tularosa pot."

"I could retire to Hawaii on that." When more creases of consternation crossed his forehead, she winked at him and raised her arms. "I give up! Now let's get back to Tocho. He's the good guy in your scenario, protecting the ruins, but maybe our man's principles push him too far. Did he think Melanie deserved a lesson? Say he followed her, knocked her around, left her locked in the cave."

"Come on! You should be writing fiction, not news stories. If he didn't have a good alibi, he'd be looking for a lawyer." He checked his watch. "How about a truce? Would you like to come out to the dig and inspect our efforts? If I know them, the gang will be back at work after dinner."

"Great. Is it far?"

"Dixie National Forest is only a few miles west of town."

"You can excavate on federal property? How's that possible?"

His hands built mountains of invisible paperwork. "First comes the State of Utah Antiquity Permit. Then the Forest Service Special Use Permit, followed by the Archaeological Resource Protection Act Permit. That nightmare's over, but if we find any human remains . . ." He gave a low whistle. "The procedure for that horror story involves prohibitive delays and more than one medicine man."

His offer seemed a great way to placate Judith and put their trip back on a positive keel. "My aunt would love to come. She's married to history. Anything Anasazi has her immediate attention."

"I'm afraid our site is Fremont. A humble second cousin sprawling across Utah."

"Why humble?"

"Small, for one. The largest village found so far is Five Finger Ridge. One hundred separate structures and fewer than three hundred people. Sadly enough, I-70 was blasting its way to I-15 right through the location. Scientists arrived in time to map the place and relocate the remains, working under incredible pressure. Time and our intercontinental highway system march on. And know what? The natives claim that Spiderwoman continues taking revenge for that destruction by causing continual problems in the concrete in the roadbed."

Terry nodded with increasing interest. "So many stories here just waiting to be told. What else sets the Fremont apart?"

"They're new. The Fremont culture wasn't even differentiated until Noel Morss's studies in 1931. Until then they were considered poor, outback Northern Anasazi brethren."

"Is there a collection anywhere?"

"Fremont Indian State Park near Richfield. That I-75 area. I understand they have some pretty nice rock art."

As they rose, she considered Tocho's plate, remnants of a puffy breadstuff. "What was he eating? It looked delicious."

"Frybread. Great with ground beef sauce as an Indian taco or laced with honey for dessert. All purpose." He pulled a pen from his pocket and grabbed a napkin. "Draw you a map to the dig."

As they parted at the cash, Terry picked up a spiral-bound cookbook on local specialties and a wrinkled copy of *USA Today*. Back in the trailer, Judith was at the table catching up on her journal. A cup of fragrant rose hip tea at hand, she nodded to the strains of Liszt. "I can't concentrate with that drumming CD of yours."

"It's relaxing. Like a heartbeat." Terry poured a four-thirty Dos Equis beer, leafing through the cookbook. "You'll never guess what I overheard in a restaurant this afternoon."

Her aunt shot her a disapproving look. "Eavesdropping, a journalist's bad habit."

Terry stuck out her tongue. "A ranger at Boulder. Pretty tough guy." She related the details.

Judith sat back in consideration, putting down her pen. "Despite Nick's endorsement, this man sounds like a number one suspect in Melanie's death. Passionate about conservation but out of control. Testosterone will tell."

Terry heard a deep growl from her navel and marked a page. "I'd rather talk about dinner. That walk made me hungry. We don't have any peppers for chiles rellenos, so let's try quesadillas. Tortillas stuffed with vegetarian goodies. Sound good?"

"As long as we still have Merlinda's salsa from Albuquerque. And we should. I bought a case." She got up, lifted the seat, and peered into the storage bin. "Only seven. We'll get more on the way back."

Terry scanned the paper, disappointed at the generic news. "Nothing ever happens in Ohio. Our history is duller than dust bunnies."

Judith cleared her throat. "The Buckeye State missed the Civil War battles, but what about the Underground Railroad? As kids, we used to climb to a tunneled staircase leading up the shale cliffs to a mansion on Edgewater Road. And don't forget the Mound Builders. And Gnadenhutton and Schoenbrunn Village. How unfortunate that our heritage is layered over by urban sprawl and the disintegration of a wet climate."

"Remember our trip to Serpent Mound when I was twelve? A snake with its jaws around an egg. You said a frog had laid the egg. Was I ever mad because the frog was gone." Gone, her inner voice repeated. Erosion or relic hunters? Again she fingered the shard in her pocket, inspecting it surreptitiously as Judith continued writing. One inch by two, it had a red glaze with stark black lines only a fine hair could have painted with such precision. Human or deer?

Her aunt closed her journal and reached into a high corner cabinet, removing a small jar. "Youth lacks perspective. You preferred lounging in the back of my Buick reading comic books."

"Dad's 1942 Captain Marvels I kept in his Kent State trunk. You threw them out when I went to college. We could have financed this vacation from a sale to collectors."

"Life is not built on money alone, Terry. And as my wise tenth graders always said when they left for the bathroom and came back to find their books gone from their desk, 'If you leave the room, you take the risk.' You should have rented a safe deposit box."

"Here's some better news. I also met Nick, and he invited us out to the dig." She paused, issuing what she knew would be taken as a challenge. "Or are your aches and pains too bad?"

Judith stopped in the middle of anointing her knees with Tiger Balm ointment and blinked, her voice charged with electricity. "Try to stop me. Those projects that take volunteers in Mexico, England, South America. They've been singing a siren song ever since I saw the end of the tunnel to retirement."

"We may get dirty."

"An Ohio State football game in the glory days of Woody Hayes. Three yards and a cloud of dust."

An hour later, sprinkled with grated jack cheese, thin-sliced onion, sauteed mushrooms, black olives and chopped green chiles, then fried like a double pancake, the quesadillas mounded onto their plates like the Seven Cities of Troy. "You may be a vitamin fiend," said Terry, "but at least you don't insist on dairy substitutes."

Judith plunged her spoon into the sour cream. "Chemistry is more dangerous than nature. Those low-fat concoctions are loaded with gelatin and God knows what preservatives. The educated palate knows."

Chapter Nine

Unsure if Tut would be welcome, they left him in the air-conditioned trailer, then drove west on Route 12. "Nick has permission to excavate on the grounds of the Dixie National Forest," Terry explained as she turned onto a dirt road that alternated between deep, sandy stretches and rutted Kurdish minefields. Only the thought that a friendly face waited at the end kept her from pulling what Judith now called a "Hole-in-the-Rock." At last they came to what looked like a trim scout camp, a dozen tents from pup to family, including a mess tent with picnic tables. Small piles of earth and yellow-taped areas testified to a regimen of purpose and organization. A battered Boler trailer hunched under the lone juniper on the plain.

Wearing a Wolverine T-shirt and cap, Nick hailed them by hoisting a narrow-bladed spade. "Welcome to the honorary colony of Michigan." Behind him, a diminutive youth followed, a shy smile on his face. "Terry and Judith, meet Walter Peebles, my executive assistant."

Walter bowed in courtly fashion, but spoke in a stutter. The women waited patiently until he completed his preamble, a blow-by-blow history of the project, punctuated by high hopes of achieving recognition for the Fremonts.

"An exam will follow, folks," said Nick with a chuckle. "Let's start the tour." He pointed toward a flagged site a hundred feet away.

As they walked, Judith asked, "How long have you been working here?"

"Since last summer," Nick said. "And for every two months in the field, estimate ten months in the laboratory."

"What interested you in the Southwest?" Terry asked, noticing that he had adjusted his sizable pace to theirs.

Nick stopped walking for a moment, eyes focused on Powell Point piercing the distance like an extinct volcano. "Ten years ago, I cut my teeth at Homolovi in Arizona, an ongoing field research project at the University of Arizona. Seven ancestral Hopi pueblos from about 1260 to 1400. Place of the Little Hills. An odd name since it's so flat that it makes this look like the Rockies."

"Sounds exciting," Judith said. "History come alive."

"I didn't think so at first. It was walk, walk, walk, or rather crawl. The crew examined thirty-three square miles in small groups. That part alone took several summers."

Blue-green sagebrush anchored the dry earth along with the clustery yellow flowers of the beeplant. Nick paused at a "wall" under excavation. On inspection, the shapeless mound revealed the definitions of mud bricks. "We'll dig through the debris to about six feet," he explained. "Sift the material as carefully as my mother treated her cake flour." He pointed to a large framed screen, where a sinewy young man with a Mohawk haircut was meticulously examining the soil, removing remnants and sorting them into piles. Bare-chested, a white bandanna around his brow, he wiped his face and saluted. Then he relocated the dirt to a finer screen.

"Looks boring, but these kids are fiends for detail, especially Eric here. He'd like to strap on a headlamp and work all night. And on our budget, we're limited to the basics. They'd love it if we could manage flotation," Nick said.

Terry wiped her brow in the languid heat. "A swim would be

great. Our last two RV parks had pools."

A corner of Walter's mouth rose, and Nick cleared his throat, summoning a polite smile. "Flotation describes a technique for securing microartifact plant remains like cotton seeds, charcoal, kernels, even pollen. With that evidence we can formulate a more precise story of daily life."

Walter broke in, his freckled face tanned but so hairless that a shave might have been a wish. "Amy found rabbit bones with knife cuts. An obsidian blade, of course. And bones offer evidence of why a people left an area. At Chaco, mule deer were hunted to extinction, leaving only rabbits and squirrels."

"Quite the detective story," Judith said, her unkempt brows twittering as she bent to inspect the emerging brickwork. "Can the stones talk, too?"

Walter's stutter vanished as his passions took flight. "Masonry style indicates not only time but influence. Higher walls use an inner core of rubble and thin veneers of facing stone, tapering as they rise. The chinking of Chaco, for example." He used his wiry arms to describe each point.

"Chaco's a stop we might make on the way back, but it's a bit off track. Is it worth a look?" Judith asked.

Walter beamed, savoring the limelight. "Chaco Canyon was the hub of the San Juan Basin. A dozen great houses, I'm talking five stories, were built there. Roads mapped aerially branch out in all directions. This might indicate a trade center as well as a political and ceremonial framework. On the other hand, it might compare to the Vatican rather than a social city. A recent book called *The Chaco Meridian* argues that Chaco, Aztec, and Casa Grandes in Mexico might be aligned along longit . . . longit . . ." His face reddened, and he looked at the ground.

"Longitudinal," Nick added in a quiet prompt.

Judith was fingering the masonry like the face of an old friend. "You mentioned chinking, Walter?"

Recovering his confidence, he knelt, and with nimble hands, assembled an assortment of stones. "It's very time-consuming. Large blocks, then tiny pieces for mortar. Sometimes a different color adds an artistic effect."

"You'll make a great lecturer someday, my man," Nick said as he spread his hands. "We'll backfill this when we finish like at that Dittert site you mentioned. That's necessary protection against . . . nosey tourists. Let's check Amy's progress, then go to my trailer."

Along a narrow path defined by wire, at the bottom of a ten-foot-wide cylindrical depression, an Afro-American girl in corn-row braids was working a soft brush against the sidewall, her chestnut brown eyes absorbed in concentration. Dressed in long shorts and a man's white shirt, she paused only to say hello.

"It's a long shot, but Amy might find the remains of a kiva here," Nick explained, smiling at Terry. "Your . . . rec room. You can see that the roof is collapsed, but there are indications of the traditional benches. If we find a sipapu, we'll be certain."

"The hole to the underworld from whence all came," said Judith with a historian's sigh.

"Yes, and quite decorative. Some kivas had plaster, elaborately painted in a fresco style. Over a hundred layers sometimes."

The last stop was a set of parallel trenches at the edge of the settlement. "The trash heaps. Middens," Nick said.

Judith nodded, closing her eyes as if shuffling mental file cards. "A medieval word from Old Norse."

"Often containing the most interesting clues, those rabbit bones Walter mentioned. And oddly, there have been burials there in some Anasazi settlements."

"Leaving their dead in dumpsites? Was there no reverence?" asked Terry with an expression of mild disgust.

"Not an indication of disrespect so much as expedience under enemy fire. High officials certainly received ceremony. At Aztec

Ruins, Morris must have hit the ceiling when he uncovered a six-foot-two warrior in one room. The man wore a turkey-feather cloak, a basketry shield, and wooden swords. Nearby were mosaic pendants of abalone and a seventy-five-foot necklace containing forty thousand beads." He clapped his student on the shoulder. "Your job would have been to count them."

Walter cocked his head, his voice rising. "Made of turquoise. Do you know that ants love turquoise? They collect it in their colonies."

"Burials in the living quarters, too. How strange." Judith said, her voice trailing off.

"Occasionally a jar interment of an infant or newborn. Many adults might indicate a siege. But they had no traditional graveyards. Or at least we haven't discovered any. Another mystery—perhaps they cremated the remains."

"Now for the pièce de resistance," he added, as he led them to the tiny trailer. Curious, they poked their heads through the door to see storage cabinets, a hot plate, and a single bed covered with boxes and papers. A case of Kraft Dinner hinted at utilitarian cuisine. "Not exactly a palace. There's barely room for me. I bunk in a tent unless the wind's up."

He removed a shoebox from a shelf, a twinkle in his eye as he gauged their interest. "Have a seat," he offered, pointing to a circle of webbed folding chairs.

Tissue paper revealed half of a small, unprepossessing bowl. "Emery gray. Pottery was not their strong point. I was hoping to find the black-on-gray Sevier or Snake Valley variety, which often overlaps this area." Then he selected a plastic bag containing tissue-wrapped objects. He opened one and passed it to Judith. "These have repaid every sore muscle."

"Dominoes. But with cross-hatches and parallel lines instead of dots," she said, passing them to Terry.

"Good guess," Nick said. "They're gaming pieces. The red pigmentation is unique to Fremont artifacts. You might be holding chips from the world's first casino."

Terry handled the pieces with the delicacy awarded a live creature. They felt almost warm. She struggled to envision a stark world, peopled by a hardy band who husbanded water-like jewels. At the ruins of Wupatki and the outlier Wukoki, the aptly named Sinaguas (without water) had occupied the desert places near Sunset Crater, at one with the elements instead of subverting them to grow grass in Phoenix golf courses. Yet they were not dour peons consigned to endless toil, their round ballcourt a poignant reminder of the human need for amusement and recreation.

With her toe, Judith rolled dry, round brown pellets toward a delicate three-petaled mauve and white blossom with a fringe of bright yellow hairs. "The rabbits witnessed this history, and certainly they're still multiplying according to reputation. What else did the Fremont eat?"

"That's a sego lily. Utah state flower," Nick replied. "The bulbous root was cooked by the natives, and the Mormons followed suit, quick to adopt good ideas. Although estimates list over twelve thousand edible plants, the proverbial trio seems to be corn, beans, and squash, a nutritious combination, provided that they got enough, which often they didn't."

Walter nodded. "The droughts from 1250–1300 may have chased them south."

"That's one theory. Prior to that, this area wasn't so dry. The streams had fish. Deer ran the hills. Hunter-gatherers could cover a hundred miles in a few days. Glyphs have pictured bighorn sheep, a cousin of the Navajo flocks. As for supplements, at higher altitudes piñon nuts were a staple. Packrats love them, leaving their own furry genealogy. Paleozoologists trace some nests back hundreds of years. Ricegrass seeds, painstakingly accumulated, may have been part of the Fremont diet as well as flowers."

"Even cactus?" Terry asked, remembering the abundant chollas.

"Nopales in Spanish. Tex-Mex cuisine uses not only the fruit of the prickly pear, but the pads. Big city supermarkets carry jars of them. Kind of slimy and vinegary, an acquired taste."

At only eight o'clock in the southerly latitudes, the sun was shrinking behind the burgundy hills and darkness was unfolding quickly. As they were leaving, Judith turned to Nick, her face alive with anticipation. "I'd like to volunteer if you need another pair of hands." She looked at Terry. "Just for a few days. We'll probably be moving on." She gave Walter a salute. "Chaco's on the list when we head back east."

"Delighted to have you. Lunch is our dubious treat, but dress for the sun."

Judith asked tentatively, "Would a dog be allowed? Well behaved, of course. Ducks are his only weakness, and I haven't seen one since we crossed the Missouri."

"I remember your little guy from Devil's Garden. Everyone will want to feed him, though. Does he like jerky? It's our favorite snack."

When Nick excused himself to answer Amy's call, Walter walked them back to the truck. Sensing that the students were a tight group, Terry asked, "Were you a friend of Melanie's?"

"W . . . well," he stammered again in social turmoil. "I liked her, even though she kept to herself. Sometimes she used pretty harsh words. 'Cannibals,' she called the Anasazi. Not too smart. Nick read her the riot act several times. You can't stay here for months and make people angry. A small community has a lot of power over visitors."

"Power? What do you mean?" Judith asked, trading glances with her niece.

He rearranged his bony frame like an itchy trilobite. "Easy enough. Out of propane at the service station. And most of us don't carry much cash. We charge gas and food, and we buy groceries often because we don't have refrigeration except for ice."

"Did something happen with Melanie?" Kaya's words at the restaurant tickled her memory.

"She told me that once at the Shell station, refilling the Jeep, the woman said her card wouldn't work. She had to leave her wallet behind for security and come back to the dig to borrow money from me. She was pretty frosted about that. The card worked fine everywhere else."

Suddenly they looked up at an unholy chortle, a flash of black above. Two ravens rose and fell together in the twilight, fighting over a long ribbon, white against the sky. It might have been the viscera of an unlucky beast.

Chapter Ten

Terry was left to her own devices the next day when Judith, fortified with a pocket of aspirins, drove out to Nick's dig after remarking that it was high time she took the wheel. Terry enjoyed a leisurely pancake breakfast and tidied the trailer. Catching up on reading, she shuffled selections from the Borders bookstore in Albuquerque and selected *100 Roadside Wildflowers of Southwest Woodlands.* A photo she'd taken at Sunset Crater in Arizona had captured her interest: dense, willowy terminal spikes like a starlet's yellow tendrils blowing in the breeze.

Not long after, a knock sounded at the door. Chris Robbins stood hat in one hand, the other holding a delicate purple bouquet interspersed with ornamental grasses. A faint, lemony perfume filled the trailer.

Terry welcomed him with a smile, burying her face in the fragile blossoms. She hadn't expected to see him again. "Irises. Where did you find those beauties?"

"No flower shop in two hundred miles. From my secret sources. Anyway, I took a chance that you'd still be here. Gave myself the day off like an indulgent boss and thought you might enjoy a hike." He surveyed the book heap with a raised eyebrow. "Wetherill, *Ancient Ruins of the Southwest.* Do you travel with a library?"

She noticed that he didn't mention *Man Corn,* sitting on top. Probably as prickly about it as were the locals. "My aunt and I are avid readers, a retired schoolteacher and a suburban journalist, so it must be in the blood. Anything you'd recommend as a westerner?"

"My guru Edward Abbey's *Desert Solitudes.* He was a ranger at Arches. Even in the Fifties he became disgusted with the commercialization of the park system. 'Natural Moneymints,' he called them. Lockstepping sheep milling around Old Faithful or bleating up the steps to the Mount Rushmore overlook. Teddy Roosevelt was a prophet ahead of his time in founding the national park system, but how could he foresee that places designed for thousands would attract millions? If you get hooked on Abbey, try *The Monkey Wrench Gang.* A bunch of eco-terrorists before the name was invented planned to blow up Glen Canyon Dam to save the mighty Colorado from Lake Powell, a playground polluted by jet skis, houseboats and *E. coli* now."

Terry scribbled the name on a pad. "I was only a baby in the Seventies, but my aunt claims I'd make a pathetic hippie. Too conservative."

Chris picked up the flower photograph. "The exposure is perfect."

"It's nothing artsy, just for identification. The guidebook says it's prince's plume. The crucifer family. Doesn't look anything like broccoli." She gave a small, self-deprecating laugh.

"A very complex plant. It utilizes selenium in place of sulphur, unlike mammals, which find it toxic. But the kicker is that selenium often accompanies uranium deposits. Ergo . . ."

"An instant mine site. How did a pilot get to be such an expert?"

"Biology major, my mother's idea. Versatile enough, but the birds and the bees don't pay the bills. I switched to business administration."

She arranged the bouquet in a plastic Taco Bell cup decorated with a grinning Chihuahua, filling it from the tap. Chris noticed the closed door to the bathroom and cocked his thumb. "Your aunt is invited, but she might find it a bit taxing. I hope she's recovered from that flight."

"Definitely. Her stamina puts me to shame. Anyway, she won't be back until dinner. So where did you want to go? I've read about those slot canyons. They sound fabulous, but they can be . . ." Realizing that she was sounding presumptuous, she let her voice trail off.

He thought for a moment, creasing his forehead. "I was going to suggest going over to Capital Reef. The Waterpocket Fold is surreal. If slots are your preference, Zion has some great ones, but the chopper's out ferrying tourists. Close on we have Spooky and Peekaboo on the Hole-in-the-Rock, but the access is a long, hot walk best made at dawn."

She glanced at the microwave clock. "It's only ten. How about if I make a quick lunch while you think about it?" At his pleased nod, she turned to the fridge and grabbed a summer sausage, a tomato, and a hunk of Swiss cheese, assembling sandwiches. She tossed oranges and bottles of water into her pack.

As she flashed him an inquiring glance, he said, "The Pine Creek hike near Box Death Hollow Wilderness might be the perfect compromise for a late start."

"Box Death." Terry shuddered. "Sounds hot."

"That's a brutal trail. There's no water for the first eleven miles, and then you're drowned for the next three. Pine Creek is gentle and inviting. Lots of shade. Trust me."

Chris waited outside while Terry dressed in loose-fitting pants, a long-sleeved cotton shirt, and sturdy hiking boots. Then they headed north out of the park, along the highway briefly, and up Pine Creek Road until Chris parked beside a faded trailhead sign. Standing on a criss-cross pattern of mountain bike treads, he shouldered Terry's daypack, then retrieved a high-tech hiking stick from behind the truck seat.

"What a beauty," she said, her eyes widening with approval as he demonstrated the spring action and adjustable length. The tip of the cork handle was angled to nestle into the palm.

"We can go as far as we like. The path meanders back and forth along the stream, so cool your toes if you feel the urge. If you're wondering why I chose the place, it's because the ecosystem is similar to slot canyons."

"Not as fatal, I hope. What about that disaster at Antelope Canyon a few years ago? It sounded terrible," she said as they began their hike, falling into step together.

He shook his head as they followed a dirt trail toward a babbling stream. On the far side, a tall cliff cast shadows over the scene. "Ten people died when a heavy rain fifty miles away rushed through the narrows. As they say, 'more water than you want in less time than you have.' The guides should have monitored the forecasts. Every tour business has crucial responsibilities. First sign of a storm, my guys never lift off the tarmac."

After they crossed, stepping on handy rocks, he pointed the stick toward a sheltered oasis in a shady corner, maidenhair fern and plush mosses clinging to the sandstone. "Beauty is tempting. To be quite literal, photographers have died and gone to heaven. When you're walking in soft, rock-muted light, you're on another planet in another time."

After another fifteen minutes, they entered a gorge where grasses and sedges, protected by the high walls, formed lush colonies. Suddenly, Terry heard a familiar drone. "Bugs," she said, swiping her neck and wiping blood from her fingers. "That mosquito hitched a ride from Ohio. I didn't think I'd need repellent in the desert." She stopped with a quizzical look. "I thought I'd find sand and sage. But the variety of landscape is amazing."

He flicked his ear with a laugh. "The downside of water. But you're right. It's what we call 'life-zones,' the changing vegetation at different elevations. The Monument ranges from forty-five hundred to eighty-three hundred feet. The desert's at the bottom, but higher up you'll find grassy steppes, sage, and piñon-juniper woodlands, even ponderosas."

She stopped and touched a bush with thistle-like leaves and small, yellow ray flowers. "Sticky," she said, wiping her hand. "It's so alien looking, isn't it?"

"Gumweed. These species have evolved methods of surviving drought and making the most of their nutrients. Miniaturized leaves, hairs to reduce air dehydration, thick, waxy surfaces, deep taproots. Plants are more intelligent than Einstein."

"I've always spoken well of them," she said with a nod. She couldn't believe she was having a conversation on the sensibilities of plants and loving every minute.

On they walked, crossing and recrossing the lazy stream, the dirt path beckoning into canyons shrinking and growing like pig-bloated boas. Ponderosa pines laddered their arms to the sky, the reddish-brown bark a roadmap. "Box canyon. Is that the idea? No way out?" Terry asked.

"Never watched old westerns? Cattle have an annoying habit of getting lost in box canyons. For my tenth birthday, Mom gave me Zane Grey's *Riders of the Purple Sage*. Read it until it nearly fell apart. Shake hands with a romantic born a century too late."

She accepted his large, gentle hand in the spirit of the moment. Strong and weathered with honest work, a contrast to Jeff's clumsy paddlings. "Tell me the plot."

He swept branches aside and guided her to a wide ledge framed by the small, leathery leaves of the Gambel's oak. Protected from the sun, they sat and sipped from the water bottles. "I'll cut it short and sweet. Guy's a stand-up character, tired of fighting lawless mobs, girl falls in love with him, and they dream of retreating into a Shangri-La canyon with a balanced rock at the entrance."

"What happens? I hope it's not tragic."

Chris's narrative slowed for emphasis as Terry clasped her arms around her knees, leaning forward in anticipation. "Final scene: as the bad guys are sighted in the distance, she turns to him. 'Roll the stone, Lassiter. I love you!' "

"Wow. And does he?" She stumbled on her words like a teenager at a prom, feeling a sudden kinship with Walter. "Roll the stone?"

His eyes misting, Chris broke off a piece of moss, teasing its velvet with a finger. He swallowed, pausing as if in disbelief at the question. "Of course. If you had all the food and water you wanted . . . and a partner, wouldn't this be paradise enough?"

A wave of heat from a downdraft broke the reverie and delivered her reluctantly back to reality. "I'll never be that romantic. Too practical, I guess." She took a deep breath. "But what a great movie."

"Exactly, and you can take your pick. A classic story reinvents itself with each generation. Tom Mix in the silent. Robert Montgomery in the Thirties. Ed Harris in the Nineties."

"Some cold January night I'll have to rent the videos. Judith and I have sworn a blood oath never to put a TV in the trailer."

Leading her past a maze of box elders, he gestured up to a flat wall that seemed pocked with haphazard marks as she shaded her eyes from the sun peeking around the junipers at the rimrock. "You saw those mountain bike tracks. And quads are standard equipment for ten-year-olds. I'm surprised these beauties are still untouched," Chris said in bitter wonderment. "Then again, the riders are probably going too fast to enjoy the scenery."

"Moki steps," Chris said, as they climbed pecked footholds

to another ledge. Circles, squares, and geometric designs of petroglyphs dizzied her as she tried to force a contemporary realism onto the montages. She found a stylized mountain goat shot with arrows, a human figure with another within. A being within a being. Hesitant to touch them, Terry took out her camera, read their features like an elusive book, written and overwritten by centuries of passersby, unknown to each other, their only tie a need to say, "I was here."

"I haven't seen Newspaper Rock near Canyonlands. Is it this good?" she asked.

"Good is relative. There are thousands of newspaper rocks, each one with unique features. Enjoy your personal subscription."

Lunchtime found them sheltered by the stream below a rock alcove seventy feet high. Far above, splashes of desert varnish trickled like paint cans spilled over the rim. Bacteria and microfungi cemented a mix of airborne dust, clay, and water, reflecting black manganese and reddish iron. The lush riparian world unfolded itself as the sun made its elliptical journey, casting eerie shadows across the hard-packed path. Cottonwoods, water birch, willow, and bushes with feathery pink stalks surrounded them in a fairy tale setting.

"I've noticed these exotic plants, but I haven't looked them up," she said as she passed a sandwich to Chris.

He laughed, tickling her face with one brushy end. "The pestilent tamarisks. Introduced by well-meaning settlers who didn't imagine that, carried on the wind, they would chase out native species. There's a movement to eradicate them in some areas. But I share your opinion. Beauty is subjective, and often the ubiquitous is considered ugly, the rare sublime."

"Pity the poor seagulls and pigeons." A canyon wren twittered its plaintive song. Surfing the thermals, a golden eagle surveyed his realm, a stranger to rocky confinement, a noble king of open spaces.

Terry leaned her head against the warm stone, a solid pillow form-fitted to her body, then closed her eyes to record an entry in her memory bank. Back in prosaic Ohio, could she ever re-summon these complex sensations, even with pictures that did slim justice? Her smile sent Chris a benediction.

"You love it as much as I do. Too bad that you'll have to head east soon," he said, forming the sentence as a question, the tracework around his eyes warm and appealing, a man of action and experience, not ledgers. He moved closer, then pulled back and stretched his arm.

"We wouldn't have stayed this long if my aunt had found an old friend." She avoided the details, unwilling to convey paranoid suspicions. "A retired lady at Sunset Years. Apparently she's moved to Washington. Then we found that girl in the Batty Caves." She shuddered, suddenly chilled despite the torpor. She didn't know why she hadn't told him earlier, but she hated to spoil the beauty of the moment.

Chris cupped a hand around his chin and nodded slowly. "So you're the tourists who stumbled on that tragedy. Your names weren't mentioned in the story. How terrible for you."

Terry looked at the Minolta, one picture left. She focused on a stalk of small white flowers, did a point-and-shoot, then waited for the rewind's hum. "My mind's like this camera. I have a mental photograph that bites like a persistent fly. Her sad little body. The dusty room. Those huge doors. Something seemed wrong about the idea of an accident. But gut feelings aren't evidence. Guess I make a poor reporter. That's why I'm stuck on the Society page."

"You're a sensitive observer. What a grim introduction to our country. I've seen more than one innocent life cut short in this unforgiving climate. And it's never pretty. But an accident? Why torment yourself? Or do you feel that the fate and chance that led you to the body gave you a special responsibility, a mission, if I can use a historical word?"

She explained her friendship with Nick and visits to the dig. "The girl made enemies with her theories on cannibalism." She found herself rattling on while Chris listened intently. Finally, she related the incident at the restaurant. "I don't know what to make of Tocho Nuvamsa. He seemed so violent. You must know him in this area of limited population."

"Tocho and I go back a long way. He used to do tricky mechanical work for me before he went to the Gulf War. Guy could repair a propeller with a paper clip. Grenade accident. With only one hand . . ." Chris sighed in resignation, brushing at a pesky gnat. "When he came home, I offered him the only job I could. Mainly cleanup. Instead, he got a grant to train as a ranger at a community college in Salt Lake. I was pleased for him. He's a bright guy."

"Was he married then?"

A stone dropped into the deep pools of his mesmerizing blue eyes, circles amid circles, and his voice grew somber. "No, but he attracted every girl in town, good-looking guy like that. He was rough on them, though. More than one sported a shiner after a weekend. Blame it on alcohol, or trying to feel like a man again after his loss by beating the hell out of someone. Kaya's a sweetheart, but she had a helluva time in the beginning. Nearly left him twice. Maybe now with another baby coming, he'll settle down."

As they packed up to go, Terry asked, "What's this flower I just photographed? It's so delicate but the perfume is delicious."

"An alcove death camus." He laughed as she jumped back. "Don't worry. Only the bulb is poisonous. Fifty thousand years of trial and error. Aren't we lucky?"

Back at the trailer, Chris said, "I hope this won't be our last meeting. I have a list of a hundred things to show you."

Hardly remembering what she had muttered, so flattered at his attentions, Terry went inside to find Judith reading about Chaco. Her legendary red clam sauce, rich with garlic, oregano and extra-virgin olive oil, bubbled in a pot, vermicelli ready to go. She glanced up with a mock pout. "Finally, you're back. I thought I was going to have to eat everything myself. Where in God's name did you go? You didn't leave a note."

Terry questioned herself with a frown. Why had she left so hastily, forgetting her common sense as soon as she'd seen Chris's handsome face? She told Judith about the afternoon and got a quick reprieve.

"Sounds like he's very interested. A quantum leap from Jeff," her aunt said with a sniff. "That boy always reminded me of Van Johnson, slightly damp in mien and attitude."

Terry tossed her a mockingly evil glare, fending off innuendos about Chris's intentions. Would she see him again? Their vacation days were limited.

Later, as they sat down to enjoy their meal, Judith assumed an expression of purpose. "While you've been gallivanting about, I've been at work on our problem. Bless that phone card."

"You called Randell-Randolph again? What for?"

"Not him. The cobwebbed synapses in this tired brain connected. A friend of mine lives in Seattle. Dick Loney, a retired Case Western Reserve librarian nearly as old as the late Queen Mother. Never married. Owned Yorkies. Probably still does. Yappy little brats with silly bow ties in their hair."

"How old? What can—"

"A bit of exaggeration. But Dewey's disciples know everything. And what they don't know, they can find out." Judith sprinkled Parmesan cheese with abandon.

Terry gave her a skeptical look and forked into a juicy clam. She was ravenous from the hike.

"I called him with that number for Deborah's alleged nephew. Track it through reverse directory or some such, he said. Then he'll go out to the address and snoop around."

"He doesn't mind?"

"Mind? He's born to serve, like my beloved Adlai Stevenson. 'Eggheads, unite! You have nothing to lose but your yolks.' Can you imagine such humility in a presidential candidate? Of course I was too young to vote for the dear man, but I worked the schoolyard." She pondered for a moment. "Dick has all kinds of connections, even in government, so I supplied him with Deborah's Lakewood Schools Pension number. That funny combination. 6666. We used to laugh about the diabolic possibilities."

Chapter Eleven

Ice cream on a blistering day transcended state lines. They pulled into the Escalante Tasti-Freeze after lunch. While a chocolate malt attracted Terry, with a rare concession to her weight, Judith opted for frozen raspberry yogurt. All the picnic tables in the adjoining park were occupied by seniors. Thelma sat alone under a sun-dappled cottonwood, notebook in hand, jotting as she shaded her eyes and mumbled to herself. Looking up as they approached, she beamed and motioned them over. Dove was nowhere in sight, but a rusted white van with the Sunset Years logo was parked on the street.

"Find the dear Poodle?" She gurgled from a large plastic cup of cola or root beer with a blob of ice cream. "Or was it a terrier? Little dogs are all alike. Even Porky has his bad moments, though Deborah loved him like a child. Coaxed Dove to let her buy him from a visitor. Even slept with him. The very idea. Do you have a dog?" Without waiting for an answer, she continued. "Now I myself owned a Bouvier. Sharpest pencil in the pack. She never would be so foolish to leave the property like they do. Did you find her, then?"

Terry swallowed, trying to navigate the pronoun maze. "Her? You mean the graves? Dove told us that the place was over a century old."

She paddled her lip, a time frame in her muzzled brain warping into a Mobius strip. "He couldn't have been at it that long, could he? How about his father or grandfather? When Jack Kennedy was killed, I was covering the mayor's daughter's wedding. Do you recall where you were?" With her mascara leaking in the heat, she resembled an ancient raccoon. She raised a stenciled eyebrow thick as Groucho's moustache and pointed at Judith. "You look old enough."

Judith choked on her yogurt, dabbing at a drip on her shirt. "Well, I . . ."

Thelma fingered a long, curly chin hair, the gobbler wattles on her neck jiggling. "Was it Omaha or Phoenix? It's not all corn pone, you know. The bluffs of northwest Nebraska are covered with picturesque sand dune sculptures like fairy castles. I was born in Crawford. Father was an officer at Fort Robinson. Then it was a state park." Her pencil drew a tic-tac-toe in the dust on the wooden table, added three x's and crossed them. "One, two, three. Deb and Blanche Boggs and Adrienne Spahn, like that ball player, unless I dropped a stitch, so to speak. And I never can in my job. I have to know who was at the party. Blanche lived longer than a Galapagos tortoise, maybe one hundred and ten. Tell the age by the lovely, old-fashioned Shakespearean name. Trey, Blanche, and Sweetheart, his dogs. *King Lear* is my favorite. 'How sharper than a serpent's tooth—' "

"Are Blanche and Adrienne still—" Judith gave Terry a nudge.

"My son James never comes to visit and thinks he's getting all my money. I saw Larry Olivier play it at the Old Vic. My third husband Michael and I sailed across the pond on the *Queen Mary*. We had the second largest stateroom. POSH. Port out, starboard home. Best for breezes." She fumbled with her ragged pad, overwritten horizontally and vertically, smeared with erasures. Her lips licked the tip of the pencil. "I didn't get your names, you know. And I must, for the record."

As Judith fumbled a reply, Terry shot her a glance, their eyes meeting. How demented was the poor soul? So far her clue had proved maddeningly accurate. But three women? Mass murder in the Southwest?

A shadow spread across the table, alarming the scruffy sparrow hopping boldly at the far end to peck at crumbs. A wracking cough announced Dove. He pulled out a handkerchief, then turned away for a moment. Finally, he produced a dubious grin. "You must be enjoying Escalante. Most folks can't abide the summer temperatures."

Judith spoke brightly. "Ohio's humidity bowls us over, and that's blissfully absent so far."

"Monsoons are coming. Gets a mite wetter then. Great sky shows, too." He settled his hat and extended an arm to Thelma, who gazed into his eyes and blushed under papery lilac cheeks. Off they strolled like a companionable married couple.

Judith shivered. "Such a nice, ordinary man. The banality of evil. Hanna Arendt was on the money about the Nazis. I'm sure he's involved in Deborah's disappearance."

"He sounds sick to me. Something worse than allergies or a summer cold." Terry watched Dove shepherd his charges into the van and drive off in a cloud of oily exhaust, then said, "Those odd names should help the investigation. When is Dick going to contact us? Maybe we should get a cell phone. How far would we have to drive to find a store?"

"Nick said they didn't work out here. Anyway, I told Dick to call the number at the booth by the laundry at eight tonight. I still see that dog at her grave. So Porky was hers. Why would she leave without him?" Her eyes misted over as she hugged herself in the rising breeze. "If only we'd come out last summer."

After a quiet dinner of Hormel chili and skillet corn bread, they toured the park perimeter, nodding at others out for modified exercise. Having peed Tut, they passed a silvery Airstream trailer surrounded by a plastic white picket fence. In hand-painted planters, sweet William bloomed along with abundant marigolds. "Amazon Village," a routed wood sign said. Two gray parrots browsed the carefully watered grass plot. "You're a bad bird. I'll pull your tail."

"Help, Mommy! Help!" The smaller bird danced fretfully, raising one gnarly claw in a defensive move and rolling beady eyes.

If dogs could suffer nervous breakdowns, Tut looked like a candidate. Ears pricked, back hairs erect, his world turned upside down as his body language signaled a lunge. Talking ducks or feathery people? With a jerk, Judith reclaimed his attention.

At five minutes to eight, they hovered around the phone, fending off a man with a cane by using anxious life-and-death motions. On the ring, Judith answered.

"Yes, this is she," she said, nestling the receiver behind one ear. A minute passed. "You don't say."

She winked at Terry, who was biting her lip. "You don't say," she added, nestling into the phone like a lover.

"What's going on?" Terry nudged closer.

"He doesn't say," Judith replied, elbowing her niece. Then she grew serious. "101 degrees? You're sure? Eighty is a dangerous age. Summer flu can be treacherous. Drink plenty of fluids. Have you tried echinacea or . . ." Nodding as she listened, before hanging up she told him to call again at eight when he had more information.

Deep in thought, Judith marched back to the trailer while Terry tagged at her heels, a black look on her face. In the kitchen, Tut began scratching with vigor. Judith lifted him by the scruff of his neck, grabbed the flea spray, ran to the door and bombed him on the steps. All three coughed until tears ran down their faces. Then as he galloped for the bed, Judith dropped into the breakfast booth and whistled a sigh of relief.

Terry felt a warm rush spread across her cheeks as her voice rose. "I'll get you for this. What did Dick find out?"

Judith put her finger to her mouth. "Be quiet. We don't want anyone overhearing. This park is a small town within a town. A few people who live here year 'round might recognize names."

"Get to the point," Terry said with a soft growl, her patience tried by her aunt's mysterious demeanor.

"Randolph. Ring a bell?"

"If you don't—"

"That Seattle number. Said his name was Randell. But the house belongs to a Mike Randolph." She mouthed the last word and nodded in satisfaction, like a spider encasing a fly. "Dick drove over on the pretext of selling AARP subscriptions. The man is . . . well, Dick's discreet. Places him in my geriatric ballpark. Far too old to be Deborah's nephew. It's clearly a plot. Did they think we were complete idiots?"

"Maybe he's Dove's brother." She watched Tut lick his rubber chili toy, eyeing them with mortification about the bombing. "But we can't tell the sheriff about the graves without looking like a two-woman crime wave detector."

"You are naive, my dear. Don't you watch television? An anonymous tip." Judith gave a casual wave. "Since everyone knows about call tracing, I'll use the phone at the Shell station. Wearing Baggies, of course."

"Baggies?"

Escalante's streets were dark and empty, only a lone bicyclist pulling a trailer heading for the local hostel. The Shell station was lit, but no one was at the cash. "Bingo," Judith said, fingering two quarters from the coin return, then stuffing her winnings into the slot. She opened the phone book for the number, dialed, then lowered her voice. "Ah tell you that a passel of bodies is layin' way back of Dove Randolph's place," she said, slurring her words and affecting a credible southern accent. "I'm talkin' graves. Just a concerned citizen doin' what's right." And then she gave directions to the Poodle and hung up. "Bad grammar should help the verisimilitude, but maybe 'passel' went too far."

Terry broke into pee-your-pants laughter, remembering that Judith had played Amanda in *The Glass Menagerie* at the Lakewood Little Theater. "But what's his motive? Where's the money? If any of the residents had the income Thelma bragged about, they'd be in Phoenix, not out here in the sticks. The ranch is no showplace, and the van's on life support. There's no reason to believe Dove's anything but a kind and generous man . . . and a sick one."

"Illness doesn't preclude criminal acts. Simple greed, gambling debts, a demanding girlfriend, even setting up for a cozy retirement. When the stakes go down, desperation goes up. Another cliché for your collection."

They spent the afternoon taking the short loop hike at Escalante Petrified Forest State Park. The "Trail of Sleeping Rainbows" rose quickly to the top of several hills, winding its way around prime pieces of rock. Taking souvenirs was strictly forbidden, according to the ranger, who also said that an estimated twelve tons of the material already decorated the backyards of Peoria and Hackensack. Buried for 100 million years, the tree's wood cells had been slowly replaced with silicon dioxide.

"A regular rock candy mountain," Terry said, taking shots of a boulder splashed with crimson and purple, egg yolk and cyan blue, and another full of burnt orange.

Judith stopped to admire a two-foot chunk of multicolored rock. "I saw piles of it for sale on street corners when we drove through Holbrook. But a tourist can't pack it out. A double standard."

Once again, Terry felt the shard in her pocket, a dumb thing that was trying to speak to her in its own way.

That evening, passing the office en route to the laundry building, garbage bags bulging over their backs like pedlars, they saw Gail talking to a triple-chinned lady, a cigarette with a one-inch ash drooping from her mouth and a familiar parrot perching on the shoulder of her Hawaiian muu-muu. Her head seemed attached without the articulation of a neck. Gail gave them a desultory wave, but her usually friendly face wore a disturbing frown. Judith left with the clothes, so Terry joined the pair.

The park owner broke off her talk. "Meet Joyce Minor, one of our full-timers. She has the Airstream by the showers. This here's Terry Hart from O-hi-o." After nods were exchanged, Gail continued.

"Poor devils dug all morning. Reggie was plenty pissed off. First time the old fart saw a sunrise in decades. Found dick all but charcoal. Dove said they have pit BBQ's there on holidays. Take the old folks out in a buckboard. Roast a suckling pig, speaking of which, guess the sheriff feels pretty near like a mortal fool."

Terry affected a sharp, surprised breath. "Dove Randolph? We went riding at his ranch. What happened? Were they looking for something?"

Gail flung the dregs of her coffee cup into the dust, her face flaming. "Some cockamanny anonymous call about bodies buried on his land. Jesus, Mary and Joseph on a saltshaker. Got to be a practical joke. Pretty mean one, though. Doesn't sound like our kids either, brats though some are."

Terry swallowed her discomfort like one of Judith's B-75 bombs. "He seemed so kind, and he takes good care of his seniors."

"Hello, good-bye," the parrot chortled in an oddly disconnected voice resembling a deaf John Malkovich's.

Remembering her sweet parakeet Winkie, whose habit of floor-walking had led to an early death, Terry reached out a tentative hand, but Joyce issued a warning tut-tut. "That beak can crack walnuts. Birdies are one-person creatures." As if cognizant, the parrot ruffled its feathers and commenced a studious hunt for mites. "Anyways, before Falco here got talkative, I was about to say that my baby sister Charmaine's been at the ranch nigh on five years. Jerk-off husband worked her worse than an ox at their Provo dry cleaners that went belly up, then divorced her and vamoosed to Vegas with a ditzy blonde hairdresser, and him bald as a doorknob." With each detail, she gesticulated with her batwing arms like a pigeon at lift-off.

Terry suppressed a smile. "How awful."

"Poor Charmy high and dry. No Social Security. Living on beans from what I could spare from my Monkey-Ward pension. Too proud to take the welfare. Not that a bird could buy sunflower seeds on that."

Gail nodded vigorously. "And Dove gave her a good home for free. Found some phoney title that gave her self-respect. Activity Director or something. Counts the Monopoly money."

"And with her as-marr, she could hardly breathe let alone work." Joyce pounded her ample chest. "Wasn't the first he helped either. Bought the old rummy Ralph Pool a wheelchair after his stroke. Dove's a pure Latter Day Saint, even if he is a Baptist." She turned to Gail with a look that could fry eggs. "Who in hell would want to cause trouble for that sweet man?"

Terry shifted uneasily, hoping the women's talents didn't extend to mind reading, then excused herself as her aunt left the laundry and they returned to the trailer. "Here's a twist about Dove," she said, relating the conversation.

Judith pooched out her lower lip. "I was so sure."

"He even told us they were graves. I didn't see any charcoal. Did the sheriff go to the wrong place?"

"Maybe. Or did Dove get there first and . . ." Judith broke off with a shudder.

"Did he play it safe after he knew we had seen the site? Did somebody warn him?"

Together they mouthed the name, linked pinkies in the family tradition and made an unspoken wish. "Thelma's mind could swirl faster than a weathervane in a Kansas tornado," Judith continued, raising an eyebrow.

"Then where could the bodies be?"

"You've seen this country. Those women could be reburied anywhere in the Monument."

Terry grew sober. "Whatever's going on, it's a conspiracy. I wouldn't be surprised if everyone at the ranch knew about it."

Chapter Twelve

Sweat and red soil stained Judith's clothes as she stripped them off, held her nose, and stuffed them into the laundry bag. "Enough dust on me to plant potatoes. I've got to hit the shower. Sorry about being late for dinner." She jiggled her poundage into the tiny bathroom, and the sound of rushing water complemented the "Fountains of Rome" CD. In quarters that demanded a contortionist, nobody could affect modesty or expect privacy. The fact that neither wore makeup other than a swipe of lipstick and a dust of powder helped keep the clutter in check.

Terry took the opportunity to run Tut to the poo-poo area, allowing him to linger over p-mail. The park was quiet, half the spaces free. Two young boys on mountain bikes rode circles in the dust, stopping to point at Tut in childish laughter. They wore tank tops and shorts, revealing scabby knees and elbows.

"Kinda dog's that? I ain't never seen such a weird one," asked the smaller. The other boy, with a familiar red cowlick, smiled at her.

"He's a Nova Scotia Duck Toller. Comes from Eastern Canada."

"Dollar?" the redhead asked.

"Duck TOL-ler. Toller comes from an old word meaning to lure. A hunting dog. The breed was developed over a hundred years ago. Its white-tipped tail entices ducks from the marshes." She asked, "Have I seen you two in town?"

"We come in from the ranch when we earn privileges. Chad's a friend of ours. He built a neat pithouse."

Now she realized that she had seen him in the store with Aggie. "Second Chance Ranch? How do you like it there?"

His companion smirked, full of bravado. "It's different from Chicago. Kids come here from all over. A few crazy ones, though, like Stevie."

"Yah, that dumb guy sees UFOs. Wooooo woooo." He waved his arms in a swooping motion.

"Knock it off. He saved your butt when you were smoking behind the barn."

Terry couldn't help grinning. UFOs? A Southwest phenomenon, even far from the fabled Area 51 near Roswell. "Where was that?"

"The night he took off from our camping trip over by Hole-in-the-Rock. Said he saw colored lights in the hills. Flickering, moving up kinda snaky, back and forth. Probably made it up to sound like a big shot after he got caught."

Anything to do with Hole-in-the-Rock claimed her attention. "When was this?"

"Uh. Day after my birthday. May 30."

As the boys rode off, Terry searched her memory. May 30, the very day Melanie had disappeared.

Back at the RV, washing down aspirins with a glass of Clos Du Bois sauvignon blanc, Judith sat on the sofa bed rubbing her hips while Terry put the cabbage rolls into the microwave, the last frozen food from the Pierogi Palace at the West Side Market. "Why did I waste my life teaching? In my time, you spoiled post-feminist, few women could enter the priestly professions. OSU's vet school had one opening. Even for doctorates in the humanities, you had to be a plug-ugly bulldog with no fiancé lurking in the bushes. I refused to play by those sexist rules."

"And you would have had a tough time finding a job or getting promoted, bumping into that glass ceiling." Terry had heard these complaints from an era as distant to her as the Renaissance. When her grandmothers had been born, only men could vote.

"I've learned more in one day than in years of graduate school. The Law of Superposition."

"Superpo . . ." Terry took a sip of wine, crisp and flinty.

"What's on the bottom is oldest."

Terry broke out in a laugh. "They're probably too tired to care."

Judith gave her a queer scan, twigged to the joke, then rolled her eyes like an indulgent parent. "Sometimes nature or utility rearranges materials. Roofs collapse. Broken jugs are recycled as chimney pots."

"I see a Nobel Prize in your future. What else?"

"Dendrochronology." Judith formed the syllables tooth-by-tooth. "Tree-ring dating of timber supports."

"So that's the secret," Terry said with a straight face.

In pontification mode, Judith furrowed her bushy brows. "Doesn't work with cottonwoods, though. Slurpy, unreliable, something about the cellular structure."

"So . . ." Terry made a camera-revving motion as the microwave beeped.

"So then they do ceramic cross-dating."

Terry got up to portion out the dinner and asked over her shoulder, more from politeness than interest, "Which is—"

"Match the pottery and masonry to other sites that use more reliable pine, allowing for trade routes. Walter told us about the differences between Chacoan and Mesa Verdean brickwork."

As they sat down to eat, Terry told her about meeting the boys and hearing about the strange lights. "Same road, same time. There must be a connection."

"But flying saucers? Probably some desert phenomenon, a trick of light. Kids will say anything."

Exhausted from the day's exertion chasing sticks, getting petted, sniffing remains old and new, plied with jerky as he wandered the dig, Tut snored on the bed, perfuming the air with a tiny bellows.

Later, as Terry poured out the Earl Grey, Judith pointed at her folded legs. "Don't stretch like that. You'll develop hyperflexive knees, and that can hurt."

"Two hundred million Buddhists can't be wrong." Terry dropped a golden dollop of honey into her mug. "Were you working with Walter? I liked him."

"He's going to lend me a book on the Fremont. Still waters, though. That boy might know more than he says."

"About the Fremont? Cannibal evidence?"

"About Melanie. But I can't connect with young people. Decades of teaching have hard-wired my brain." She drilled her cornflower blues across the table. "It seems that they were friends. Or from what my intuition whispers about our shy fellow, he could have been smitten with her."

Terry set down her cup with a curious and wary expression, her motions slowing. "What exactly are you . . ." Her voice trailed off.

Judith's finger outlined the male and female symbols on the table. "So you will ask him about her. 'Pump him' in the vernacular. It'll be easy. Start with his name. I'm sure there's a town called Peebles in southern Ohio. And look sharp. I'll choose your outfit."

"What?" She stood and banged her knee against the table.

Chapter Thirteen

Reluctantly, Terry tagged along with Judith to the dig the next day. Silver-edged cumulus clouds were massing for a shower, humping their backs like the Buckeyes at a goal line stand. Halfway to the site, drops spattered the dusty windshield, lightning slashed a curtain of purple, and minutes later, the sun peeked out like a tardy debutante.

"Mother Nature. As changeable as a woman. Wouldn't it be magnificent to see this place when a real thunderboomer hits?" Judith pointed to a deep arroyo under the wooden bridge, a few trickles fast disappearing into the sand. "But I wouldn't want to be caught down there in a flash flood."

In the parking area, Tut leaped out, running toward a student who called to him. Judith led Terry to a roped-off area around an unprepossessing slab. "Metate," she said. "The grinding stone. Broken ones were recycled as hearths or building material."

"How did it work?"

"Simple. With a mano, a harder material, they reduced dried corn into meal. Basalt for coarse grain, graduating to sandstone for finest." She knelt in demonstration. Judith was famous for making history come alive through costumes and drama. Her annual description of the fall of Constantinople and the slaughter at Hagia Sofia brought other faculty to stand in the rear of her class.

"Took a toll on their teeth, provided they lived past thirty,"

Terry said, running her tongue behind her incisors. "The men went hunting. We stayed home to pat tortillas and crack pine nuts. What a grind."

Rising with a grunt, Judith squeezed her arm. "Nice pun. Now you're liberated, so let's do our own cracking. Have a tète-a-tète with Walter and find out more about Melanie. You're a bit seasoned to be a sex symbol for a mere lad, but who knows? Pick me up at five, will you?" With a snicker and a hitch in her walk, she set off toward a small group working at a wall.

Terry smarted at the tease. The fashionable concept of mature women with young lovers sounded like child molesting. Yet Walter had to be nearly twenty unless he'd entered college as a prodigy.

She found him perched on a canvas camp chair, hunched over a notebook, before him a table of bagged specimens in neatly sorted piles, each labeled. "Looks interesting." With a stretch, she adjusted the white halter Judith had suggested. Her legs were trim and muscular under her long shorts, but she hid the scars of the accident like a reproof at survival.

Walter's large Jersey calf eyes saucered when he turned, and his face colored before he put down his hovering pen. "Days and days go by without much." He indicated a page entitled "Universal Data Form," which appeared to be a cross-section of ground.

"Tell me more." If she ever wanted to cover more than social events, she'd better practice investigative journalism.

"Each layer has a legend. Lines, dots, crosses, they all indicate a different strata, even rodent intrusions or sandstone slabs. The scale is one centimeter to ten centimeters."

"Very precise. What's the purpose?" She tried to lean closer, but lost her balance, grabbing another chair in a clumsy attempt to sit down. Being a femme fatale was hard work. Walter reminded her of an innocent rabbit.

He coughed, edging aside to make room. "Helps us determine the time line. Did something fall in naturally after it was abandoned, or was it destroyed?"

Forget about asking him about the name Peebles. Time to broach the hard part, using a subtle segue. "My aunt's become a convert to the Fremont cause, and her enthusiasm is getting me interested. I never realized how much effort went into a dig. And now that you're a hand short—"

"A hand short?" Behind round, wire-rimmed glasses, his face assumed an owly look accented by tiny, pointed ears. Calf, rabbit, owl—was she constructing a menagerie?

She cleared her throat. "Melanie. Or maybe she didn't make much of a contribution."

"Oh no," he assured her, polishing his glasses with an optical tissue pulled from a pack and peering through them until he was satisfied. "Melanie was a bear for work. She took it to bed with her." He added with an embarrassed smile, "I mean that she was always examining fragments, writing field notes, studying maps and books to correlate patterns of movements. Her hope was . . ." He stopped and looked away.

"What, Walter?"

His face contorted in disgust. "She wanted to find cannibal evidence here, too. The Coombs Site at Boulder was considered by Turner, but narrowly dismissed. Certainly there was more than one murder, though. Blows to the head with a blunt weapon. One burial had arrowpoints under the ribcage, and the leg bones lacked internal cancellous tissue, which often means—"

"Cancell . . . you're losing me here, professor. I flunked anatomy." That lie came easily. She hadn't even taken the subject.

He swallowed in discomfort. "Reaming or scooping indications. A sign of cannibalism. Melanie felt Turner had been too conservative. Ran to Nick with what turned out to be a deer femur. The gang had a big laugh over that, and she didn't talk to anyone for days."

"Sounds humiliating." Terry wiped sweat from her brow as a morning breeze failed to appear to temper the heat. "Didn't any of her friends offer support?"

His voice broke as if unable to choose a register. "One guy really had a case for her. Told everyone to lay off."

"Who was that?" Forget the coy, co-ed mode. Terry returned to reporter style. Short, declarative sentences like Thelma's " 'And who was there?' " She felt a sudden kinship for the woman whose dedication had outlived her gray cells.

"Danny Romero." He shrugged, studiously bland, but one eyebrow twitched like an itchy trilobite. "He . . . left the day she disappeared."

"The same day? Strange."

"I thought so, but if her death was an accident—"

"You're probably right, Walter." She looked across the site, young people working in purpose and harmony. "Everyone here seems so intense. Why did he leave the dig? A slacker?"

"It wasn't the work. His dad was laid off from the Ford plant in Detroit. Danny needed to earn more to help his family. He's the oldest of seven kids. We aren't paid much, just pocket money. He got a good job at Ruby's Ranch in Bryce Canyon. It's a real tourist trap. Have you been there?"

Terry recalled the punishing miles of trailer hauling, timeless blurry panoramas with her bleary eyes flicking from the berm to the center line, white-knuckling the wheel, her mind oblivious to the visual feast. "We passed it coming here. My aunt and I aren't keen on bumping shoulders with mobs of people. But I've been thinking of returning for photos ever since I saw the landscape from a plane ride."

"Hey," he said, snapping his fingers in a memory jog.

"Melanie's sleeping bag. Her parents only took personal stuff. You could give it to Danny. He may be back next summer. His boy scout model was so old that the filling was leaking, and the zippers didn't work."

Her luck was too good to be true. "Great idea, Walter."

Leading her to a sagging pup tent heaped with supplies, he dived in, wiggled his slim butt like an eager minnow, and rummaged around, emerging with a tight green bundle. "A brand new Marmot three-season. Perfect condition. Melanie took good care of her gear."

Sure that she had pumped innocent Walter of his usefulness, Terry excused herself, told Judith where she was going, then went to the truck to check the map. Forty miles west of Escalante, Ruby's Inn, a town in itself, served as the commercial entrance to Bryce. If nothing worked out, a well-stocked tourist supplier might provide some unusual salsa.

Along Route 12, Terry passed first through the richly colored Cretaceous shale badlands of the Blues, a spectacle of ridges and melting ice cream sundae mounds, stopping at a viewpoint to admire the heights of Powell Point in the distance. She drove quickly through Henrieville, Cannonville, and Tropic, tiny duplications with refurbished motels signaling the burgeoning visitor numbers. Nearby Kodachrome Basin State Park was another attraction they hadn't explored. Freed from the nerve-wracking shackles of the trailer, she marveled at the changing vistas, from junipered plains to the tempting parfait of the sandstone layers. Then climbing onto a plain, she approached the Paunsaugunt Plateau, guarding the treasures of Bryce.

Ruby's Inn, a giant complex covering many acres back into the tall red pines, boasted a gas station and service area, restaurants, a rodeo entertainment center, an RV park, motel, and the central store. Busses massed like flatulent dinosaurs, spewing diesel fumes, downloading buzzing tourists who swarmed out to snap at anything that moved. Terry pulled up for gas, a good place to ask about Danny.

The silver-haired, brush-cut woman at the pump shifted a toothpick around the corners of her mouth. Bone-thin, dressed in a tank top and wheat jeans, she wielded the nozzle like a bionic extension, her skin tanned to the durability of a boxing glove. A Bullwinkle tattoo added lively color to one forearm.

"Is it always this busy?" asked Terry, coughing at the exhaust.

"Weekends are even worse. Never should have paved that park road. Give me the old days," she said, knocking the last drip from the pump and swirling the gas cap with a flourish. "Ruby's started out, took 'em in by horseback. Needed a good week to hit the high spots. Now it's a racetrack blow-by in an hour. Don't see nothin' but the ass end of another vehicle. On to Grand Canyon, Yosemite. Thanks be to God that they're finally banning snowmobiles."

She recalled Chris's commentary on their plane ride. "I hear winter's the best time. Maybe we'll return then."

The woman grinned, a generous gap-toothed smile as broad as a mare's, and accepted Terry's fifty-dollar bill, thumbing change from a belted metal apparatus. "Now you do that, sweetheart. If I'm not in Frisco with my grandkids, meet you at this pump. I'll tell you what's worth a gander."

"You must know everyone at Ruby's," Terry said. "Does Danny Romero work here? I have something for him."

"Sure does. Isn't he a charmer?" The woman squinted her eyes in reflection as she flipped away the toothpick. "Find him at the main building in the grocery area."

Surrendering to tourist mode, Terry browsed the huge store like an elk in heat, admiring T-shirts, swimsuits, books, records, tapes, expensive jewelry, camping equipment, cups and gourmet items. Into a handbasket, she scooped flavored piñon nuts, four salsas (a brandied cherry dessert variety, two five-alarm habaneros, and a roasted chipotle), mesquite potato chips and a goat cheese herbal chip dip. Finally, she urged her gluttonous self to the back of the store. Stacking fruit at a bin was a handsome young Chicano in pressed Dockers, form-fitting navy T-shirt, and a spotless white apron. He flashed her a dazzling smile, and she saw one large bicep flex. His neck was massive, his chest sculpted like a bodybuilder's. "Help you, ma'am? These oranges just left California. Ripe and juicy."

Terry returned his greeting like a slow pitch. "Danny Romero?"

He nodded, searching her face in question as she introduced herself. "I've come from the dig. Walter gave me Melanie Briggs's sleeping bag in case you could use it. It's out in—"

"Jesus." His dark, sculpted brows flashed lightning. "I still can't believe she's gone. All that energy, hair like cornsilk." He balanced himself against the stall, and his coal black, liquid eyes grew moister. She reached out a tentative hand, but he shook himself like a stunned dog, groping for words inadequate to his feelings. "I'm OK. Shi . . . stuff happens."

Maybe she should explain. Otherwise she'd look like an interloper. "My aunt and I are tourists. We saw the Batty Pass Caves on the map and got curious. So we—"

"Someone should have cleaned up that old site. Padlocked the doors. Why the hell was she . . ." Endearingly childlike, he swiped his hand over his nose as he leaned on the bin. A few oranges tumbled from the pile, but he ignored them. "I made her a descanso there. Up in the hills."

"A descanso?"

"Mexican custom. You see them along the roads in the Southwest. A place to honor her with a few favorite things. A Tony Hillerman paperback. Juicy Fruit gum. An Avril Lavigne CD. A Koko charm for her bracelet. She was a Tigers fan, so I got a stuffed animal. Some people leave money. That wasn't her style."

Terry's heart melted at the tender gesture. Suddenly Melanie came alive, wearing that bracelet Judith had seen, one palpable detail in a life snuffed out. "It sounds perfect, Danny."

He leveled wounded eyes at her. "Her parents took her back east. This way I can still . . ." His voice cracked like tinsel. Then a customer ambled through the doors. His sweatshirt read: "Don't Trash Texas." Danny's strong chestnut hands began repiling the oranges, capturing the errant ones juggler-style.

"The bag's outside in my truck."

He checked his watch, a no-frills Timex model like hers, as a girl trundled a box of peaches through the clear plastic flaps at the entrance to the storeroom. "Break time." He considered Terry's full basket. "Go through the cash, and I'll meet you outside."

Ten minutes later in the parking lot, Terry said, "I can see that you were close to her. What a blow."

With his emotional storm in check at last, he shrugged. "The pretty senorita didn't have much time for me. She liked my poetry, but Nick was her hero."

"Nick?" To hide her astonishment, the sudden heat on her cheeks, she gazed over at three huge women mounting cow ponies. The air was filled with "ach's" and "mein Gott's."

"He's a bit . . . old for her, Danny. Besides, he's supposed to look out for his students, not sleep with them." Her voice trailed off at the naiveté. A middle-age math professor at Ohio State had put the moves on her roommate.

"You've got it wrong. Nick's a stand-up guy. So she had the hots for him. Which girl didn't? Doesn't mean he did anything about it." Danny's tone reflected genuine respect, and she felt suddenly guilty about suspecting the professor.

Terry opened the truck door and together they reached for

the bag on the seat. Danny stroked it with undisguised tenderness. "It's soft and warm. I'll smell her scent for a long time," he said. "Maybe forever."

His mildly erotic statement was so ingenuous that Terry felt like hugging him. An odd lump in the bundle made them pause in the transfer. They knelt on a spot of clean pavement and probed the satiny folds. The tight roll concealed a small notebook.

"What's this?" Terry asked.

Danny opened a page with reverent hesitation. "A diary. I saw her writing every night in her tent."

Letting a hunch override her better judgment, she took a chance. "The sheriff should have this, but I have the worst compulsion to read it."

He yanked the book to his chest, closing his hands around it like shielding a newborn baby. "What kind of a person are you?"

"I'm not on a fishing expedition, Danny. I'm a reporter for a paper in Ohio, accustomed to probing for details." Like corsages and wedding cake styles. "The accident seemed wrong from the beginning."

"The bar on the friggin' door slipped into place in the wind. That's what people are saying."

Terry waved off his analysis with a gentle sigh. "Escalante doesn't have the personnel for a comprehensive investigation. It's a credible theory, and the sheriff's sticking to it. But I've heard that Melanie made enemies with that Man Corn fixation."

He squinted against the sun, then looked at the journal as if he wished to read it, too, yet knew he'd find only sad witness to an unrequited love. "True enough. Once she got her teeth into something interesting, she was like my old Rottie Bumper. 'Enemies' is a strong word, though."

Using a reporter's talents wasted on inane details about

bridesmaid's bouquets, she gave him a long, serious stare to assess his body language. He seemed calmer. Could his volatile nature indicate steroids? Or merely the unbridled emotions of a young man in love? Taking no chances, in the welcome spaces of a parking lot in full view of a gabble of tourists heading for the restaurant like a hungry herd, she folded her arms and zeroed in on a hunch. "I heard about your family troubles, but I have to wonder why *you* left the dig so quickly."

His face reddened under an invisible slap, more hurt than angry from the waver on his full lower lip. "The day she disappeared, I took off at dawn on my motorcycle. Stopped for breakfast in Henrieville. Got here about nine and started orientation. Ask Camilla, the manager." He pointed to a smartly dressed lady in a trim tan suit greeting a bus offloading Japanese tourists.

Terry leaned against the tailgate. "I sense a story here. I'd like to read this and track her activities. Give me a few days." She raised an index finger as his nostrils flared. "I'll deliver it to Nick, and he can take it to the sheriff. Call his office if you doubt my intentions. No way I'm cruising for an obstruction of justice charge even if the case is closed."

He exhaled slowly and surrendered the diary, shaking her hand in a firm bargain. "You seem like an honest lady. If someone did hurt her, I want to know."

Her pride still tweaked by the honorific "lady" clearly shoving her out of his age group, minutes later she pulled onto the highway. Danny's cooperation signaled his innocence. Why else would he have turned over the diary? She returned to the dig to find her aunt sitting under the awning of Nick's trailer, cradling Tut. Next to her was a thin brown book, *Exploring the Fremont.* Terry picked it up. "This looks interesting. I have something to show you, too. Melanie's diary was in a sleeping bag that—"

Judith's eyes brimmed with tears. "Our boy started limping

around noon. Then he couldn't even stand." When she touched Tut's left hind leg, he issued an unusual warning growl. "I can't see with these damn bifocals. Too much reflection in the sun."

"He's definitely in pain," Terry said, all thoughts of the diary dissolved. "Let's get him to a vet. In cattle country, someone must treat animals."

"Nick suggested the Pet Corral on Main." Judith's voice broke, and a tear rolled down her cheek. Terry had never seen her cry, not even at her own parents' funerals twenty years ago.

Though the sign indicated six for closing, Rita Kinsolving's office was still open at seven. A gray-bearded man with a yowling tabby under his arm "howdy'd" as he held the door for them and tipped his straw hat. Giving their names and situation to the youthful assistant, they asked if they were too late. The blonde girl in a bright blouse with puppies smiled proudly. "Rita never shuts her door if there's one person left. Mom keeps dinner waiting some nights. But I love it."

They sat alone in the waiting room, Judith stroking Tut's head. Growing more agitated, he nearly bit her hand, entirely out of character for the happy dog.

"A visitor in trouble?" asked a plump brunette in faded green scrubs, her hair gathered in a long ponytail. After introductions, Rita the vet ushered them into the examining room, freshly mopped, the smell of antiseptic floating in the air.

"Let's have a look." She let Judith lift Tut onto the immaculate steel table, then buckled a black fabric muzzle over his mouth. Tut *grrr*d as Judith frowned in embarrassment, but Rita's gray eyes were cool and analytical. "I'm a stranger, and he's in a strange land, not that animals don't hate clinics on general principles. Take no chances. I learned that my rookie year when a 'friendly as a kitten' Lab took offense to having his anal glands expressed. Twenty stitches." Her muscular forearm bore a jagged white scar.

Stepping out of the way, Terry inspected graphic posters of veterinary health problems, fluorescent eye closeups, skin eruptions, view-from-above diagrams of cats and dogs from emaciated to morbidly overweight. Tut was at the indulgent end of the scale.

"What's wrong?" Judith asked as her chin trembled. "He was fine until a few hours ago."

The vet used a scope to peer into his eyes and ears, then ran capable hands and fingers over his body, even the belly and tail. "Have you been walking in the desert?" Rita asked, reaching for a pair of surgical scissors and clipping around the toes of the foot he favored. Eyes rolling wildly under duress of confinement, Tut began a slow, plaintive whine, a canine song of fear and helplessness.

"We've been at a Fremont dig in Dixie National Forest. For a change, he's had free rein, wandering about," Judith said with a nuance of guilt.

Rita applied herself to Tut, a question on her brow smoothing as something caught her attention. "Hold on. Here's a clue." Using tweezers, she probed gently, then in triumph drew out a small particle, dropping it into a white enamel bowl. "Prickly pear cactus. Dogs love to step on them."

"Did you get it all?" Judith asked, her creased face relaxing in a hopeful smile.

Rita set the instruments aside and turned to wash her hands in the sink. "That's tricky. Sometimes bits of the thorn stay hidden until the flesh suppurates. Gets infected. I'll give you a bottle of peroxide to treat the wound. He'll be sore, but the paw should heal quickly. I don't want to cut into the pad unless I have to. Bring him back if he isn't better after two days. And watch out for ticks near any thick vegetation. They're wicked out here."

As Judith thanked her, Rita poked Tut's undefined ribcage.

"He's rather overweight. Too many snacks?"

Judith nodded, patting her own belly. "It's hard when routines are upset. He gets off his food, and then the blackmail begins."

"You're here to enjoy yourself, and I give you credit for including your dog instead of leaving him in a kennel. Have you seen much of Escalante?" Rita asked.

"More every day, but never enough. We took a plane ride at Robbins Aviation to get an overview of the area," Terry said.

The vet's jovial face chilled like the first September frost. Then her smile returned as she lifted Tut from the table.

Chapter Fourteen

"And that's this morning's weather. Have a Kokopelli day," the announcer chirped as Terry and Judith groaned in unison.

"A mythical figure, a hunchbacked medicine man or a carrier of seeds. Now he's a mockery like that ridiculous happy face." Judith had Tut pinned on the couch over a towel while she dabbed his foot with cotton balls soaked in peroxide. "They downplay the penis concept, but fertility extends to plants, animals, and people, too." He moaned histrionically until she released him, then ran to his place on the queen bed.

"What a phallic interpretation. Koko is merely playing a flute," Terry said.

"Flute indeed." Judith demonstrated her point with an unsubtle mime. She moved to the table, picking up a pocket calendar. "Time's slipping by. I've called Dick three times with no answer. His fever has me worried. Have you finished that diary?"

"Our enchanted evening at the vet's wore me out. I got as far as the end of the semester in Michigan. Final grades. Packing. Routine stuff. Her handwriting is worse than mine. I'll get back to it today."

Judith turned on the stove to reheat the coffee, clicking the large BBQ lighter without effect. "What's going on? The burner won't ignite."

"That's impossible. That stick-on patch read half-full. We filled up in Tucumcari. Let it go for now. The fridge, air, and lights are on electricity, and we certainly don't need heat."

Her aunt tapped the stove in annoyance. "What about cooking? The microwave commits sacrilege upon bacon. I'll help you haul out the tank. If it's empty, it should be easy for two healthy women."

At the Shell station, they pulled up with the cylinder rolling riotously in the bed. After parking by the propane weigh scale, they entered the store. Pork rinds for Terry and sunflower seeds for Judith joined another loaf of Wonderbread. Kaya from the restaurant stood behind the cash. From the size of her belly, surely this would be her last week.

"I'll take these, and we need a propane fill on a thirty-gallon tank," Terry said.

"Sure," Kaya said, moving toward a door to the bays. "Chuvio! Propane fill!"

A short, dark man with a droopy Pancho Villa moustache emerged. His mouth worked a substance more complex than gum, cheeks bulging in rhythm like a sack of stuffed toys. He wore greasy overalls, shirtsleeves rolled to reveal huge tattooed biceps, an eagle on one, a bleeding heart on the other. "My brother-in-law will give you a hand," Kaya said as the phone rang.

Terry took Judith aside for a second, whispering, "That's Tocho's brother. What does he know about Melanie?"

Outside, hoisting the tank from the truck bed, Chuvio plopped it onto the scale and screwed the connections. "Empty as a beer can on Sunday morning," he said as he adjusted the dial, the gas hissing. As he disconnected, Terry watched, making small conversation about the weather, the tourists, then adding in a sad voice, "What a shame about that girl they found in the desert."

"Huh," he said with a snort. "Bitch had it coming. Calling us . . ." He arced a splash of tobacco. Dark and oily, it splattered a Rorschach blot on the cement an inch from Terry's shoe.

Judith planted her feet, her hooded eyes shooting rivets. Many a rowdy class had found their ears pinned back by her imperial bark. "How dare you! An innocent young woman is dead. Show some respect."

Terry joined into the spirit, her heart tripping with excitement and fear. "I heard a ranger in Boulder had a grudge against her."

Cursing under his breath, Chuvio dropped the cylinder into the bed like delivering a bomb, denting the sidewall. He scribbled a bill and dropped it onto the pavement. "Fifteen bucks. Pay up inside and clear out. Get your fuel down the road. We don't want your nice white business." He swiveled on his boot heel and stomped to a service bay, where he grabbed a slider and in one easy motion, nestled under a truck on a lift.

The women stood in disbelief, wondering if this scene represented the dregs of the civility gene pool. In the next bay, Terry saw Tocho maneuvering an engine block on a chain. Even with the prosthetic, his movements were deft and effortless, a model of ergonomics. Then he went outside to an ancient robin-egg blue pickup and reached in to retrieve a Thermos. The vehicle had seen rough years, but someone had started bodywork, judging from the scrofulous application of Bondo.

Judith observed with a caustic voice, "Who said Neanderthals died out?"

Terry nodded and cocked her thumb toward the blue truck. "Check out Tocho Nuvamsa. And I wouldn't call him handicapped. He can throw his weight around."

"So that's the man. All it might have taken to overpower a girl was one good hand and a cartload of bravado. Knowing Westerners, he probably has a gun."

"I hate to condemn him on first impressions." Terry shaded

her eyes to locate through the glass window the shadow of Kaya serving another customer. "Why was his wife so nervous at the restaurant? Was there a conspiracy to arrange an alibi? I wish we could talk to her."

Back at the RV park, a new neighbor stepped out of an elephantine forty-foot Panther bus a mere foot from their kitchen, diesel fumes filling the air. He saw the women with the propane cylinder and rushed up to help them locate it in the outside cupboard.

"Need a hand reconnecting, ladies?" the burly man asked, introducing himself as Mitch. "Arkansas Traveler" was painted on the side of his mobile apartment.

Terry pulled an adjustable wrench and a pair of pliers from the tool kit in the tote box. "Thanks, but no problem. I've done it before."

Inside, Judith was peering out the window at the shiny leviathan. "That rig must have cost over two hundred thousand. Some retirees sell their houses to buy them. Can you imagine?" she said with a whistle as Terry came in to wash her hands. Then Judith lit the stove. "All A-OK. We're stalled in Seattle, but you need to get back to that diary."

"I feel like a voyeuse. You never read mine when I was a teenager."

"Didn't it have a cute little lock?" Judith assumed a look of innocence.

"I wondered how you found out about that keg party my senior year. Did you use a paper clip?"

Threatening thunderstorms kept them inside until dinner, when the tardy sun dried the drops from the picnic table. A salad seemed a quick option, so along with avocado, lettuce, tomatoes, ripe olives, shredded jack cheese and slivers of ham, Terry added garlic toast on the grill. As they were finishing, Gail strolled over with a foil-covered paper plate.

"Have a beer or a glass of wine," Judith offered.

"Can't stay. Latecomers arrive about this time. Thought I'd drop off this apple pie. My friend Joyce stuffs me and Jason like piggies." She patted her round stomach with a guilty moan.

"You're generous. Fresh baked goods are worth their weight in gold." Terry placed the warm gift on the table.

"Neighbors gotta share. And you've been here so long, it's like you're a regular." She patted Terry's arm, then turned and walked over to help Mitch, who was having trouble with the cable hookup.

The pie was piquant with tart cinnamon apples and a rich, flaky crust. "Must be lard like Mother's," Judith observed, forking it in with a smile as juicy as the fruit. "Crisco never darkened our door."

After the meal, Judith read up on Chaco Canyon and Terry returned to the diary, using a small spiral notebook to record key facts. Within a few minutes, she reached the Utah entries. "Nicky's so hot," it read. "Wish I'd been in his Anthro 350 section last year. He teamed me with Walter, kind of a geek but OK. Today we set up camp, making up menus and stuff like Girl Guides. Yucky food, though. Oatmeal is boring, and if I see another baked bean, I'll barf. Anyways, we're picking up where last year's group left off. This week the walkover of the new section. Site Survey, Site Recording, Mapping. The gridwork will be wicked. When are we going to get to the fun part, the excavations? Sure takes a long time, but Nicky's the boss." Here she had drawn a smiley face. "All the better to get to know him."

Terry gulped, then turned a page. Darkening her end of the trailer, her aunt called, "Anything yet?"

"Doesn't look great for our man Nick."

Judith's loud yawn signaled her intentions as she pulled the curtain, and Terry continued, trudging through each page, aggravated by the sloppy handwriting. So small, too. Did she need reading glasses at thirty-four? Sometimes the entry held only scientific data, as if the dig had assumed more importance than Melanie's crush. Then other notes confirmed a rising interest. "He's not married, Wally said. Took him a morning coffee in his little trailer. Two sugars and one cream. Woke him up. Did he ever look cute with his hair all mussed. Would I like to run my hands through those curls. He sleeps in his briefs, too. Lots of chest hair. Thirty-eight isn't that old. Does he date students, or is he uptight? I'll have to ask around, carefully, of course."

Chest hair. Wally. Terry ground her teeth. Half the diary remained. A blind alley, she guessed, but she'd never see Nick in the same way again. Then came the incident with Tocho at the Boulder museum. "I was telling a couple of history teachers from California about Turner's thesis and how the Coombs site evidence nearly passed the test for cannibalism. Then this native ranger guy barged in and started to hassle me. Some people can't take the truth. I nearly reported him except that the whole thing was so pathetic. Like I should make trouble for a cripple." Terry snorted at the term. Melanie's credit line took a major blow.

Suddenly a beep from the center of the trailer made her jump. In a grumpy voice, Judith called out, "What in God's name is that? I was nearly asleep. Now my damn back's throbbing again."

"I'm not sure." A minute passed. Then another beep, or was it a chirp? Flicking on the kitchen lights, Terry tried without success to home in on the sound. She waited, poised to pounce, peeved at the distraction. Another chirp sounded.

"It's coming from the floor. Are there crickets out here?" She dropped to her knees and scanned the bottom of the cupboards. Beep!

Finally, she zeroed in on the sink area, spotting a small white plastic box attached to the bottom of the cabinet. "Gotcha. It's the propane alarm."

Judith flung open the bed curtain, sniffing pointedly and fanning the air. "I don't smell anything. Didn't you make the connections properly? Check the book."

"Listen, Aunt Judith. The stove's working, isn't it? Give me a break. I didn't major in Electrical Engineering." Opening the utility cupboard, she rummaged through piles of manuals, flinging them every which way. Finally, she unearthed the guidebook, thumbed it, and sat back with a groan. "We need new batteries."

"Not at this time of night. If you don't disable it, I'm going to clock it with a hammer. At my age, a good sleep is way better than sex."

Terry pulled a multiselection screwdriver from the silverware drawer and removed the offending unit, tucking the parts into a Ziploc bag. "Deed done," she said. "Nighty night, Judith."

Tidying up, she returned to the diary. Melanie and the gang went to the show in Panguitch. Amy cut her hair with nail scissors (not much to her liking, but free). "I'm sure N's . . ." What was that scribble? "Interested. He put his hand on my shoulder to get a closer look at Room Two's wall. My heart was beating so loud I thought I'd die."

Terry tried to recall her youthful crushes, that French horn player with the penetrating eyes who sat near her in the Buckeye Band. They'd worked on his fraternity's float for Homecoming, but he hadn't called again. Apparently contemporary college girls weren't as bold and free as one would imagine from television and films. Despite her flirtation, Melanie seemed fairly innocent, though Judith would not have approved. In *Father Knows Best* days, even kissing on the first date was taboo.

Getting up to go to the bathroom, she heard Judith and Tut snoring in operatic tandem. Cumulative days of long labor in the field was catching up to them.

Back at the diary, Terry yawned. It was after eleven. She

sympathized with her aunt. Eight hours of sleep was her mantra, too. With only twenty pages left, reading the wretched script was crossing her eyes. She placed the diary into the cabinet over her bed, arranging the covers, fluffing the pillow, then flicked off the light. If Nick had been involved in a love affair with Melanie, she didn't want to know the sordid details. Or did she? Was it possible that he was involved somehow in her death? Minutes passed while her brain whirled. Despite the yawns, the Sandman was dragging his heels. She tried the old blackboard trick. Write down your thoughts, then erase them. Nick and Melanie inside a giant heart-shaped lasso. In the distance a coyote howled, answered in a different timbre. Mates on a hunt, calling in the night? Staking out territory? Then she sat bolt upright and hit the bed lamp. She had to know the truth in this deadly soap opera.

Chapter Fifteen

As Melanie learned more about local geography, she used all of her free time touring the area. Money for gas was her greatest complaint. She had plans to join a dig the following summer in the Yucatan, and then begin her master's degree. Nick would be awarding one of his crew a full scholarship, and she was hopeful of being the lucky one. But lately a problem had arisen. "Big trouble. That bitch Amy erased my sign-out the day I went to Covered Wagon Natural Bridge. I know it was her. Who else would pull such a rotten trick? I think Nick believed me because you could see that something had been written there."

That action seemed not only low, but dangerous. Terry shifted back into Melanie's camp, felt a tear cool her weary eyes. So much promise cut off, a dedicated young woman prone to a bit of silliness and the occasional hurtful slang. Hadn't she called a schoolmate "retarded" and received a tongue-lashing from Judith, who told her to use a more creative epithet, preferably from Shakespeare?

Melanie had been forging farther and farther into the wilderness. She'd taken every secondary road in the Monument area, from the southern reaches of Stevens Arch, then over to the elusive Egypt, and back to the northeast, taking the Burr Trail Road to Wolverine Loop Road through the Circle Cliffs. She'd come nose to nose with a faded midget rattler as she climbed over a chokestone in Spooky's mini-slot canyon, but knew enough to keep out of its way. On another occasion, the Jeep wouldn't start twenty miles from the nearest dirt road. Luckily the engine was merely flooded. Despite the blast from the air conditioner, Terry broke out in a cold sweat, remembering the shameful but sensible surrender on Hole-in-the-Rock Road. Judith would have approved of the girl's initiative.

On the most harrowing trip, after climbing the crumbling talus below a steep cliff miles down Reservoir Road in search of what appeared to be a small lookout wall, Melanie fell, landing upside down with her foot locked into a narrow cleft. The sturdy hiking boot prevented a sprain or break, but she dangled for heart-stopping minutes, blood pounding in her temples, until she could right herself and free the boot. "Nick would have had a cow," she wrote. "He warned us not to try anything risky without backup."

A page later, Terry's interest was piqued by a moonlight walk and a kiss or two, noted only with capital *D*s instead of the *N* for Nick. She had told him she didn't want to get serious, but the "silly guy" kept writing her poetry. "And the moon never beams without bringing me dreams," she quoted. "Cool rhyme, but I think I heard it somewhere. Mom's Elvis albums maybe." Danny had been right to assume that he hadn't captured much attention. Terry remembered his sweet ingenuousness . . . and his quick alibi. With those winning looks, coaxing a middle-age female manager to bend the truth might be easy.

In the final pages, Melanie had started talking to people in the area. "Local yokels," she called them, after receiving nasty comments about her Man Corn theories. Finally, one nice old prospector called Hick had spun tales about his mining days, mentioned possible ruins west of the lower Cockscomb, one of the Monument's most signal features, a double row of steeply tilted fins running from near the Arizona border north to Canaan Peak. Melanie had driven the Cottonwood Canyon Road, paralleling the stunning geological fold, then on another day come in along Johnson Canyon Road to Skutumpah. Terry checked the map, chuckling at Mollie's Nipple. But where were Raven Roost, Eagle Hill? Was the girl naming the sites herself?

The diary ended on the next page with Melanie getting the Jeep again. Nick had been a "sweetheart" to choose her over Amy, who wanted to drive to Bullfrog Basin Marina to rent a jet ski, apparently a frivolous plan getting a thumbs-down. Melanie was headed for Nicky Bench and then Dead Fox Hill. She'd been there before but planned to take more water. Nicky Bench. Dead Fox Hill. More games. Where was that in relation to the Batty Caves? Terry decided not to wake her aunt by map flapping. She was crabby when she didn't get enough rest.

Eyes burning with fatigue, she jotted the last notes into her records. Just because the diary said that Melanie was going to a certain location didn't mean she had. People change their minds. Terry also entertained second thoughts about Tocho. The diary hadn't mentioned him after their initial argument. Maybe suspicions about the man were as groundless as Nick implied, though Chris had suggested that he had an alcohol problem. Terry fell into a restless sleep.

Chapter Sixteen

Nick was parked in a lawn chair under a gigantic beach umbrella more suited to Acapulco, a mug of coffee in his hand, on the ground a gnawed toast crust attracting a carnival of red ants. Consulting a sheaf of papers, he glanced up at Terry's arrival and swallowed so quickly that he coughed. "Coffee's fresh. Want some?"

"No, thanks. Caffeine overload already."

"Where's Judith?"

"Her back was sore, and she didn't want to push her luck." She mulled over her approach. "Nick, I have a confession. Chalk it up to journalism," she said in an offhanded manner.

"I was wondering when you were going to tell me about that shard." A pious smile formed on his lips. In his collarless black shirt, he might have been a casual Jesuit priest.

How did he know? Was she that transparent, or had he put two and two together in their conversations about the Dittert site? "This isn't a joke. I found Melanie's diary when Walter gave me her sleeping bag to take to Danny Romero at Ruby's Inn." She paused, gauging his surprised expression. "And I read it."

He scratched behind his ear. "I couldn't figure where that went. Saw her writing in it every night. It wasn't with the personal effects her parents took. Anything we don't already know about? Did she mention why she went to the caves?"

Terry shook her head. "The usual teenage angst. Never

mentioned Hole-in-the-Rock Road after the first week of exploring. It's puzzling all right."

"You know the sheriff gets it pronto as a matter of course. He'll probably send it on to the family. I won't tell him you've been a bad girl."

Stinging over the gibe, she handed over the slim volume with relief. As their eyes met, she wondered if he would read it, too, and how he'd feel about Melanie's crush. Surely nothing had happened between them. Danny hadn't thought so, nor had the diary recorded an affair.

"Terry?" He received the book awkwardly, then placed it on a table and offered her a chair.

Sitting with her legs crossed in a business-like pose, she folded her hands on one knee. Then Nick took a deep breath and exhaled. All was silent in the still air until the tink of a pot from the cook tent. What was the matter with him?

"I, umm, have a great local source for Black Angus steaks. May I bring some over tonight? Around six?"

"Sounds super." Why the hesitation? He sounded more nervous than Walter. And the "may" was so prim. Inviting himself to dinner was no big deal, especially after being so gracious about Judith's joining the crew. She should have made the offer herself long ago.

Back at the trailer, Terry found her aunt doing stretching exercises on the picnic table. "I think I got to that muscle strain in time. If they had a masseuse in five hundred miles, I'd treat myself." Judith eased into a chair. Next door Tut was playing ball with a friendly male dachshund from the Michigan Upper Peninsula.

"Finish the diary? I was still snoozing this morning when you left. And where have you been all this time, anyway?"

Terry had a hard time keeping exasperation from her voice. "Finished is right. The more I read, the more confused I got."

She summed up her notes about Melanie's travels.

"Made up names? How irritating."

"The last place mentioned that I could find on the map is Telegraph Flat. That's on Route 89 by the Arizona border. Very rough territory." She swung one leg over the other like an irritated cat. "And as for Nicky Bench . . ." She told Judith about the crush.

Judith let loose a wild laugh. "That poor man. I won't be able to look him in the face."

"Yes, you will. Guess who's coming to dinner?"

Late that afternoon, Terry ran in to the grocery for cream and water, and met the Sheriff at the cash, buying cigars. He motioned her outside after she had paid, his face plum purple, the veins a roadmap to apoplexy.

He stuck a rum-soaked crook into his broad mouth and lit it with a Zippo, puffing noxious clouds. "Hear you've been muddying up my territory, little lady, and I don't appreciate it. The investigation is over. What are you still doing around here?"

Terry flicked back her curly hair, wishing it were longer to add to the effect. Did he mean Dove or Melanie? Better play it safe. "I can't imagine what you mean, but your tone isn't very friendly to tourists."

With a frozen smile, he rested a hand on his gun in a theatrical posture, tapping his fingers. "Let's start with the diary. Nick brought it over this afternoon."

"An innocent discovery you should have made yourself in a more careful search. I was trying to comfort a young man when I found it."

"That case is closed. An accident pure and simple. But that's not all you're up to. What about the phone call from the booth outside the Shell Station? Give us some credit." He watched her like a human lie detector, but she kept her face passive. Then his voice softened as he shook his head. "Dove told me about your friend moving to Washington. So what? I can't for the life of me figure why you're bothering the man. Like you have a vendetta."

"Ven . . . what a great imagination." She checked her watch, raising her arm to punctuate the gesture. "If that's all, I have a guest for dinner and some other stops to make."

"Best slip eastbound to Ohio before you meet a rattlesnake meaner than this old lawman. Even the dead ones can bite."

Back at their site, as they sat outside, the picnic table covered with a festive cloth and the Bryce Canyon appetizers arranged in tempting array, Nick arrived with three bottles under his arm. Wearing a brown chambray shirt, slacks, and desert boots, he passed a huge, bloody package to Terry and presented Judith with the wine.

"Stocked up last trip to Flagstaff," he said, twirling an imaginary moustache. "Thought it might come in handy to relieve women of their inhibitions."

"Splendid," Judith said, examining the labels. "Never could pronounce Grgich Hills, but a fourteen percent cabernet doesn't box with velvet gloves."

The steaks browned up succulently on the grill, causing Tut to dance, waving his white-tipped tail. Cubed roasted sweet potatoes and cole slaw rounded out the meal. The chocolate dessert salsa made an interesting topping for their Cherry Garcia ice cream.

"This is a nice change," Nick admitted, as Judith brought out the decaf. "Camp cuisine is filling but routine. I could cook more elaborate meals in the trailer, but I don't like to pull rank. Wrecks the team idea."

The word "team" stuck in Terry's mind, though she nodded acknowledgment. After clearing the picnic table and refusing an offer from Nick to wash dishes, Judith removed herself on the pretext of laundry. Terry blinked as she left. Hadn't they just put away the clean clothes? Or was that Sunday? Without the discipline of deadlines, time assumed a life of its own.

Alone and mellowing from the hearty meal and the wine, they made desultory conversation about the progress at the dig and the possibility of a kiva. Terry's lips were tingling, an unusual but pleasant sensation. The breeze had stirred as temperatures fell. The park was peaceful, half empty in the usual midweek slowdown. She reclined pasha style on the folding lounge, head tipped back to admire the star show, one arm trailing on the patch of grass that had started flourishing beside a dripping waterline.

In a nearby chair, Nick had been quiet, a blazing comet riveting their attention. Then he stood abruptly and blurted something with his head lowered. "I read the diary, Terry, before passing it to Reg. And I want to explain."

In her growing haze, only the last word poked through. Robotic repetition seemed the likeliest response. The wine had hit her hard. She coughed to conceal her fuddled state. "Esplain?"

"Melanie's comments about me."

She waved her hand at the stars, conducting their symphony. "Oh, I never gave any cree . . . cree . . . thought to that." Her head began swimming, and she shook it until it behaved.

"When I read about the damn coffee she brought me, I nearly choked. Sounds like she was trading favors to get the Jeep." He rubbed at his chest, then seemed to remember that intimate detail that had intrigued Melanie. "Jesus. This is embarrassing. Nothing, and I mean nothing, happened between us." His voice struggled for control. Nervousness or guilt?

Returning her gaze to the sky, she attempted to focus on Orion's belt. "Of course not, Nick. There was no mention of any . . . young girls are silly." She tried a reassuring laugh to disperse the tension, but it emerged like a giggle. "Of course I wasn't, but—"

"Please let me finish. In Arizona . . ." He drained his glass and poured more, then set it aside as a second thought. "Twelve years ago, when I was a grad assistant and handled the labs for the professor, I had an affair with a student, I'm ashamed to admit. At twenty-six I should have known better."

"I imagine it's common." Regretting the choice of words, at his abject posture, she felt a shift toward sobriety as a chill breeze made her shiver in her peach linen shirt and cotton pants.

He traced a finger around his neck as if he wore a choke collar. "This girl, Cheryl was her name, had been in my class the semester before. Physical Anthro."

Tempted to joke about the "physical," she shrugged instead. "Long time, small crime. Ancient history."

"A humiliating one. The story gets complicated. She'd received a C. Smart enough, but caught up in sorority functions. Her research project on genetics had been a shambles. Then she tried to blackmail me into changing the final mark. Some hoax about a missing assignment. If I didn't agree, she'd claim that she'd refused to have sex and lost her A."

Terry's sympathy was aroused by the tawdry details. Another case of a decent man trapped by university conventions? Yet a good liar would have denied everything or prepared excuses. "Sounds messy."

"Could have been, but I had a wise old chairman. As a grad student, I was powerless as a kitten. The upshot was that he asked around in other departments." He laughed grimly. "I was the third TA Cheryl had tried this on, including one woman."

Terry felt a rush of relief. "No problem then. You were lucky."

"Don't I know it." His puppy eyes blinked, and with a gulp, he took her hand and leaned forward. Suddenly Judith emerged in the darkness, whistling "Some Enchanted Evening," Tut at her heels. With the laundry bag humped over her shoulder, she resembled Koko's mother.

Nick backed off, stretched, and captured a light shard with his watch. "Nearly ten. I'd better get back to camp. Hitting the hay early is more my style. Thanks for a terrific dinner. If you're not leaving too soon, maybe we can try it again." He turned toward his truck, then stopped. "OK if I use your washroom?"

Minutes later, he emerged, gave a quick wave and stubbed his toe on a rock without flinching. As he drove away, Judith looked at Terry with an amused smile. "Two men? An embarrassment of riches."

Following Terry to the rig, Judith carried in the bag, stuffed it into a closet and sighed. "I couldn't bother folding neatly like you, and don't blame me if your whites turned pink. Must have been that strong wine. Liquor and laundry is a devilish combination." She sniffed twice, putting a finger over each nostril. "And I'm so stuffed up. Who gets post-nasal drip in the high desert?"

Joining the diagnosis like a susceptible fool, Terry found herself breathing through her mouth. Judith brought out the Benadryl pack and they took two tablets each. Still on a befuddling high, trying to sort out Nick's story, Terry fumbled to close the windows and lower the blinds. When the breezes rose, the plastic ends on the cords tick-tack-clacked in random torture. Tonight at last in the cool, the noisy conditioner got a furlough, leaving only the screen door for ventilation. She spent seconds in the bathroom, leaving her teeth unbrushed, her hair and face unwashed, then undressed in clumsy motions and flicked out the light. In the darkness, a precise voice broke her trance. "And I hope you appreciated the privacy."

Terry worked her words around an uncooperative tongue the size of a grapefruit. Would she have a royal hangover in the morning? "I'll return the favor when you find a man. So far, it's Reg or Dove."

A low growl rolled her way. Cuddling into her pillow, welcoming the quiet, enveloping blackness, soon she was dreaming of the soft, cool reflected light of the box canyon. What would a real slot canyon be like? A mystical planet, to paraphrase Chris. She drifted on the tide, barely marking diffused sounds of distant coyotes, like the trains that bisected Lakewood, far enough away that their lonely whistles seemed a neighborly passing in the night. Her mind voyaging, making sense about the diary didn't seem so urgent. Where Melanie had gone, whom she'd met, whether Nick was . . . She flipped onto her side. Easy to sort the stubborn facts in the sober clarity of morning. Terry swam like an eel, slipped up and down from the dark velvet world to the bright surface.

But despite the easy rhythm, a smear, a muddle, a palpability emerged, worrying her dream like a persistent terrier, chewing on the edges. A ticking. A click. Damn cords, but hadn't she closed all the windows? Fixed the door? A squalid atmosphere pressed her chest like leaden weights. A reaction to the Benadryl? Her mouth was so dry. She groped for the nighttime glass of water on the table. Forgotten. In a hazy reflex she shucked off the sheet, fighting it with scrabbling feet until she lay in her panties, sweating alcohol like an alley wino, the bed damp beneath her body. Sympathy for the hormonal stutters Judith had endured a few years ago rose with each breath. To steal from Mark Twain: If this is menopause, give me tea.

Then Terry's lungs exploded in a crushing spasm as she came alive to a sickening, gut-wrenching smell like being parked over a sewage lagoon. She elbowed herself to a sitting position and shook her head, struggling for breath in a poisonous prison as her hands raked her throat. Had the septic hose disconnected? From far away she heard coughing answering her own gagging noises. Rolling off the bed, she banged into the kitchen table, then with blind fingers, lurched toward the door, expecting fresh air through the screen. A solid barrier! Both doors were shut. Unsteady, she braced against the stove like a trapped animal as acrid fumes buckled her knees.

"Judith! Wake up! We have to get . . ." Working desperately at the latch, she overbalanced and half-tumbled down the metal stairs, straining her wrists, but blessing the soft sand at the bottom. After several punishing deep breaths, she held the last, and crashed back inside, crawling up to the queen bed, dragging her aunt with one arm, pitching Tut with the other. Outside she propped Judith against the picnic table, relieved at the integrity of movement that signaled consciousness. The night was moonless, shrouded in clouds, and only the glow of feeble sodium lights illuminated the campground.

In the blackness, Terry reached inside the RV to hit the exterior light switch, then stopped as instinct whispered a warning to avoid anything electrical. Instead, she retrieved a flashlight from the nearby utility cabinet. Its strong beam played around the stove. The burner nearest the door was turned to high. She flipped it off, then as a chill hit, looked down at her panties. She scooped a blanket from Judith's bed and hustled out, gulping like a beached salmon, enfolding herself in the covers.

Judith had crawled to a lawn chair, moaning and retching. "What happened? That terrible smell had to be propane."

Terry knelt beside her, heartened to feel Tut licking her hand, putting weight on his foot again. She suppressed the urge to vomit that exquisite cabernet, a sour, rotten taste plastering the back of her raw throat. "A burner was on. How could that have happened? I never got up . . ." A giant headache clamped her forehead. In her stupor, could she have made a trip to the bathroom and bumped against the control?

Judith looked ghostly in the yellow light, her eyes swollen and streaming with tears. "I'm sure I didn't. But accidents need only to be possible, not probable. Add the pills to the wine, a very deadly interaction."

"Come on. If an accident could happen that easily, how many of these rigs could they sell? It was our fault for disconnecting the alarm." She urged strength into her voice in an effort to clear herself.

Judith groaned, leaned forward to rub her niece's blanketed shoulder. "Sleeping nude again? That'll learn you." They both laughed in mild hysteria.

Lights flashed next door, and their Arkansas neighbor stomped down the steps of his shiny aluminum bus. He wore a Razorbacks T-shirt and briefs, and his unshaven face puckered at the smell.

"For God's sake, don't light any matches! The gas will take awhile to clear," Terry called.

"Propane! I'll check her out." He marched to the outside panel, opened the door, cursing at the darkness.

As he grabbed her flashlight to peer into the cabinet, Terry said, "The stove burner was on. The rest of the system should be—"

"Let this mule skinner take a gander." He aimed at the top of the cylinder, tested the connections. "Seems nice and tight. We'll turn her off for now. Come morning we'll do a Snoop test."

"Snoop?" Terry asked.

"Detergenty stuff that bubbles up to show a leak. You oughta carry some in case," he said with masculine satisfaction.

Dressed in a fuzzy chenille robe, her silver hair in foam curlers, his wife waved from their door. "Come up for a coffee. It's nearly five anyway. We're early risers."

Judith rose stiffly and followed Mitch upstairs. "Best we can do is breathe. Good air in. Bad air out."

Ice water as their preferences, Terry and Judith sat together on a pillowy sofa in an area plush as Air Force One. CNN blared the news, more suicide bombings in Tel Aviv. Beneath a black velvet painting of Elvis, Mitch munched a sweet roll, his brow creasing, then shook his bald head. "Usually these accidents happen because of poor ventilation. Dumb-ass campers using heaters in tents. You ladies must have a guardian angel. 'Cause you sure ain't got a propane detector."

Silence fell as the two women exchanged glances. Terry said, "I'm afraid that we . . ."

When dawn broke, Mitch sprayed the connections and pronounced them safe. With the windows open, the fan cleared the air but not their sense of unease. Judith hunched in dismay at the breakfast nook, once so cozy and intimate, ignoring the cooling coffee, her hands trembling. "It's like vacationing in a gas chamber. If I don't get over this, we'll have to sell . . ." Her voice broke into a small sob.

This was no time to make things worse by agreeing with her aunt, but it frightened Terry to see her vulnerability. In deference to their residual nausea, Terry portioned out small bowls of Grape Nuts. "We need a break. Let me ask Gail about an easy drive up into the mountains. Tut seems back to normal."

She returned shortly after with a makeshift map. "We'll take a circle route, but first she suggested a Genesis panel only a few miles west. Very secret. Only the locals know."

"Origin of the world? It does sound interesting." Judith's eyebrows, a window to her world, lifted as she picked up her notebook.

Half an hour later, parking on the highway in Kane Springs Canyon, they followed Gail's directions. Monoliths had fallen from the mountain, some landing in Stonehenge collections, providing a smooth surface for ancient writings.

Terry pondered the scene, removing her sunglasses to better admire the color and contrast. "How desperate they must have been to express themselves without paper."

With an entranced smile as she sat on a rock, Judith placed the notebook on her knees and began to duplicate the panel. "They would have seen paper as a poor and temporary substitute. These images were for all time." She explained that the horned figure represented a shaman, often associated with snakes and lightning power images.

Terry followed the shaman's arm to a circle where a dozen people joined hands standing around its perimeter like enclosing the planet or buying the world a prehistoric Coke. Not all figures were the same height. A few were small enough to be children. "The dots spraying from the shaman's rod might be rain. What are those ladders?"

"Zipper glyphs. Snakes, centipedes, maybe a primitive calendar. Possibilities are endless. Polly Schaafsma seems to be the leading expert on symbols."

Reluctant to leave the magical display, but wilting in the heat, they returned to the truck. Main Canyon Road to Griffin Top climbed gradually through thick, secondary growth forests with the occasional viewing pullout. Gentle switchbacks masked the height of the hills. As they drove, the breeze purified their lungs. Old lumbering roads and foot trails beckoned into the woods.

Finally, they reached the navigable heights of the magnificent Aquarius Plateau, which approached 11,000 feet. Scenic pastures opened at intervals, a little Switzerland with alpine meadows. Tall and narrow spruce and trembling aspens had replaced the desert landscape. Miniature lupine spread their blue flowers across the meadows along with the brilliant reds of Indian paintbrush, silvery sagebrush and sheep fescue.

They descended a few hundred feet, captivated by the vacation within a vacation, finally detouring into the cloister of a piney grove and got out to relax under the sun-spotted canopy. Terry leaned against a massive ponderosa. Judith lay peacefully in the grass while Tut roamed at will, scampering after pouch-packing chipmunks and the curious Englemann squirrel with its telltale floppy ears. In the absolute silence, resident voices emerged. The tapping of a downy woodpecker sculpting hollows in the dead wood. The papery skitter of an upside-down nuthatch probing bark for insects. The resinous air made artificial perfumes seem rank and cloying. Terry felt the timbre of a reviving heart. Judith placed her glasses on a stump, closed her eyes and soon began snoring. For a timeless hour in nature's spa, their battered souls rejuvenated.

Finally, the harsh squawk of a Stellar jay broke the reverie. Judith woke with a snuffle, peering about in disorientation, then in wonderment, her gray pallor replaced by a healthy pink. "I was dreaming of Elysian Fields. Exactly like this paradise." With a smile, she ran fingers through her hair, dislodging pine needles.

Terry toyed with strands of grama grass, entwining them like Judith had done for her every morning in seventh grade, fashioning braids so tight that her eyes felt slanted. The horror of the night had vanished. Here was the healing clarity she needed. "I feel safe out here. The West has such wide-open spaces, but that seems to magnify the evil."

"If you mean Dove . . ." Judith blew dust from her glasses and polished them against the sun. "I'm calling Dick tonight. Whatever he has, we'll pursue until time runs out. If he doesn't answer, we'll make plans to leave. I'm not going to miss Chaco."

"Back to your cantankerous normal now?" She gave her aunt a hug.

"Meaner than ever. And I suggest dinner in town. Maybe at that fancy place that nice fellow took you. I wonder why you haven't heard from him? He can't call, but he could—"

"Chris runs a business, and this is his peak season. I'm sure he thinks we've moved on like other tourists. Don't make a big deal out of it." Standing up to brush herself off, Terry felt mildly defensive, as if she'd been a boring date.

"A federal case, we used to say." Judith wagged a finger. "But you are getting sensitive as you approach middle age."

Back in town, the line of tourists outside the Cowboy Blues sent them to the Promised Land Café for hot beef sandwiches with mashies and ubiquitous canned green peas. "Can't beat comfort food," Judith said. "Mother made this with roast leftovers. Then we'd watch 'I Love Lucy.' Sitting in their living room, Lucy and Ricky would hawk Phillip Morris cigarettes in commercials. Imagine that now."

"We've come a long way, baby. Smoke-free at last."

At the trailer, Terry unlocked the door carefully and peered around with suspicion as if someone might have folded himself into the closet or lurked behind the shower curtain. "I've been thinking about last night," she said as she manipulated both doors and inspected the mechanism. "My head hurt so much that I forgot something."

"It's obvious. Someone . . ." She paused in maddening fashion after using her annoying substitute for "you." "Got up and brushed against the stove cont—"

"Before the damn Benadryl. I left the outside door open. And I made sure that the clip fastened tight so it wouldn't bang if the wind rose."

Judith played with the two latches, logistics and possibilities racing through her quick mind. "Yes, but the night was calm. Even unsecured, it couldn't have clamped itself together."

"I had to press the lever to separate the doors."

"Are you saying . . ." Judith's face radiated sudden horror as she sat down heavily on the carpeted stairs.

Terry paused and felt icy hands circle her throat. "Somebody familiar with the layout slid open the screen panel, reached across to turn the burner dial, and then shut both doors to make a nice little Texas-style execution chamber."

Chapter Seventeen

Late the next morning after a trip to the store, Terry knelt, installing fresh batteries on the alarm. "If this had been working," she said, gritting her teeth, "we'd have wakened immediately, even in a semi-stupor. According to the guide, this baby has an ear-splitting siren. Tut would have barked himself nuts."

"The smell probably confused him until he blacked out. So whoever did this might merely have intended to scare us away from Escalante," Judith said, sitting on the sofa, stroking the dog at her feet.

"Merely! How reassuring to think that someone knows all about RV alarms in order to be that solicitous of our health." Terry gave a crooked smile. "This kind of reasoning is like a self-serving perpetual motion machine. I'm at a dead end on Melanie's story, too. What say we cut and run? We'll have more time for Chaco and Mesa Verde. I've aged twenty-five years. Now I'm nearly as old as you."

"No wiser. Younger women should never twit older ones about their age. That's how men retain power." Judith grabbed the phone card from Terry's wallet. "Let's call Dick again."

Their librarian detective had spent three days in the hospital semi-conscious with a raging fever. But the love of the hunt had revived him, even if he'd been limited to armchair sleuthing via phone and computer. Judith let Terry share the receiver at the laundry phone to enjoy his precise, Clifton Webbish tones.

"Deborah Winters is alive and well," he began. "Her Lakewood pension checks are arriving on time."

"Of course," said Judith. "In Seattle."

"I daresay not," he replied with smug satisfaction, citing a friend in the credit check business. "In Salt Lake City. Direct deposit in the Zion Bank. Opened the account last November."

"At Christmas she was still writing me from Escalante. This is senseless. She would have sent me her new address. Besides that, Dove said she was living in Washington."

"I'll bet my ticket to the Westminster Dog Show that she isn't living period. There's an automatic deduction of two thousand dollars each month to Sunset Years. A gold mine."

Judith's mouth gaped. "How could someone get away with this?"

"The country's going broke. Ask yourself if the government has time to root out this shameful kind of fraud. My colleague's son collected his dead father's Social Security for five years. Luckily he's in jail now thanks to the wary eyes of a neighbor who felt that an Infiniti was rather pricy for a Wal-Mart clerk."

"Dick, you're an angel. Work your magic on these two names." She told him about the other women Thelma had mentioned and kissed the phone with a smack before hanging up.

Back at the RV, Judith turned to her niece. "I want to see this matter settled for Deborah's sake. It seems only a matter of time before we have enough evidence to go to the authorities about Dove. But perhaps we should switch parks. Make a base at Ruby's Inn. You said they had facilities."

"Word gets around," Terry said. "It would be evident that we're still in the area. We're safe enough if we lock the door. The combinations were too lucky. But I feel like getting a gun." She rubbed her brow at the impure thought. "Downtown Gallup had blocks of pawn shops, but how much red tape would there be and what kind of delays? We have no permanent address out here. Maybe a Saturday night spec . . ." Her voice trailed off at the thoughts of back alley deals.

"That sounds like a bad movie script." Judith trundled to the back of the trailer and lifted the bed, which rose magically on struts. From underneath she pulled a small bundle, unwrapping a tea towel to reveal a derringer. She glanced down her bifocals, flipped the chamber and removed a tiny bullet. If guns had genders, the silver winked in the sunlight from the window like a naughty lady.

"Aunt Judith! You advocated strict gun control."

"Think of it as a historical artifact, my dear. I bought it at Guns-R-Us on Prospect Avenue before we left. Yancy Derringer was my hero in late-Fifties television. That theme song is branded into my brain. 'They say that Yancy Derringer had ruffles at his wrists, brocade and silver buckles and iron in his fists.' " She blew on the barrel and polished it with her sleeve.

"Ruffles at his wrists?"

"Picture a riverboat gambler. And as for my sensible version of gun control, the older and weaker you are, the bigger your weapon. Young men get zip guns. I deserve an Uzi."

"I'm getting nervous watching you play Annie Oakley," Terry confessed, sweat breaking out on her brow. She cringed, expecting the weapon to blast a hole in the flimsy aluminum ceiling. "And what's a zip gun?"

"A devilishly creative carved wooden model. Youths were more inventive in those innocent days. *Rumble on the Docks.*" She replaced the ammunition and tucked the gun away. "Forearmed is forewarned. The motto of the information age."

"Speaking of information," Terry added, "we might be able to learn more about what's going on at the ranch without another visit."

"Surely not Thelma." Judith rolled her eyes.

"What about Joyce's sister, Charmaine? The one with emphysema. Surely she visits here every now and then. Maybe we'll get lucky."

Nick and his students had left for a four-day trip to the McElmo Canyon in Colorado, so Judith's work at the dig was for all purposes over. Recalling the pleasant memories from their drive to the Aquarius Plateau, they started the day with another hike. Terry decided on Chris's Pine Creek trail. On familiar terrain, she felt in control. Barring an attack from a wild ass, nothing could endanger them in that blissful, shady canyon.

"I can see why you raved about it," Judith said, blinking at sunlit revelations as they ambled. In wild abandon, Tut plunged into the creek between methodical tick checks.

Having started at ten, they reached the petroglyphs for lunch. In stunned silence, Judith surveyed the wall with the appreciative eye of an armchair expert, copying the figures into a notebook. Then she turned to Terry with reverence in her voice. "Notice the Barrier Canyon style, the horned man, his body a rectangle widening at the shoulders. Typical Fremont headdresses, hair-bobs and necklaces. Space men, the stuff of science fiction. And that sheep within a sheep. Koko's theme is everywhere," she whispered. "Reproduction was the essence of survival. Without it, what was the point to life?"

"Times are changing. No stigma on being childless, which suits me since I don't feel very maternal."

Her aunt laughed bitterly. "At your age, I heard short-sighted fools blather on about how selfish it was not to have children. Yet replicating yourself seems the ultimate egotism. This shrinking world's hardly short on population, despite ravaging plagues of HIV/AIDS and systematic genocide. Unless we fly to the planets soon, Malthus will be off by two centuries, but he'll be right."

"No one can ever call you sentimental. Must have been tough sticking to your beliefs." She opened the backpack and portioned out hummus and crackers, adding a dill pickle. Finally a use for that can of chickpeas.

"Plenty of role models, my dear. Your old-maid great-aunts, Nora and Beth, who raised Angora goats, corraled your mother and me each summer on their farm in Coshocton."

"Then they weren't childless, and neither are you," Terry added with a wink.

The trek had been so energizing that they decided to hike another hour. "We'll be back before dinner. Joyce often walks around that time. Let's hope her sister drops by." Judith touched a pale pink flower with five petals, crushing a leaf under her nose. "Heavenly. It's wild geranium."

Terry gulped from her water bottle, watching a small seep emerge from under a rock and marry another, forming a larger stream bubbling lazily toward the creek. "Tocho and Dove. Wouldn't it be funny if the two threads were related?"

"Just like in archaeology, surfaces under surfaces. But don't count on it." Judith wakened Tut and gave him a cautious fingering, discovering one puny tick that hadn't begun its meal. With an "ugh," she flicked it into the brush. "Find a squirrel, laddie."

Later, as they were turning back with reluctance, Judith spotted a small alcove fifteen feet up one steep cliff. She craned her crepy neck. "I spy with my tick-baned eye. A granary. Or part of a wall. And a couple of pecked footholds where the surface hasn't eroded. Moki steps. That's from the Spanish *moqui* after the Hopi *mookwi,* a tribal name."

Terry ran a fearful gaze along the precarious rock face and mumbled to herself. She could almost hear Judith's curious mind changing gears. "I'm not climbing that. A spider would think twice."

Deaf to all pleas, Judith tramped around to inspect the scene, finally dragging over a large branch, gray and barkless. Leaning it against the slick sandstone, she said boldly, "No problem." With one foot between a cleft in the log, she tried once, twice, three times to haul herself up. "Ooof." She stepped back, turning a resolute face toward her scowling niece. "Too much ballast. Not enough liftoff, Cape Canaveral. Give me a boost."

"This is crazy. You're going to strain your back . . . or mine. What if you fall?"

"Nagging doesn't become you." Judith inched up, testing her grip while Terry labored under the load of 150 pounds. She shouldered Judith's ample butt to hoist the woman to a safe perch, dodging small stones that dislodged from the symphony of guttural grunts above.

"Lafayette, we are here!" Judith trilled in triumph, waving her arms, mixing Churchill's victory sign with Rocky's pumping fists. Terry stepped back in momentary relief and watched her aunt's graying head disappear into the alcove.

"Anything?" she called.

"Not so far." Silence for a minute. A rustling sounded, an echo of feet in the acoustical miracle of the natural amphitheater.

"Don't touch any rocks. Rattlers love to slither into crevices."

"No walls," Judith said with an audible pout as she peaked over the edge. "Every alcove doesn't contain ruins." She paused, her voice brightening. "But there are cliff swallow nests higher up, an apartment of mud daubs. And someone camped here. I found the date 1934 and the initials NEMO on one wall. 'No man.' Jules Verne's submarine captain. Rusty Heinz bean cans. Now they're probably protected relics."

"Risking your life to 'discover' garbage? I hope your tetanus shots are current. Come on down. And be careful."

Following the laws of physics, descending was trickier. Judith groaned, scuffed her hands searching for purchase, and flinched at a prickly pear nest. As Terry watched in mute horror, six feet from the ground, she lost her grip on a root clump and plummeted like a flailing marionette to the hard path, lying prostrate, mouth slack, her eyes closed.

"Jesus!" Terry said, kneeling at her side, shoving Tut, who was nosing Judith's face.

A whimper merged with a laugh. "Not my hip, not my head, not my back." With Terry's help, Judith sat up and touched her foot gingerly. "My ankle, rather, Achilles heel. I wrenched it playing racquetball in college. Vomited my lunch from the pain. A sprain's worse than a break."

Terry stood with a gesture of helplessness, wishing for a cell phone to dial 911 but wondering if an ATV would serve as an ambulance. "How in hell are we going to get you back?"

Judith nuzzled into Tut's fur. "Doggedly, I would imagine."

"Let me think." Perched on a hummock of grass, her heart pounding in the rush of events, Terry massaged her temples as flies buzzed. That anyone else might wander down the canyon to lend a hand seemed a remote possibility. Eternities to limp back, even with a makeshift crutch. How did the natives rescue their wounded? No wheels, no horses until the Spaniards. A wagon train of westerns galloped across her brain. *Little Big Man. Dances with Wolves.* Moving those tents. She considered the deadwood by the creek. "Could we make a travois?"

From their oversized heavy twill shirts and two sturdy poles, she fashioned a rudimentary stretcher. "Nothing fancy. Your poor foot might drag, and you'll get soaked, but it's the best—"

"A steer can do. Aunt Nora's favorite expression. No excuses. I overreached my capacities, a venial but hardly cardinal sin." Judith examined her sagging breasts with chagrin. "Pass the sunscreen. I'm fishbelly white. And why ever did I ever burn my bras? They would have come in handy."

Most of the canyon trail was level enough, except for fording the stream. Five times Judith rolled off and dragged herself across the sand and gravel as Terry hoisted her shoulders. Panicked by the abnormality, Tut kept butting in to lick Judith's abrasions with his raspy tongue.

"Stop that, Tut," Terry said.

"Don't worry about it. Far more germs in the human mouth, so they say."

As darkness fell, they reached the trailhead. Next to a Lexus SUV, a silver-haired man, knobby-kneed in shorts, and his blonde arm-candy wife gave odd stares to the pair hunching along.

"Women have every right to go topless in this enlightened age, don't you agree?" Judith called, summoning a bold smile despite the pain. The man broke into laughter, and the blonde said, "You go, girls!"

By the time they returned to the park, the evening was lit by a host of stars across the cloudless sky. Gail answered Terry's knocks at the small house next to the office and shook her head. "The poor old doll. Thank God you got back. Emergencies get sent to Panguitch, or Page, Arizona. If the ankle's not broke, tough it out until morning and see Doc Fred Muldoon on Main. He keeps an x-ray machine in his office. Circa 1945. God knows what kinda toxic radiation, but it works."

Sitting sideways in the truck, Judith removed her sock and stroked her foot, fast bloating into purple. "Tonight the poor old doll hits the Tylenols."

After helping Judith into the RV, Terry heated Manhattan clam chowder, laced with bobbing croutons. Propped up in bed, Judith gulped the pills with a quart of water for a chaser. After a few sips of soup, she handed the cup to Terry. "I'm too nauseous. Eat for the both of us. You worked like a dray horse."

Rubbing a knot from one throbbing thigh, Terry said, "We're safe, and that's what counts."

Judith closed her eyes, hugging Tut until he squeaked. "When

I was in that luminous alcove, centuries melted away. I could have been living when man first walked the earth, bathing in the same sunset and sunrise, drinking the same sweet water."

"Sweet, nothing. With all the mining in this area, who knows what residual chemicals lurk in the creeks? Don't I recall some arsenic by-product of silver production? And let's not forget giardia from animal dung." She winced at Judith's bloody elbows and knees. "You need some Bactine on that. Here comes my revenge for the times you swabbed me with iodine."

Her aunt began to laugh until tears soaked her pajama top. "I'll have to dangle this ferocious animal off the bed."

Chapter Eighteen

In the bright morning, Escalante was becoming as familiar as Detroit and Warren, Lakewood's hub. Exiting from a frosted-glass door bearing the name Muldoon etched in copperplate script, Kaya Nuvamsa stood aside as Judith hopped past. The small storefront had a waiting room with six easy chairs, coffee tables, lamps instead of overhead lighting, but the usual antediluvian magazines featuring Bush Elder, a grinning Clinton, and pamphlets on high blood pressure, HRT, and Alzheimer's. No receptionist was in evidence, but the atmosphere was homey, including a toy corner. A chubby, pregnant teen burping at intervals flapped through a *National Enquirer.*

Judith selected a *Reader's Digest* and turned to the vocabulary quiz. "I always score nineteen out of twenty," she told Terry with a sniff. "They do it on purpose. Always one tricky question."

Fifteen minutes later, a medium-height, full-chested man in a light-brown three-piece suit emerged from an inner door. Except for rather prominent ears and thick, steely hair, a vintage Anthony Hopkins might have been his twin. An unlit corncob pipe clamped in his broad mouth, he had a wry expression. Terry and Judith looked at him with curiosity.

"Foolproof quit-smoking system. It's been empty since my last year in medical school." He handed the young woman a bulky envelope and said quietly, "Instructions for the medication. Drink two percent milk instead of pop, quit the Cheetos and Ding Dongs and come back next week." She shrugged as a young man in jeans and a mesh T-shirt ran in mumbling apologies, helped her to her feet, and out the door. The roar of a blown muffler echoed down the street.

"Iron pills and folic acid samples. The latter prevents Down's syndrome. If only we'd known years ago," he said. Then his gaze fell upon the swollen ankle. "That's a hot potato. Let's get you into the examining room." With Judith's arms over their shoulders, they fumbled down a hall into a Victorian diorama.

While her aunt eased into a chair, biting her lip, Terry noted the floor-to-ceiling bookcases with a wheeled ladder, the mahogany desk, the leathern globe. Heavy brocade curtains framed the windows, lending a claustrophobic effect to the large room. Only a shiny steel examining table and a huge adjustable lamp added a modern touch.

After a brief introduction, Dr. Muldoon removed his coat and rolled up his sleeves. Then he placed the pipe into an ornate wooden holder with a briar and a Meerschaum. Judith blinked back tears as he manipulated the blackened ankle and foot. "I don't think it's broken, Doctor. There's some move—"

"I'll be the judge of that. You sound like a teacher. Act like a patient," he said, testing the tendon. "Don't know what an x-ray will show, all that engorgement. But it's standard procedure even in the hinterlands."

While he hustled Judith into another room, Terry scanned the shelves. Many books were early twentieth-century medical volumes bound in calfskin. Others were new, an encyclopedic range from babies to geriatrics. A framed diploma showed that he had graduated from the Ohio State School of Medicine. Instantly she trusted the man.

As time passed, Terry grew bored. Why not learn more about Dove's condition? From a shelf she picked up *The American Medical Association Home Medical Encyclopedia.* Turning to "cough," she traced a flow chart. "Is the cough dry? Are you short of breath? Are you hoarse? Is your temperature over a hundred degrees?" Having seen Dove only a few brief times, she closed the book in frustration.

Half an hour later, Judith returned, ankle bandaged expertly as she thumped along on metal crutches. "For heaven's sake, Fred. We might have rubbed elbows in Pomerene Refectory. I ate lunch there when I had geology across campus."

"Remember Mirror Lake with tiers of stone benches? And the submarine races?" he asked, leaning closer, his brown eyes twinkling.

"Submarine?" Terry felt like a third wheel, or was it a fifth?

"Ancient Buckeye joke, dear. I'm sure you christened those moonlight activities with a more modern name." Judith poked Fred, and they chuckled in conspiratorial fashion.

"Tylenol will do the job for such a Spartan lady," he said, putting on his coat with a sigh. "I suppose you'll be on your way, and I'll never caress this trim ankle again. My loss."

Judith blushed and batted her eyes, a strange apparition for her niece. "Perhaps we'll be back. Escalante must be breathtaking in the winter, a dust of snow across the canyons."

They were nearly at the front door when Terry recalled that they hadn't paid. She took out her wallet and cleared her throat. "What do we—"

He cut her off with a snort, shooting his creamy cuffs, gold scallop shell links gleaming, as he snugged a blue striped tie. Her father had used that complex Windsor knot. "Too crass to accept payment for a trip down Memory Lane. Professional courtesy. Perhaps I'll need a history lesson."

Terry shook his hand, well manicured and baby smooth. "It's a social sin to pick a doctor's brain, but I have a . . . friend with a persistent cough."

One jagged iron eyebrow rose in clinical interest. "How old's the . . . friend?"

She tried to recall Dove's creased face, overexposed to the sun, perhaps appearing older than he was. "Early sixties."

"Heavy smoker?"

"Maybe." Realizing how inane that sounded, she added, "We just met."

His smile was indulgent, accustomed to irrational patients. "Not to diagnose hastily, but throat cancer's a slow but sure killer. Takes a few decades to develop."

"Dove." Her lips formed the name without sound.

"Dove Randolph?" His face grew solemn as he pressed his hands together. "He had an operation five years ago in Salt Lake. Radiation, too. A painful process, but he took it like a trooper. We'd hoped for the best, but survival percentages are against him. Haven't seen him in months. I'd ask him to come in, but he's his own man."

Heading back to the RV, Terry stopped for takeout fried chicken, the usual assortment of mashed potatoes, gravy, cole slaw, and buns. When she returned to the truck with the savory bags, Judith remained in a reverie no pill could induce.

"As a callow freshman, I went to a fraternity party of med students. The Beatles were on Ed Sullivan that night, and we were as excited as puppies. Later I danced with a young man wearing a Nehru jacket. He asked, 'Do you believe in love at first sight?' 'Certainly not,' I said. Then he raised my palm to his lips. 'Neither did I . . . until tonight.' The world's most prosaic opening line. Never thought about it until now. Do you suppose that was Fred? People change in nearly years. All I recall were those smooth hands."

Terry cocked her head with interest. "And did you—"

"Did I what? Romance was not on my agenda. Never even told him my full name. I went home at nine to finish my paper on Bismarck."

"Another family trait. So how did an OSU boy get out here?"

As they hit a bump entering the campground, Judith eeked and adjusted her foot on the bench seat. "His Uncle Will from Dallas was the town doctor, took over from a practice started in 1900 in that very office. No Mormon, just dedicated to healing. Fred joined him. And they worked together until the old fellow died years ago."

"I like him." She gave her voice a seductive edge. "And so do you apparently."

"A gentleman, *rara avis* these days. And did you see those cuff links? The devil's in the details." A saucy smile crept over her face as she peeked into the bag, her nostrils pricked in anticipation. "My voracious appetite's making a reappearance. So much for good intentions. I had intended to bide on soups for seven days and get back into my favorite jeans."

As they pulled in, Terry noted that Mitch's bus had been replaced by a tent trailer with an air conditioner on top. With leaky plastic flaps, a waste of electricity. "A week's our limit if we want to make any more stops before heading home. Your ankle should be better by then. No walking for awhile. You'll probably get pretty bored. The grocery rents videos. Maybe Gail can tell me where to buy a cheap combo TV."

Judith pounded her small fist on the dash. "I'm not breaking our rule. I can still read and write. And of course, the crutches must be returned."

Chapter Nineteen

To savor the sun and escape the confining trailer, Judith had marched her crutches out to the chaise lounge. Beside her on the picnic table sat a sweating glass of iced tea with a lemon slice. She sipped quietly, absorbed in Walter's Fremont book, jotting information into her journal as her eyebrows rose and fell. Between her legs, Tut snored, head on the bandaged foot.

At the picnic table, Terry rotated the Escalante map, reading her notes about Melanie's travels. "Doesn't that pressure hurt?" she asked.

"Camaraderie is more powerful than nerve endings. Pets are the ideal tranquillizer . . . when they're not stepping on prickly pear." As she stroked the silky head, he burbled, tongue lolling.

" 'Read the signs,' you say. Somewhere in here . . ." Terry flapped the map, beginning to tear at the creases. "Is the key to Melanie's death. Intuition is stronger than optical proof."

Judith turned a page. "I hadn't expected to find these Fremont cousins so fascinating. Do you know that four distinct artifacts distinguished them?"

No use interrupting her aunt in lecture mode. "Do tell."

"A rod-and-bundle basket style. A gray coil pottery. And listen to this, a one-piece leather moccasin using the dewclaws of a mountain sheep or deer. How ingenious and advanced, actually. The Anasazi used yucca fibers."

"They both sound uncomfortable. What about Melanie? Don't you care anymore?"

Judith's face mixed weariness with resignation. "Of course, but I feel helpless and humiliated with this ankle. Maybe it was an accident after all."

"Like the propane disaster. Merely a bump in the night."

"Remember how sweet Dove was to Thelma at the ice cream place? If she knew about the bodies, everyone at the ranch did. That boy Craig seemed so nice. It's hard to imagine one of them creeping here in the middle of the night. And how would they have known the layout of the RV?" Judith pursed her lips and scanned the campground. An older couple with canes made the circuit. Their comfortable Lincoln Town Car with an Illinois license was parked in front of one of Gail's rental cabins. "When is the other proverbial shoe going to fall? Maybe one of us should start carrying my little friend. Or is it 'packing'?"

"Don't be ridic—"

An ear-splitting shriek filled the air. Tut leaped off the lounge, threw back his head and started to keen.

Striding purposefully down the road came Joyce Davis, parrot on her shoulder, trailed by a thin woman with an oxygen tank bumping its wheels on the gravel. "Charmie, here's these nice Ohio folks," Joyce said. Introductions were made, the parrot secured on a low branch of a scrubby pinyon, and Tut banished to the trailer after the bird shot him evil glares and managed a screech that lifted the hairs on the back of Terry's neck.

"I saw you at the ranch," said Charmaine. "Craig said you came back to ride. Nufflo's my little man. He could eat a bushel of our apricots, provided I take out the stones." Her glance fell upon Judith's bandaged foot. "Lordy, did you fall off your horse?"

"Twisted my ankle climbing up to an alcove on a hike. Dr. Fred told me to keep off it for awhile."

"Isn't he a gem? He visits us once a month. All the girls are in love with him."

As she engaged the woman in easy conversation, Judith smiled, her voice nonchalant. "The scenery at the ranch was breathtaking." She paused and touched one finger to her long, sharp nose. "I came the first time to visit Deborah Winters. We taught at the same high school in Ohio. What a disappointment to find her gone to Washington."

Charmaine smoothed the wrinkles in her shapeless cotton sundress, its colors washed to pale imitations. After a quick intake of breath, a crimson flush brightened her sunken cheeks. "It seems only yesterday she was with us."

Judith spoke with deliberation, her head angled like the parrot's as she homed in on Charmaine. "April. That's hardly yesterday."

Her tongue tracing the bottom of her upper lip, cerise suckbacks highlighting the grooves, Charmaine stumbled for words. "I, I mean, her memory is still fresh."

Terry traced a line in the dust with her sneaker. "Memory. Sounds like she's dead."

A spasm of coughing stopped the conversation as Charmaine staggered to the picnic table, Joyce urging the tank forward. Alarmed at the effectiveness of their tactics, Terry poured a glass of iced tea from the pitcher, regretting her poor hospitality. Goodbye to another pie delivery.

Charmaine gulped noisily, dribbling brown stains on her dress, then twirled a dial on the tank and tried several agonizing breaths, her nostrils flaring like a racehorse broken down at the finish line. Finally, she sighed in relief. "I get a . . . spell every now and then. What were you saying?"

"We were sorry to miss seeing Deborah. Were you good friends?" Judith asked.

Charmaine tossed feeble glances at Joyce, who was twisting her fingers like Chinese party crackers. "Truth to tell, she was kinda better educated than me. Chummed up with the bridge crew."

"Bridge was her passion. She clipped every Charles Goren newspaper column for her scrapbook. Her letters mentioned two other partners. Blanche and Adrienne," Judith said in one smooth, unbroken dialogue.

With a shudder, Charmaine began to weep, tears leaking from the corners of her bulging, codfish eyes, as if her face had shrunk around them. "My allergies. I'm a martyr every summer."

Joyce massaged her sister's back and tsked. "Soon as the rains start. Damn that mold."

"We'd love to talk to Blanche and Adrienne. They sounded like interesting ladies. Maybe they could tell us more about Deborah." Terry glanced at Judith. What fun to work in tandem, reading each other's thoughts. "Perhaps we should make another visit."

"Those dear souls were well past ninety." Charmaine placed one hand on her chest. "It's lovely and peaceful out there, but we're not equipped for the very elderly. The time came when—"

"They died?" Terry tossed a surreptitious wink at her aunt.

Charmaine summoned a sad smile, only a shaky finger on the tank control betraying her nerves. "My heavens, no. But they needed more care than Dove could provide, God love the man. They were taken to Salt Lake City where the families arranged for nursing care. Sure is lonely without them."

After they had left, Judith said, "A poor liar, wouldn't you agree? How did you like my improvisation about Goren's column?"

"Brilliant. Blanche and Adrienne. Gone to glory. Two more accounts in the Zion Bank." She frowned, her jaw line firming. "If only someone would take us seriously."

"Like an FBI agent? Don't they get involved only if crimes

cross state borders?" Judith considered the foot anchoring her to the park. She tossed her crutch onto the gravel. "Charmaine will probably head straight back to Dove and warn him. You know, I should ask Fred about the women. He's the only doctor in fifty miles. Meanwhile, I want to finish Walter's book."

"I'm still thinking about Melanie. Help me with this," Terry said, bringing the map to Judith's lap. "Maybe you'll notice something. Hole-in-the-Rock Road was the first place she went, an easy drive from the dig. She never mentioned returning, nor any interest in the caves. Next came the Griffin Top Road by Dixie National Forest, and the Burr Trail Road east of Boulder. Down the Smoky Mountain Road, she had a close shave with a washout on the way to finding dinosaur tracks on the Collet Canyon Cutoff."

"I'd love to see those. What's the road like?"

" 'Washout' speaks volumes to me." Ignoring Judith's contemptuous puff, Terry trailed her finger along the map, a mass of bluffs, buttes, benches, and measureless canyons. "A week before she died she went down to the southeast. The Cockscomb. That's near the Vermilion Cliffs that start the staircase. Rough country. Telegraph Flat is the last place on the map. Then this stupid Dead Fox Hill in her final entry." She blew out a frustrated breath and rapped the table lightly as if summoning helpful spirits.

Judith snapped her fingers. "Didn't she mention meeting some man?"

"The old prospector? Hank, no, Hick. You're right. He's the only one who gave her any directions. But where would I find him?"

"Isn't there a picturesque false-fronted saloon still standing after a hundred and twenty years?"

"In Mormon territory?"

Judith turned a page in the Fremont book, and her voice

Chapter Twenty

Terry scribbled a map. "Prospectors have to buy groceries somewhere. Here's where I'm headed. Kanab's the nearest town in the area she was searching." Then she placed her camera and water bottle in the daypack. Making little fuss was important. Judith felt bad enough about her helpless condition.

Her aunt aimed a crutch tip in her niece's direction. "If you're not back by seven sharp, I'm calling Gail, and then that oaf Reg. Don't get into trouble. You're not quite the same girl who left Cleveland."

Heading west on 12 and south on 89 for an hour, she stopped for gas in Hatch, a quaint hamlet. A tall, erect graybeard in a white shirt and bolo tie marched out with a salute. "Full service here, lady," he said, as he washed her windows, checked the oil and water. "Ever since I got back from World War II, I'm still at it."

"I was born when self-serve was invented," she said as he polished the side mirrors. "Maybe you can help me in another way. I'm looking for an old prospector."

He guffawed, nearly dropping the nozzle. "Check the cemetery."

"Is there a live one called Hick?"

"Hick Jacet? That old rooster lives south a piece. Not sure where exactly. Stop at Rusty's in Kanab. He handles the mail."

Traveling aimlessly was guzzling time and gas, but paved roads were a safe adventure. Terry recalled Judith's glee at their harrowing trip to Hole-in-the-Rock. If her bold aunt ever got used to driving the truck, no telling what risks she'd run. Terry continued down 89 to Kanab. With no other stores in the vicinity, Rusty's stocked everything from groceries to tires and hardware. Coleman lanterns lined up by battery-operated flashlights. A strange mixture of old wood, dust, and vinegar greeted her. Beside a pickle barrel, the crimson-haired owner, his name embroidered on his shirt pocket, propped his well-darned stocking feet on a battered steamer trunk, huffing "The Yellow Rose of Texas" on a mouth organ.

For the sake of custom, Terry bought a spicy beefstick and a plump dill, munching at the cash. "I love harmonicas. And you're good. Any coffee here?"

"Ain't got no capo-chino," he replied, heading for an enamel pot steaming on a single burner. "Do you okey-dokey with home brew, though. Don't hold with them prissy filters. Getcha a bitta calcium crunching a few egg shells. Cheaper than vittymins."

Terry accepted a ceramic cup and paid the tab. The coffee was dark and strong, yet not bitter. She tongued the shards to one side of her mouth, then felt foolish and swallowed. "Beats Starbucks."

"What bucks?"

"A big national chain. You can't imagine what they charge." She hoisted the cup in mute praise. "I'm looking for Hick Jacet," she said.

He scrutinized her with a gimlet eye. "Revenoor?"

"What's a revenoor?"

"Guess nowadays they calls them the ATF fellows. Keepin' an eye on everthing what makes life fun." Rusty clacked his dentures and wormed a gnarled finger into his hairy ear with undisguised pleasure. "Hick sells a bit of shine on the side. Hard to catch, less'n he wants to hole up in the pokey in a winter cold spell. Frets about leaving his ladies, though."

Terry did a double take. This was Mormon territory. "His ladies? You mean he—"

A wheeze like a broken accordion came from Rusty's thin chest, passing for a laugh. "See, ma'am, where some Utah men have too many wives, Hick's married to his Indian motorcycles." He pointed to a faded road map tacked on the wall. "Head about forty miles east along the Shinarump Cliffs. Then turn left at the leaning telephone pole and drive 'til you hit Paria. He has a cabin across the river in Pahreah." He pronounced both words Pa-rya.

Terry's eyes crossed with confusion. "Are you talking about two different places? The name for a wild dog? A cur?"

Rusty decided that his privates deserved a thorough scratch. "Past cure for that old Mormon town. That's P-A-H-R-E-A-H. Near fifty families there in the 1880s. Cattle, vineyards, nice little spot. Then floods kept washing 'em out. Place was doornail dead except for tumbleweeds until the movie folks built a set about two miles closer. Called it P-A-R-I-A, easier to spell. Used ta shoot oaters there. Tourists like to take photos. Washed out in a storm, but got rebuilt by some historical society."

Terry pondered the mental jigsaw puzzle, afraid to mistake the directions and become buzzard bait. "Are there any signs? Where does Hick live? Paria or Pahreah?"

"Hell, lady. You're not going to find anything else moving other than a scared lizard. Drive over and look around. It's not rocket science."

Down the road, eye on the map at her side, she passed Telegraph Flat, Melanie's last destination, turning at the leaning pole onto a rutted dirt road. Minutes later, she approached an assortment of wooden buildings with the characteristic squared storefront above the roofline and porch, far too similar to be anything but imitations. Getting out, she crouched like a gunfighter, hunching her shoulders to survey with mock wariness the dead-quiet scene, imagining Gary Cooper stone-still on the main street, an army of one, Grace Kelly peeping from a window, once glassed and lace-curtained instead of an empty, broken eye. The buildings were dwarfed by a mountain of sandstone built at the bottom of a sea once writhing with life. "Do not forsake me, oh my darling," she hummed, accompanied by the insistent tickings of grasshoppers. Remembering that Melanie lay in a cold grave waiting for the snows of Michigan sent her back to her mission.

Returning to the cool cab, she stepped on the gas, quickly reaching the end of the set. Ahead lay the shallow Paria River glimmering and rippling in the sun. How deep? She got out and walked to the edge. Twenty feet across, perhaps a foot in the center. Suppose a hidden sinkhole bogged the truck? As her eyes wandered, Terry shook off the imagined dangers, observing single tire tracks crossing in several places. With renewed confidence, she switched to Four-Low to navigate the rocky route, holding her breath for interminable seconds, then bumping up a slope into the scattered remains of old Pahreah.

An abandoned cemetery with only a memorial plaque sat on one side of the road, farther along the skeletons of starveling fruit trees. Remnants of stone foundations and a few chimney stacks were all that remained of the historic town. Yet someone stood on guard. Incongruous as Lady Liberty in the desert was a flagpole flying Old Glory in front of tarpaper shacks with metal roofs. One tilting, doorless shed displayed motorcycles in states of deconstruction, wheels, frames, seats, and engine parts assembled with care on makeshift shelves. A rusted metal advertising sign on the outside wall featured a tweedily clad young man, legs in puttees, striding a thin-tired motorbike, its long, angular handlebars embracing him. In one corner, a chief's head sported a long feather, and in the background, robed natives stood stoically beside their tepees, arms folded, observing his progress across the plains.

From underneath the cab of an ancient, round-fendered Ford 100 pickup, a junkyard Shepherd cross wearing a stars-and-stripes bandanna raced up barking, lowered its head for a pet, then groveled to expose its belly. Terry stoked the dusty fur, unable to resist a friendly animal. His muzzle was white with age, and a piece of his ear was missing.

"Geronimo don't have teeth enough to hurt you none. He's Gerry for short," said a voice from the sagging porch of a clapboard cabin supported by cement blocks. A bird feeder with a pecking sparrow hung from one roof support, beside it a short, muscular old man in patched workpants, red long underwear, and a black cap with the chief's head logo.

"Hick Jacet?" Walking over, she extended her hand to an arm thick with curly white hair, survived a few pumps, and gave her name. "Rusty says you're the King of Indian motorcycles." She knew nothing about motorcycles, but could she wing it? Getting on his good side was job one.

His face lit up like Times Square on New Year's. "You a collector? Got me a 1939 Chief with a Princess sidecar great for kiddies. Slap on fresh paint, and you're riding in the Easter Parade."

She flashed a wedding cake smile, then lowered her gaze like the ingenue she'd never been. A little flattery might go a long way. "Mr. Jacet, I need expertise more than wheels. You know this area like the back of your hand, I've been told."

"Don't mister me. Cut out the soft soap and come on in 'fore the blasted sun fries ya." A grizzled, unshaven porcupine of a maitre d', he held the screen door and jabbed his thumb, missing the last joint, toward two wicker armchairs. With padded seats, they were soft and accommodating.

From rough-sawn rafters, a ruby glass oil lamp hung bordello-style, a hurricane lantern on a scarred pine table next to a pile of dog-eared motorcycle magazines. Near a shelf of canned goods and an open sack of flour, a cookstove sat in one corner, its pipe piercing an asbestos square on the ceiling, two warming ovens and side rack, nickel trim shining proudly with the name: South Bend. A hand-pump was bolted to a soapstone sink, and a crank radio confirmed the absence of electricity.

Hick sat stiffly. "I've blistered my butt and busted my knees crawling over every godforsaken inch of this territory."

"Uranium?" She recalled Chris's history lesson.

He guffawed. "Do I glow in the dark? No truck with that toxic crap. I mean Queen Silver, girlie." His browned face, a roadmap of creases, shifted into sadness. "Not worth dogshit now since the damn Hunts broke the market, but to me it's pretty as a woman in a *Playboy* calendar."

With an inner laugh about the archaic but endearing "girlie," Terry made conversation to pave the way to serious questions. Creating a rapport had been a tenet of Journalism 101. "I've admired those turquoise bracelets."

"Pawn's your best bet."

"Pardon?"

"Like in pawn shops. Natives hock the family jewels to buy a happy weekend when money's short. The old stuff's a bargain if you know where to go. Not in Utah, though. Mormons frown on that traffic near as bad as liquor. Head across into lawless Colorado. Cortez or Durango."

"To be honest, Hick, I'm looking for a location in the desert near here. A student's diary mentioned you."

"Me? That so?" He narrowed his eyes, hobbled to a burnished oak sideboard, the only discordant touch in the rustic cabin, and picked up a quart Mason jar and two jelly glasses. "What's this all about?"

"A young woman died in . . . a so-called accident in the Batty

Caves near Escalante." Terry related the discovery and her suspicions as a reporter.

"Don't get no papers, but I heard about that one, wondered if . . ." He poured generous portions and passed her a glass, then sat back, removing his cap to rub a bald pink dome like polishing a prize bowling ball. "Gettin' ahead of myself. Shoot."

For a moment, Terry hesitated, her hand frozen in midair. Despite the hospitality, his wary interest spooked her. Had this geezer been involved in a more sinister fashion with Melanie? For that matter, why had she waltzed in here alone? Predictable perils of the solitary female sleuth. Then he winked, toasted her with a gallant motion, and drained his glass, squeezing his eyes in satisfaction. Returning the gesture, she sipped the clear, innocuous liquid, puzzled at its harmless trickle down her throat. Spring water? Then liquid fire exploded in her belly. She wiped away a wash of tears as a pleasant warmth rushed through her core. Whatever cocaine offered, this was close enough.

"What is it?" Realizing her rudeness, she added, "Packs a punch, but . . . smooth."

"Tater brandy. Brew it myself. Old oak bourbon barrels from Tennessee double the fire power." He offered her the jar. "Top-up?"

"Wheeoow. Chased out the cobwebs. But I have to drive." She cradled the glass like a time bomb. "Melanie Briggs was on a dig in the Dixie National Forest. Drove all over in a Jeep on her days off. Telegraph Flats was the last destination I could identify. She mentioned other places I can't locate. Making them up, perhaps, or they might mean something to you."

His rheumy eyes flashed with recognition, then sorrow creased his brow. "A Jeep? What did this here girl look like?"

Terry leaned forward, hopeful at the spark, willing herself to recall the newspaper photo, not the mummified reality. "An attractive blonde about twenty."

"That's her. A real beauty. Never done told me her name. Met her over to Kanab gassing up. Passed the time of day. Asked me the best place to scout for ruins, relicts, whatever the hell they call 'em." He swirled the brandy in his glass like a liquid crystal ball, his eyes creased in sad reflection.

"Did you give her any directions?"

"Christ on a cactus, it's a crapshoot." He pointed to a window where torn calico curtains flapped in the hot breeze. "Go up Hackberry Canyon this side of the river, or Molly's Nipple to the west. Drive if you got four-wheel, but sooner or later you burn boot leather. If you can stand the heat, roll seven-elevens, and don't end up as a coyote's supper, you might find a shard or two. Not legal, damn gov'mint says, but who cares out here? I'm from New Hampshire. 'Live free or die.' "

From her pocket, she retrieved her notebook and leafed through the pages. "Raven Roost. Eagle Hill. Mean anything?" She omitted Nicky Bench for obvious reasons.

He doubled over with laughter, snorting through his mottled purple sugar beet nose. "Sounds like the villain's hideout in a movie shot in Paria or in Kanab. Used to call that area 'Little Hollywood.' My old pal Bert was an extra. Sawbuck a day for falling off horses. Wrecked his back some wicked. Wore a leather corset 'til he croaked at ninety-five."

She tried a second sip of the liquor, holding it in her mouth in connoisseur fashion to appreciate the subtle flavors. Oak, blackberry, lemon? A miracle from a humble potato. Then she turned to the last entry, holding her breath, her hands folded in resignation. Another nonevent, as Judith would say. "Dead Fox Hill."

One bushy eyebrow wavered like a fussy caterpillar. He slurped from the jar, savoring the brandy like mother's milk, then swiping his broad mouth on the back of his hand. "Dead Fox. Yessir. Now that might signify. Not on no maps, though."

"Surely foxes die all the time. Who notices?"

"Die all the time natural. Don't die all the time poisoned." He steepled his hands, cracked with wear, the fingers knobbed with arthritis. "Had us a rabies scare here year or two ago. Guv'mint dropped poisoned bait from planes. Could be the girl found what's left of their sorry carcasses."

Against her better judgment, Terry's nose for the hunt took over. "I have a 4 × 4. If it's not that far, could you point the way? If I can find what she was doing around here, then I—"

He grabbed a fly swatter and dispatched a buzzing bluebottle. "Kitchen Corral Wash is another place to start. But not alone, partner. And I ain't promising jackshit. Spin the roulette wheel, we got a barrel of numbers to guess where she headed."

Terry stood in excitement, shaking his weathered hand in impulse. Then she grimaced at her watch reading five o'clock. "We'll need an early start, and it's so far back to Escalante."

He scratched his nostril with the truncated thumb, an illusion of the entire digit entering one bulbous nasal cavity. "You're welcome to share vittles with Gerry and me. Chili's a prospector's middle name. Like it hotter than a griddle in Hell?"

Terry made the sign of the cross. "Where's the nearest phone?"

Chapter Twenty-One

Despite the furnace of Hick's chili, spiced with flakes of ruthless dried habaneros and sluiced with quarts of warm Utah beer, Terry slept sounder than a citizen of Pahreah's graveyard. The small back room with pasteboard walls, a metal cot with a lumpy mattress, mismatched sheets, scratchy army blanket, and an orange-crate bedside table transported her to an evening in *Riders of the Purple Sage.* Called to the park office from Rusty's, Judith had assessed the logistics and conceded without fuss. The good doctor had dropped by, inviting her to "sup" in Panguitch at Grandma Tina's where the angel hair pasta with Alfredo sauce had won kudos from *National Geographic Traveller.* Companions of the Sixties, they were lamenting the passing of Woody Hayes and the close of the Kahiki, Columbus's legendary theme restaurant.

The smoky smell of bacon set Terry's mouth watering as her eyes flickered open, confused at the darkness. "Coffee's boilt! Heat's going to beat us to the trail!" yelled a gruff baritone. Yanking on her shirt and jeans, shedding fastidiousness under the realities of life ad Hick, she finger combed her hair, soaped and splashed her greasy face with the water pitcher and basin her host had placed unseen like an offering on an army trunk along with a tiny wrapped bar of Ivory. A threadbare but clean folded towel had a Manger Hotel logo, a national chain anchoring downtown Cleveland, RIP courtesy of Motel 6.

Hick was whistling "Dixie" at the stove, flipping bacon bits out the window into Gerry's slavering mouth as the dog gave obliging howls. A steaming cup sat on the oil-cloth-covered table beside a brown beehive crock of dark honey and a punched can of evaporated milk. Terry doctored the coffee, blew on it for caution, and drank deeply, jump-starting her groggy nervous system. The smell of burning piñon perfumed the kitchen, and the glowing lamplight gave the room a warm sepia wash.

With a clatter of pans and dishes, onto the table slid two enamel plates of scrambled eggs, home fries, bacon, and baked beans, followed by a gargantuan pyramid of hot biscuits. A jar of Welch's grape jelly and a bottle of Tabasco finished the parade as Hick sat down in faded army fatigues, arranging a huge napkin underneath red suspenders.

"Do you cater often?" Terry asked, wondering where to start. Could she taste everything at once?

"Dearie, you couldn't afford me. Not all the money in the US of A Treasury could divorce me from my solemn obligation to these motorcycles. They're my faithful ladies."

As Terry forked into the savory meal, coaxing Hick for his biscuit recipe (bacon grease the magic ingredient), he related his service in the Korean War as a motor pool sergeant, where he fell in love with the Indian machines. How he raged against the yuppie Harleys, the "furrin" Honda Goldwing and other "sissy" Japanese and German lines. Marshaled on the wall in simple frames were photos of a 1926 Scout, a 1934 Sport Scout (a Pennsylvania police bike), and a 1952 Vincent Rapide.

"So the Indians ended production in the Fifties? My aunt might have seen one." She remembered his commentary from the night before and was beginning to feel genuine nostalgia for the sleek steel harem.

His eyes flashed and cold disgust flooded his face, scrapes and white residue from a styptic pencil showing an effort to shave. "No, ma'am. They're making 'em again, retro something whatever. Don't prime my pump on that ball of wax."

Keeping a serious expression amid the mixed metaphors, she admired the feminine lines of the Rapide, a panther sculpted in metal. "I see your point. A poor imitation is an insult. Why remake *Gone With the Wind*?"

His gaze fell fondly on the picture, a gnarly finger tracing the cowling, lingering on the leather seat and feathering the headlamp as if revisiting the face of a lost lover. "Designed like a fine watch, but strong enough to beat to the end of the earth," he said with a catch in his voice. "Build cars like these beauties, we'd still be driving Grandpa's Model T."

Terry's crotchety '96 Ford Probe, pricy Japanese underneath an American skin, sat on summer vacation in the garage, having required a wiper motor, alternator, catalytic converter, front wheel bearings, and CV boots, all at tax time. "Wringing five years from a vehicle is a miracle. They either rust to pieces or nickel and dime you to death."

Hick drizzled more honey into his mug. "Saw your loaded-up Chev. Wait until you have to replace those computer gizmos. Gotta have a Ph.D. to fix that stuff."

Reaching for a fourth biscuit, Terry smiled. "I shouldn't have to worry for years and years. GM sold me an extended warranty." She hesitated to mention its $2,000 price tag.

"And you paid the shot?" He crunched a rasher of bacon, gestured with his knife to drive home the point. "If'n they're such hot stuff, how come you had to ante up beforehand?"

Remembering the Dutch uncle salesman with the picture of an adorable Schnauzer on his desk, she wrinkled her brow and spooned a blob of jelly onto the flaky biscuit. The plates emptied, and Hick rose for coffee refills, draining the pot.

As Terry rounded up the plates, he directed her away from the sink like cutting out a wandering heifer. "Them dishes'll bide. Time we were going." From a corner, he shouldered a lumpish khaki canvas pack with leather-buckled pockets, then filled two canteens at the hand pump. "Nothing fancy. Jerky and cornbread."

As she watched the sky's peach-Melba glow, Terry had second thoughts. They could drive the truck only so far, and then . . . Would this haphazard search bring answers? She retrieved her prim straw hat from a peg, took a long drink from a bucket and dipper, and followed Hick like an uneasy pup.

He disappeared into the largest shed, while she visited the tilting outhouse. The night before, she'd approached with trepidation, expecting spiders' nests, mice, even a sharp-fanged rattler coiled below. But the walls were freshly whitewashed, the hole complete with polished oak seat, demurely down, a fresh roll of baby-soft paper on a nail, not a rude comment penciled on the walls, and only a faint aroma of lime. A well-thumbed *Reader's Digest* honed her vocabulary, but she missed two questions. Par for the course, Judith.

When she returned, a clank, a cough and a rumble sounded, and out chugged a metallic blue Indian motorcycle with matching sidecar, red plastic container of gas strapped behind the seat along with the canteens. "A Princess for a princess," he said, mock-punching her arm as she stood slack-jawed. "Didja think I was gonna get chauffeured in your motorized living room? All those bells and whistles like tits on a bull. Rather have a mule, but Buster Brown died at twenty-two climbing the Scorpion. Hope to cash in that way myself, 'stead of rotting in a nursing home having some sour old broad wipe my ass."

After collecting the binoculars from the truck, with apprehension she lowered herself into the sidecar, nestling her feet around the pack, which was stuffed into the nose. Snapping on goggles and a worn leather helmet that might have served at Dieppe, he handed her duplicates. "Gallup army surplus. One-stop shopping." To join the drama, Terry sailed her straw hat across the yard onto the porch, where it landed conveniently on a rocking chair.

The sun was blossoming onto the horizon, a molten egg against a palette of mauve and brown, dissected by one bright bloody streak. For an hour, they drove up Kitchen Corral Wash, a bumpy ride, despite the cushioning pillows leaking feathers into the air like a downy ticker tape parade. Terry sneezed several times while rearranging the bolsters. Up a draw they continued, climbing switchbacks until they reached the plateau leading to No Man's Mesa. In this technicolor moonscape, sandstone forms rose in all directions, an eroded seabed more navigable underwater. Blackbrush, sage, and narrowleaf mahogany clumps injected green into the auburn wasteland. Where shade provided succor, whorled milkweed and scotch thistle eked out a bare existence.

"How did anyone survive here?" she asked, licking her lips against the caking dirt, wishing already for another drink, trying not to sound whiny.

"I'm no history prof," he said, "but we puny whites came in the Spanish explorations. Back ten thousand years, the natives camped or cached food in every solitary mile."

"My aunt sees granaries everywhere," she said as they rounded a curve and paused at an overlook to settle the dust. In the distance, folds of sandstone turned on their sides, beaching like a pod of distressed whales, their sparkling pink and gray layers ribbons of contrast.

Hick spit on his goggles and rubbed them on a checked handkerchief. "The Paria drainage system. Part of the Chinle badlands."

Terry translated. "Badlands. Malpais. Bad country for travel, but devastatingly beautiful. No one could imagine these images in a nightmare, nor capture their colors in a dream."

"Guess I take her for granted, but I wouldn't live anywheres else. Nature's a killer, though. Stay on her good side, you'll see another sunrise." A striped lizard leaped onto a rock to gauge the danger, swiveled its tail, and scuttled off faster than the eye could follow.

"I guess you're no stranger to stories of death in the desert, especially with naive and unprepared tourists."

"Heard of Everett Ruess?" At her blank look, he continued. "College boy came here before the war, the Big One, not Korea or 'Nam. Got him pack mules and tramped into the wilderness."

"After gold or silver?"

"Naw. That was the crazy part. Sort of a writer fellow. He just plain liked to wander. After he went missing, some of his stuff got printed. Understand it's popular now that folks are getting interested in our history. Pretty words, some say, but not a lick of sense. Worked his poor beasts until they dropped. I can't abide a man who mistreats animals, even out of ignorance." He took a drink, swirled the canteen to assess their supply, and passed it over. Another gallon had been wedged beside the gas can. Hick took no chances.

"Missing? And presumed dead?" She took frugal gulps, moistening her dry lips.

Hick gave a lopsided smile, then chuckled. "He'd be over ninety. Disappeared in 1934 in the Escalante Davis Canyon area. Never upturned a shred of him or his belongings. Lucky mules were found in a brush corral."

Terry shuddered. "Sounds like my aunt and me breaking down on the Hole-in-the-Rock. Discovered in 2060 during construction for a Wal-Mart. Only the rusted body of our Sierra and melted Mozart CDs beneath a mound of blowing sand."

He scratched under his chin where the strap rubbed. "No stopping so-called progress. Damn paved roads write a death sentence in asphalt. 'Course I'll be watching the buzzards circle my bones by then, looking up or down's gonna depend on my currency."

After another sweltering two hours, resting momentarily to munch a handful of jerky and cornbread, they rousted a piñon jay from the shade of a juniper bush. Terry's long-sleeved cotton shirt was plastered to her skin, and there was no prayer of locating a fabled plunge pool. Stretching her legs as Hick relieved himself discreetly behind a clump of blackbrush, she chafed at the thought of continued confinement in the sidecar coffin. "How far could Melanie have come on this trail . . . if she came at all?" she asked as he remounted.

He gestured toward a massive rockfall from a crumbling butte in the distance. "Mile past that turn, she'd go on foot. 'Course she could have packed a tent and a blanket. Stayed another day if she hauled enough water."

"I don't think so. The professor kept a careful eye on his students. She would have been expected by supper time, nightfall at the latest."

At a spacious, level spot that invited parking, Terry paced the area like a bloodhound, peering under rock overhangs and bushes, wherever evidence might have blown. She wiped her brow, crusty with salt. "Wind would have erased any tracks of her passing. Stupid of me to hope for a scrap of paper or something personal."

Hick scratched his chest, then grabbed the jerrycan to gurgle gas into the tank. "Just like Ruess. You'd a thought something would have remained. A watch, belt buckle, pieces of leather."

Uncapping the binoculars, Terry scanned the nearby hills with eyes untrained for an immense vista. On the printed page they could ferret out a lone typo, an errant apostrophe, but in this vast, alien world, which punished the brain with information overload, how could she spot the anomaly? At last her gaze settled on a promontory. She squeezed her eyes against the idea of an object out of place. With a hopeful expression, she turned to Hick. "I think I saw something. Give me a minute."

With distances as hard to gauge as a mirage, her minute stretched into half an hour. Terry groped up the hills and slid down, scuffing her boots and bruising one knee. Then she hiked a sandy ridge to the subject of interest, her calves aching in the effort. The sun bore down like a drill bit. This was no time to travel the desert. Ancient feet avoided high noon. Protected by sparse three-leafed saltbush were piles of small bones resembling cat skeletons. A tip of fluttering red fur in a creosote clump waved a gruesome flag.

"Dead Fox Hill. Your hunch was right," she explained when she returned, panting like an animal, hands on her hips as her temples pounded. She promised her parched lips a Vaseline application before bed as she took the canteen he offered. "I'm betting she came this way."

"Got you a keen eye. Nice going."

As they proceeded, the trail became rutted and irregular, and at last narrowed between rock cuts, squeezing the sidecar and rubbing paint from one corner. Hick said nothing, but she saw his knobby fingers grip the handlebars. "Opens up in half a mile. In a Jeep, she couldn't pass here unless it flew," he advised, his eyes straying toward the wound on the sidecar.

Surrendering to the blazing heat, any concept of further activity an exhausting prospect, Terry hung her head. "I think the fat lady just sang. Sorry to have wasted your time. You've been generous and patient. It wasn't rational to imagine we could find anything. This isn't a Hollywood film."

Hick thumped her back like an encouraging uncle. "Hell, best fun I've had since Christmas in jail, 1989. Sheriff's wife gave us Wild Turkey, roast turkey and all the trimmings."

At the overlook near Dead Fox Hill, they stopped to drink before the final push. Hick was describing his overhaul of a

1914 Indian single, from a reverie about the original saddle stamp to the trouble finding a headlight shield. But he'd sold it for $9,500, eating off the profits for two years. His words were disconnecting into fractals like her DirecTV transmission during spring solar interruptions. The sun had stunned her into submission, and she grew faint with only the tight leather helmet for protection. Despite regular drinks, she hadn't had to urinate, a sign of dehydration. Never again would she complain about Ohio humidity.

Before they remounted, circling ravens croaked conversation. One feathered down, hopping indignantly, pecking at the ground. Suddenly a glint appeared. The brazen bird juggled silver in its beak, then a speck of green. At Terry's approach, it waddled away, blinking wary yellow eyes. She called to Hick. "Any food left? I have an idea."

With a grin, he rummaged in the pack and tossed a sliver of jerky to the bold bird. It cocked its head, gave a warble that let the object fall, swooped up the titbit in fair exchange and flapped off in noisy triumph, leaving jealous cohorts shrieking.

Terry stooped for her prize, struggling for focus in the white glare. "A piece of jewelry?" She shielded her eyes as blind fingers probed the delicate object. "A girl with a green pompon. It's a cheerleader charm."

"Pretty trinket. Mean something?" he asked.

If Terry weren't struggling against collapse, she would have done cartwheels. "We saw a bracelet in the cave. And she was a cheerleader in college." She placed the bauble into his large paw, and he considered it mutely like King Kong examining Jessica Lange. "We don't know when she lost it. Maybe weeks before her death."

"Don't think so." Hick made a grocery run to Kanab once a month on the last Friday. Their meeting at the gas station had been only a few days before the girl's disappearance.

She placed the charm securely in her breast pocket and buttoned it over a slowing tympanic symphony. Heart attacks didn't run in her family, or she'd have been expecting one. What now? Back to the Batty Caves? She never had seen that descanso. Would the accident site contain clues that the sheriff had missed?

Against the pitiless sun, she shielded her eyes to read the ever-present five o'clock. Was her watch frozen in time? Then she gazed transfixed across the barren, surreal Martian landscape, shimmering waves of heat almost palpable. "What's out there, Hick? Where did she go?" And if we know where, she thought, we'll discover why.

He shrugged, sucked at the canteen and wiped his mouth on his sleeve. "You could fan out in all directions, spend months trying to second-guess her path. More like she gave up here, like us."

On the return drive, stoically enduring the bounces jolting her spine and bruising her hipbones, Terry ruminated about showing the charm to the sheriff. Another instance in which to feel foolish. Yet taking a risk was the secret to life, Judith promised. Those fearful of upsetting the status quo had an easy but unimaginative ride from cradle to grave.

"Bless those brave Mormons," she whispered, her aches a shallow imitation of their rigors. With the roar of the motor, Hick hunched forward as if poised to liberate Panmunjom.

Arriving at the cabin gritty and sweat-stained, Terry accepted the offer of a shower. At the rear of the shack, an elevated fifty-gallon oil drum with a showerhead promised tepid but cleansing relief. "Like on MASH. Loved that Hawkeye and Radar. And that Hot Lips. Whooee! Ever met a lady like that in my hitch, I would have re-upped," he said as he brought her soap and a towel. "Used to watch it at my buddy Bert's house."

"My aunt bought the tapes. And speaking of nicknames, how did you get yours?"

"Might not know it to look at me, but my family weren't no low class. Dad was a Classics professor at a prep school. Same one I got kicked out of three times. It's Hector. But 'Ah, Heck.' drove me nuts. My brother Paris answers to Parry."

Later at the truck, a desiccated sponge restored to normal weight, she leaned out the window. "I feel bad about scraping the sidecar. Would you take something—"

White whiskers returning to his cheeks, Hick pooched out his lower lip and waved a fresh jar of brew in dismissal. "Gotta whole gallon of that color. Gives me a project to pass the time. Young folks wouldn't understand that, fast world they live in. Listen now. See some jim-dandy scenery if you head east to Big Water, then take Smoky Mountain Road to Escalante. It's rough, but you can put your baby through its paces."

"This baby's had enough for one day," she said, declining another opportunity to be stranded in a remote location. "One last request for my memory bank. Say 'jerky'." With her camera, she snapped shots of Gerry with his grinning old pal.

Fifteen miles from Hatch, she approached a dirt road with a sign pointing east to a place called Alton. Skewed at the crossroads was a familiar robin's-egg blue pickup with signature patches of Bondo. A half-opened jack and a spare tire sat uselessly beside a rear flat. Terry slowed in curiosity, expecting to see Tocho, wondering if his prosthetic was unequal to the tricky mechanics of tire changing. As she accelerated, her mirror framed a slender brown arm dangling from the window.

Chapter Twenty-Two

Terry jammed on the brakes, then reversed, tires squealing on the boiling asphalt. As she charged out to peer into the truck, she found Kaya lying in the back seat, panting like a dog, her face contorted and sweat trickling down her high-boned cinnamon cheeks. Clutched in one hand atop a distended belly was a small leather medicine pouch on a rawhide string. "I thought no one would ever stop," she said, fighting back tears. "Water broke an hour ago. My husband was at work. I didn't want to bother him. Thought I could make the hospital in Panguitch with plenty to spare. But the tire blew, and I tried . . . until the pains hit."

Terry nodded, her forehead icing with fear, as if she'd stumbled from the wings into an absurdist play without having read the script. What did Kaya mean about water? Then she gave herself a mental swot upside the head. Grade ten health class when she had kept a copy of *A is for Alibi* inside her book for the tedious lectures about STDs.

Grunting, Kaya pointed at her slim watch. "Five minutes between contractions. Three weeks early." Another stab rolled back her eyes, and she bit her lip until blood trickled onto her white cotton blouse. A zia sign was embroidered on one breast, the four directions, winds and seasons. The balance of life.

Terry opened the door and eased into the passenger seat, shoving aside an overnight bag. Unclear as to how to proceed, except to offer mindless Samaritan platitudes, she tried to force confidence into her shaky voice. Why hadn't her mother let her see Mimi deliver those kittens? Forget the miracle of birth. This looked like sheer hell. "I can take you to the hospital." With unease, she wondered what the volatile Tocho would say about an Anglo ferrying his wife around. If Chuvio had told him about the incident at the gas station where Melanie's name had caused an ugly explosion, he might connect the dots.

"No time. I've helped the midwife since I was twelve, and Shuman was an easy delivery. Stay with me." She tried to swallow, licking her bruised lips. "My mouth is so dry."

Terry felt her adrenaline hit overdrive, a disturbing instinct she'd been happy to avoid in a quiet, uneventful life. Yet running or fighting wasn't going to bring this baby home. "I have water in my truck. How about towels? I always carry a few in case our dog—"

Kaya cut her babble with a shriek and a pound to the window. Galvanized into action, Terry stumbled from the cab, legs as elastic as Olive Oyl's cartoon pipestems. Her vision narrowing into a tunnel of pitch, she knelt in the dirt and took deep breaths, slapping her face to avoid fainting. Rising in humiliation, she reached the GMC, upturning clean towels from a bag under the seat. She grabbed her water bottle, freshly filled at Hick's. Why wasn't she feet up and fed by now, sharing a tall, cool beer or two or three with Judith? That wish was as far from reality as a pennant for the bridesmaid Indians.

"Hurry!" Kaya called, the urgency in her voice underscored by a subtext of agony.

With no handy extra doors on the venerable truck, Terry stretched over the bench seat into the back, positioning herself around Kaya, her legs cramping into a space fit for midgets. Readying the towels like an overcaffeinated masseuse, she felt vague abdominal pangs in a weird autonomic sympathy. Her great-great-grandmother Ann had had seven children, all boys.

In the name of God, how, and more to the point, why? She passed the bottle to Kaya, who sucked against the stifling heat in the truck, a portable easy-bake oven. The woman closed her eyes, folded slender brown hands like a Madonna, and went limp. Minutes became millennia. No rise to the ample chest, no flicker of eyelids. Terry choked back the possibility of death, her pulse throbbing in her temples. Should she leave for help? Try to shift her into the GMC? Then Kaya's smoky eyes snapped open, and she said as if ordering a work crew to dig a ditch, "Let's go. This baby wants to greet the day."

Without the slightest hesitation, Kaya yanked up her skirt and fumbled with her soaked panties. The world spiraled into a tiny circle as Terry stared mesmerized, eyes widening in tandem with each millimeter of soft, pink cervix. A wet crown of jet urged outward, forced into breath with the heaves of Kaya's stomach and sinewy thighs. A being within a being. The rocks had spoken. A partner in the dance of life, Terry moved in rhythm, humming to herself, easing the slippery cocoa head, stuffing towels mindlessly wherever space appeared. A metallic reek of blood filled the cab, primitive, essential, mingling with their pungent sweat. Only then did she decipher siren words singing in her brain: "Give me two piña coladas."

Suddenly a swirl of dust devils rocked the truck, then moved off. Terry was gasping like a marathoner in the last mile. With sharp white teeth, Kaya nipped the umbilical cord, tied it with the dexterity of an animal balloon twister, and began scooping the afterbirth into a plastic bag. A squalling female lay next to her, working surprisingly muscular legs in protest against being jerked into a loud, bright universe. "Wrap up Maska, will you?" she asked politely. "According to family tradition, you're her godmother, but maybe you don't want the honor."

"I'd be proud. Does her name have a special meaning?"

Kaya grinned, pointing to the churning arms. "Maska means

strong. Shuman means rattlesnake handler."

Terry swaddled the squirming child in her favorite blue towel, a lion cub on one corner, and nestled her into Kaya's eager embrace. She peered at the bag. "Why did you—"

"It will be buried to give power to the weavers. Some tribes dry it for medicine pouches like mine."

Terry moistened a towel and gently cleaned Kaya's hands. Then she turned to marvel at the miniature human, shriveled face expanding and contracting. What awaited this baby? Abject poverty or a share in an enlightened community inspired by the hope of the new century? Tiny fingers grasped her thumb with astonishing power, sending a warm, nurturing message to her loins. Nature's tricks. This little innocent would demand 24-7 service for the next decade and a half.

"I don't even know your name," Kaya said as Terry helped her out of the seat, and they headed for the GMC, "but I've seen you in town."

Aware of the woman's pain and exhaustion, reluctant to broach the sensitive situation about Tocho and Melanie, Terry told her about their trip from Ohio while they drove toward the setting sun to a quiet street in Henrieville.

A dozen tires anchored the roof of an old trailer, enlarged by plywood add-ons. Neatly swept, a homemade brush broom by the front door, the yard was planted with shady Russian olives. As they entered a narrow room cooled by window fans, beside a crib with a sleeping child, a wrinkled, bow-backed woman in a simple cotton dress rose from a small loom. The grandmother, probably Judith's age but bearing the burden of a harsh and demanding life. She hugged Kaya and exchanged words in lilting, musical cadences. With a toothless smile that could melt glaciers, the woman gave Terry a universal gesture of gratitude. Uncovering the newborn, then nodding in satisfaction, she disappeared into the kitchen area and returned to press a package into Terry's hands.

As Kaya settled into a rocking chair to give Maska her first meal, her steady, almond-eyed gaze met Terry's. "Thank you," she said.

Shortly after nine, still shaking, Terry pulled up to the RV beside a shiny hardtop Jeep with a bumper sticker: "I Support the Right to Arm Bears." Outside, chatting companionably with her aunt was Doctor Fred, wearing a white Huarache shirt and blue slacks, Corona beer in hand. An ice chest with an army of bottles and an assortment of cold cuts and salads sat on the picnic table, under which Tut snored contentedly.

"Sorry I'm late," she said to the parental atmosphere. "You'll never guess what happened. I'm a godmother, and I need a beer!"

Judith's mouth opened soundlessly as she stretched awkwardly for her crutches. "Allow me," Fred said. Prying off the cap with a silvery instrument, he handed a bottle to Terry. "Church key," he said. "Probably Greek to such a youngster."

Terry dropped heavily into a chair, leaned back and drained the bottle in four gulps, cooling her head against the frosty glass. "Entirely copacetic."

Judith asked, "So you were saying before this old codger interrupted?"

"I've lived a week in two days." With no idea what Judith might have shared about Melanie, she spun a story about meeting Hick, exploring the Chinle badlands in a punishing sidecar, then rescuing Kaya. Expedition of events would pave a fast track to bed.

"I splinted a wrist for that old sidewinder Hick years ago. And Kaya has a healthy girl, does she? I suspected she might deliver early. Have you considered a second career as a midwife?"

"I nearly fainted. Not a promising sign for a rookie. Besides, it's far too messy." Shoving back bloody memories, she browsed through the food on cruise control, constructing a gigantic sandwich from homemade rye bread and opening another beer.

"Aren't we the chosen people? Joyce came by. Probably wanted to see if we were still here. I gave her a bottle of wine for her thoughtfulness." Then she peered at the bread. "You don't suppose there's anything wrong with . . ." As her voice trailed off, Fred gave her a strange look.

Recalling her gift, Terry went to the truck, retrieved the package and placed it onto the table, opening it to release a heavenly fragrance. "Tamales!" She added several to her plate and ate until her stomach ached. Spicy shredded pork inside fresh maize puree. Nothing since breakfast but jerky and cornbread. A desert monk's diet. "Kaya's a strong woman. I hope Tocho treats her well. But certainly if he keeps drink—"

Fred reared like a bee-stung bull, crashing his bottle to the table, foam flowing over his hand. "Lord God, my dear girl. The man's allergic to liquor. One pissant three-point-two beer makes him puke like a poisoned pup." He shook his hand dry, then bent to stroke an alarmed Tut. "Apologies for the crudeness. Where in tarnation did you hear that malarkey?"

Had Chris been listening to town gossip? She shook her head, still disoriented after the long trip. On an empty stomach, alcohol added a potent buzz. Suddenly she felt the heavy heat of the evening sink into her aching muscles. "Maybe I misunderstood what someone said. It doesn't matter. Mother and child are safe. I'm glad I could help." She yawned faster than she could cover her mouth, then to her embarrassment, hiccoughed.

Judith's mouth flickered a smile, but her unusually soft voice registered concern. "Go freshen up, relax, and leave the old folk to carry the shank of the evening. I'll be back on my pins any day now." She rotated her foot, rose hesitantly to test the weight.

"Careful, girl," Fred cautioned, reaching out an arm.

Terry excused herself and dragged into the trailer like a mobile sack of potatoes. With the adrenaline high dissipating faster than smoke in a wind, she felt drained, unable to think straight. Soaping in the shower, she turned the wrong dial for a cold shock, then nearly burned herself into a lobster. "I'm dangerous," she muttered.

She shrugged into an oversized Cavaliers T-shirt and fell onto the bed, suddenly aware of the return of the air conditioner blast. *White noise in my private retreat. I won't be bothered by Fred and Judith, just drift off.* A glass of cool spring water at hand, she opened the map she had nearly memorized and retraced Melanie's final travels. From the timeline and her own judgment of distances, it would have been not only impractical but nearly impossible to have eaten breakfast with the group, then driven over to hike the Paria area for at least six hours, judging from where the charm had been found, finally trailing back to Hole-in-the-Rock Road to the Batty Caves. She furrowed her brow, wanting to think and hardly able to. What about that rough Smoky Mountain route Hick had mentioned? In the dark? Even Melanie wouldn't have been that foolhardy.

She folded the map. And Melanie hadn't lost the charm on an earlier visit, according to Hick's dates. Another thread to follow. Nick's crew would be back tomorrow. If Danny had known about the bracelet, surely they had seen it, too, and might have heard about the missing bauble. Stretching like a weary cat, she cozied the light blanket around her aching shoulders, tormented by a rib cage of pain. Sidecars should be outlawed. Maybe they were, for all she knew.

Terry closed her eyes, reflecting on Tocho. By now he'd learned about his new baby. Would he resent her help, connect her in paranoid fashion with Melanie through his nasty brother at the gas station? As her body relaxed, her stuttering mind took the reins. This new flurry of activity and Fred's entrance into their life had shifted the propane incident to a cobwebbed corner of her memory. Maybe they shouldn't have stayed in Escalante like sitting ducks, even if they did own a Toller. Who was the predator and who was the prey, she wondered, her eyes lead sinkers. From outside came a titter from Judith, a hearty roar from the doctor, then "Shhhh. She . . . her rest." OSU nostalgia. Her aunt in coquette mode was a revelation. If this turned serious . . . As she lapsed gratefully into a heavy sleep, images of submarines with bridal bouquets festooning their periscopes floated in a rippling pool.

Chapter Twenty-Three

"Hell, yes, I remember that stupid charm. Once a cheerleader, duh," Amy said, pulling a tube from her pocket. She joined Terry at a table in the mess tent. Behind them, Walter chopped lettuce and assembled sandwiches. Amy rubbed sunscreen on her long, shapely legs, then down her muscular arms. Her motions were leisurely, as if admiring a work of art. Capping the tube, she wrinkled her nose. "Yuck. Can't get the unscented kind in the boonies. Perfumes are criminous."

"And the day Melanie disappeared?" Terry asked. "Did you see it then?" She nestled the charm back into her shirt pocket.

Amy flipped back her braids. She furrowed her tweezered brows, pulled a Virginia Slims from a pack, snicked her mini-lighter and let smoke drift from her nostrils like hot breath in January. "I didn't like Melanie from Day One. Little Miss Sabe-Lo-Todo. That's what my Spanish prof called a wiseass. Every morning, noon, and night. Flap, flap, tinkle in our faces. Reason I know that the cheerleader was still there that morning was 'cause that green glinty glass from the pompon always smacked me in the eye."

Terry assessed her coolly. Her Cleveland naiveté vanishing by the minute, she had learned that people could lie. "I'm surprised at your hostility. Her diary said that you cut her hair. Sounds friendly enough."

Amy's ripe plum eyes widened, and she biffed her cigarette onto the ground near Walter's foot. With a *tsk,* he toed it out.

"You were reading her diary? That's pretty damn nosey."

Terry sat back with a casual smile, ignoring the challenge. A higher power guided her, the goal of finding Melanie's murderer. Or murderess, she wondered, noticing Amy's strong mahogany arms, probably able to crack walnuts faster than Falco. A six-foot Amazon fond of weight training? "The diary . . . dropped into my hands, so to speak. If it reveals any information about her death, bad manners are the least of my concerns."

Amy gulped a Diet Coke, then snorted through her long, aquiline nose. "I saw her dick with that park ranger in Boulder. Mouthing off statistics. Pointing her stubby little finger at him. Babbling about the human myoglobin found in coprolites in Cowboy Wash being proof of cannibalism. As if the poor jerk could understand scientific data. He should have clocked her on the spot."

Terry managed a definition of coprolites from the context. "Is Cowboy Wash near here?" Melanie's unpopular opinions might have won her enemies elsewhere.

"Dolores, Colorado."

"I hear she was kind of a loner. But you know, Amy," Terry said, arching an eyebrow Judith-style, "someone around here tried to get her in trouble by erasing the sign-out sheet."

Amy pursed her shimmering lips, a look of absolute unconcern washing over her face. "Probably invented the story herself. Short people are so insecure."

Something was simmering here. Terry stirred another pot. "I wondered about her friendship with Nick. He seemed devas—"

Amy stood abruptly, crushing her pop can and dropping it onto the ground with a clink that twitched Walter's angular neck. "Nicky was never, and I mean never, interested in that twit. Now pardon ME." She stalked off, oblivious to the narrow-eyed look Walter flashed her as he piled the last of the sandwiches onto a paper plate and covered it with a towel.

"Just jealous. She's been trolling for Nick ever since we left Michigan." His voice cracked as he took off his apron.

Terry shifted self-consciously, glad that she wasn't wearing that provocative outfit from their last meeting. Judith had compromised her in that melodrama. "Don't tell me they . . ."

"Nick's strictly business. I noticed that he avoids being alone with any of the girls, especially her. And she's very competitive with all of us. Now that Melanie's . . . gone, Amy will probably take the graduate school scholarship."

"It's certainly a stroke of luck for her, sad circumstances aside." She wanted to believe in Nick's innocence, past and present. The soul of ethics, Walter didn't know or wasn't telling. "Anything new on the dig?"

"Unbeeelievable! I'm surprised Amy didn't tell you. We might have a kiva here. That's rare for a Fremont site, according to Madsen. But this crossover area could be Fresazi or Anamont." He noticed her confusion. "A joke around here. Those are Madsen's terms. The book I gave your—"

"She's devouring it. Out of commission with a sprained ankle, or she would have spent every last minute of our trip here."

"Aren't those figurines totally awesome?" he asked, his eyebrows fussy bees.

"The fig . . ." Terry looked into the distance where a hawk traced ellipses, zeroing in on a tiny prey below. Nick stood with a notebook in hand, looking one way, then the next, as if laying out a plan. "Excuse me, Walter. Catch you later." She moved off toward the far end of camp, but as she approached, a student rushed up to Nick with a roll of marking tape and they began a conversation. Working hours were a bad time for a chat. Shrugging, she turned aside to let the man do his job.

If she went back to the RV, Judith would be napping, better left undisturbed. Time apart healed the small scratches that built up when two people traveled together. What could she accomplish before lunch? As she drove out of the park and along Route 12, she saw a descanso with filigreed metalwork. What about Danny's, fashioned with loving hands? Perhaps the caves had a few more secrets to whisper.

Terry gritted her teeth against bad memories and looked both ways before turning toward Hole-in-the-Rock. Thumping along to the beats of Chakira, music Judith didn't appreciate, an hour later she was following the dirt track toward the Kaiparowits Plateau as if led by a siren song. Relaxed about the distances, she drove slowly to enjoy the scenery.

The miles toward the hills soon disappeared, and she began the gradual climb toward the Batty Caves. She stomped on the brakes at a sudden movement in her peripheral vision, realizing as her heart thrummed that it was a frightened jackrabbit, large pads springing him into the shelter of black sagebrush. Parking nearby the "Capone" car, mute witness to a young girl's death, she left the truck and entered the late morning heat. In her surprise at discovering the diary, she hadn't asked Danny exactly where the shrine was, but why erect it miles back at the highway? Surely he hadn't placed his tribute at the rough wooden doors of Melanie's tomb, she hoped as she turned the corner to the caves. With an eye to caution, someone in the justice system had padlocked the doors. Terry didn't want to revisit that scene. She'd replayed the image like a stuttering film, the bundle on the bunk, a doll, a person, Melanie with her dreams turned to dust as her remains winged back to frigid Lansing.

A lone insect from some nearby seep troubled her ears. "I heard a fly buzz when I died." With a minor in English, Judith loved to quote dear Emily. Impatient in the punishing torpor, ignorant of the fine points of the tradition, Terry wondered if Danny had collected the descanso. She followed a steep trail up a rocky wash where Nick had said the Jeep had broken down.

With his strong legs and bruised heart, had Danny trudged to some more desolate corner far from prying eyes?

After ten minutes, sorry that she hadn't brought her water bottle, slightly nauseous from dehydration, she encountered a boulder garden and forced her legs across the irregular terrain, stopping at last to ease the burn. Oil stains smeared the ground, and rocks bore the scrape of metal. A broken plastic "eep" caught her attention. She picked it up like an artifact and placed it on a rock. The washout headed upward at a 45-degree angle, an invitation for a mountain goat. As her sore feet in their useless runners protested, she found a flat place to sit, then jumped up as the yellow tail of a giant hairy scorpion scuttled into a crevice. "Where is it, Danny, or were you inventing a convenient story?" she asked aloud.

Returning to the caves, on a whim she turned to follow a small draw, the soil hard-packed, as if a water course had packed it into mud. Near the woody bush of an orange globemallow, she saw Danny's offering and approached in quiet admiration, kneeling to inspect it. A plastic wreath anchored the paperback, gum, CD, and Koko charm. Some crass tourist might take the objects, and she could have enjoyed Tony Hillerman's classic southwest mystery, but it would have been sacrilege to despoil the fragile ceremony. No sign of the stuffed tiger, a coyote's playmate perhaps.

Danny had set sandstone slabs on their sides to form an enclosure of about two square feet. One rock had fallen over. When she righted it, she noticed an odd tire track with a lightning pattern cut preserved in the hardened mud. How many weeks had the descanso been here? Time for wind and sand and the occasional shower to obliterate other evidence of police cars, an ambulance, a local reporter. Even Danny and his motorcycle. She shrugged, then photographed the touching site for Judith. Had anyone written an article on the phenomenon?

A Mexican Catholic tradition, were descansos limited to the Southwest? What was the origin of the word? Desolate? Disconsolate? She took shots from all angles, including close-ups, using a filter so that the brilliant sun wouldn't whiten the contrast.

Half an hour later, back down the road near Devil's Garden, a figure bent over a bicycle passed her. It looked like Amy, smartly outfitted in lycra shorts and top, and a streamlined neon helmet. The bike was a modified mountain model, able to handle rough roads but lightweight for better speed. The girl was in top shape, Terry thought, watching her work the pedals like pistons. The dig was only twenty-five miles away. It was possible on a day off that she could have reached the Batty Caves, but how in the world would she have lured Melanie there?

Before returning to camp, Terry went to the grocery for water. They were using nearly three gallons a day. Annoyed at the mundane chore, she poked a cart between the cramped rows, selecting chicken wieners, rolls, cheddar cheese, a withered cabbage, a bag of hoary carrots, a jar of mayonnaise, and a pound of bacon for Hick's biscuit recipe. Heading for the cash, she spied Dove in labored conversation with a portly, bald man wearing Coke-bottle glasses. A box of groceries sat on the counter between them, and they seemed to be pulling it back and forth. She positioned herself behind a Doritos display, snatching a jumbo Cool Ranch package and then a bottle of Naya, opening them both for an impromptu picnic. Thirsty from the parching wind, she craved salt like a steer heading for a blue block.

Dove rubbed his hand across his forehead, his face ashen. "Trust me just a bit longer. We'll settle up."

The bald man pulled on the box. "Let's get down to brass tacks, Dove. You owe me back to May. We been friends since

LBJ left the White House, but you're plain presuming now. What if all my cus—"

"Have a heart, Phil. We got two more seniors come in from Grover and Teasdale. Not a single, sorry-ass relative to give 'em a pot to piss in. I'm trying to put clothes on their backs, get their Social Security coming regular, sign up for Medicaid. The red tape's fierce. And you know I need that new septic system sooner than later. Fifteen grand for a place with as many people as mine. The health inspector could shut us down. You wouldn't want that. Where would your Uncle Bud go?" He leaned away from the counter to cough. From the agonized voice, it was evident that he was laboring against a spasm.

With a grunt, Phil rang the brass cash register, pulled out a ledger, and made a precise entry as he peered at the figures. "You're no businessman, Dove. You're an unpaid social worker. Tell you what. I'll handle you another two weeks, and that's 'cause you're my sister's husband's cousin." He peeled back the wrapper on a GooGoo bar and took a thoughtful bite, working his dentures around the caramel. "Hate to sound so hidebound. There's talk of a big grocery chain coming in when the new park gets cracking. I'm hanging by my fingernails until my granddaughter finishes college or marries a millionaire."

Terry waited until the screen door snapped behind Dove's bent back. How beaten he appeared, years older than when she had last seen him. If he had been working a scheme for gain, this was telling evidence to the contrary. The septic problems jived with the odd smells they'd noticed at the ranch. Instead of rolling in money, he was having trouble keeping the business operating. Despite the questions surrounding the propane disaster, maintaining suspicions against the man was taxing her conscience.

Judith was enjoying a rare noon beer at the table inside when she returned. "I took shots of Melanie's descanso up at the caves on our favorite road," Terry said, unloading the water and placing the gallons under the other bench seat.

"Really? Next time Fred and I are in Panguitch, we'll get them developed." She winked at Terry. "I'm proud of you going back there after your experience. It mustn't have been easy."

"No patronizing, please. And here's some more information on Dove." She related the grocery store encounter.

Judith crinkled her eyes. "I called Dick. Blanche and Adrienne are getting their pensions through the Zion Bank in Provo. That's near Salt Lake. He's going to make some enquiries through a retired judge. There's a snitch line for this kind of fraud. It's out of our hands now. Whatever happens, I feel that we got some justice for Deborah."

Terry grimaced. "I'd still like to know where the bodies went. If only I had a bird's-eye view of the ranch."

"Not without a helicopter. Do you know anyone who flies one?" They both grinned.

That night after baked potatoes, grilled wieners, and a carrot salad that challenged their teeth, Terry took a stroll to collect her thoughts. The gibbous moon sliced the clouds like Poe's falling scimitar. The absence of birdsong called attention to itself. From the threatening pewter sky, another shower looked possible. Thunder rumbled beyond the hills, a cloudburst flooding distant arroyos. Too far to help Escalante, where the arid ground would suck the blessed moisture like the balm of Gilead. At the vacant end of the campground, far from the bustle of late diners bickering over cable television selections, she perched on a weathered split-rail fence. She tried to read the witches' brew of roiling clouds, mesmerized at what lay hidden in the shifting layers, a snail, an armadillo, a . . . cheerleader?

The scrape of a boot nearly tumbled her from her seat. Feeling foolish, she braced and turned to see a towering figure backlit by the jaundiced sodium beams of the campground. He wore black jeans and a luminous white shirt with a turquoise belt capable of choking a horse.

"I'm Tocho Nuvamsa," he said.

Her hands gripped the rough rail, finding little comfort in the substance of wood, short of a handy baseball bat. Saying as little as possible was her plan, yet she couldn't deny knowing the name. She should have known that sooner or later they'd cross paths. "Kaya's husband. How did you know where I was staying?"

His voice was low and gentle as he stepped forward, removing his Stetson. Darkness hid his eyes, but she felt their steady contact. "Folks who need propane don't stray far from town. I asked Gail. She saw you taking a walk." He paused, toeing the ground with one boot like a restive horse. "Sorry about my brother. He's a hothead like me. Doesn't mean nothing. I owe you a favor, if you ever need one."

Terry's tripping heart slowed. "I was glad to help. Maska's as beautiful as your wife."

"I'm a lucky man, and I'm going to make them proud of me." The simple pledge sounded so boyish that she understood the softness that bound Kaya with velvet chains.

Though Terry had relaxed her guard, she couldn't help remembering the angry man at the restaurant. As she rethought the scene, his actions reflected a smouldering resentment rather than a hair-trigger temper. Either way, Kaya didn't have to stay with him. With a job and a mother to help with childcare, she could have been independent. Hearing an approaching putt-putt, Terry tried a calculated risk. "If you owe me, tell—"

"Anything." He looked over his shoulder as Gail made her leisurely rounds in a golf cart, giving them a friendly wave.

The scene seemed benign enough. If she suspected anything truly dangerous, she and Judith would scorch pavement heading out of Dodge. Terry took a deep breath and plunged forward, describing her actions since finding Melanie, her newshound's implacable nose. "Everyone heard about your argument with Melanie Briggs. The sheriff must have cleared you, but for my satisfaction I'd like to know where you were when she disappeared."

A deep breath expanded his broad chest. He walked forward, one hand in his pocket, the other dangling useless at his side, and gazed up, as if seeking enlightenment from the purity of the fleeting moon. In the distance, more growls threatened, and a crooked flash of lighting silvered their faces. "I was out of the state, handy as it sounds. Kaya doesn't know the whole truth because . . ."

Terry waited, arms folded, sensing the advantage of learning something private and forbidden. Her heart tripped at the tension. "Go on."

"Sure I had words with the girl about that damn book. Nothing more. But it set me up later for a row with an ignorant tourist wearing our people's legacy around his neck like a cheap souvenir." He stopped and turned away, straightening his shoulders. She could have sworn that he wiped the corner of one eye. "We traded insults, and he raised a stink with my supervisor. I was suspended without pay for a month. The baby was coming. We don't have much put aside. My mother in Page, Kaya's family, too, they depend on me. I went to Vegas to gamble. The American way." He smiled engagingly, his large white teeth gleaming. "Cleaned up at blackjack. Over two thousand dollars. Enough to get us through if I work a bit at the garage. Kaya thinks I collected a debt from an old army buddy."

"Sounds like a handy story. How did you prove that to the authorities?"

He pulled out his wallet, full of Visa slips. "Kaya makes me keep all the credit information. Thank God for that fleabag motel."

Terry brushed a hand through her hair. "I'm glad, Tocho. But I'm still confused about Melanie. Too many unlucky coincidences."

He shook his shoulders like a massive steer. "Her ideas were evil, and she paid with her life, accident or not. Perhaps the spirits were angry at her disrespect. The sheriff's honest, but he's a lazy bastard. If you've got something—"

"Something and nothing." She related her experiences with Hick. "Dead foxes in the Chinle badlands. A charm. The land's so vast." She gazed at the fearsome silver bolts that fenced them like an electric prison.

"But the population's so small." He extended his left hand and gripped hers warmly. "Use your advantage, Easterner. Who else did she offend? Or what did she learn that needed to stay hidden?"

The scree of a nighthawk made her turn, the whitened flicker of its wing trailing on the updraft. When she looked around, Tocho was gone.

Plodding back to the RV, she started to reconsider the Man Corn idea as a motive for murder. Perhaps blinded by the obvious, she had failed to probe into every last corner, risk finding a scorpion surprise. Yet what could Melanie, an absolute stranger to Escalante, have learned that led to her death? So far the only local fraud involved Dove. But the diary mentioned nothing about him, not even horseback riding at Sunset Years. Was something more desperate aboil in town? The answer always lay one canyon over. "Judith," she said as she opened the door and tapped red dust from her shoes. "Cross off one more suspect."

Chapter Twenty-Four

"The mint's from Uncle Will's herb patch," Fred said as he engineered three juleps. "The sovereign remedies worked wonders." To Judith's inquiring eyebrow, he added, "St. John's wort for depression. Comfrey for bruises. Aloe for skin eruptions. Even in the desert, nature is a bountiful storehouse."

"With a soupçon of alcohol. Lydia Pinkham's straight-laced hormones. Don't tell the pharmaceutical companies," Judith said, fingering the yellow, bell-like flowers on a tall stalk.

"Some can be toxic, though," he said, laughing as Judith pulled back her hand. "That's monkshood. Source of digitalis. Don't nibble the flowers."

"To my old next-door-to-Kentucky home." Terry toasted them with the julep, milk-mild compared to Hick's brandy. Still, it was cooling on another scorching evening baking moisture from the monsoons and keeping humidity at bay.

Fred's house was on the street behind the clinic, a solid brick model circa 1920. In the thriving back garden, they sat around a fieldstone barbecue while a succulent sauce bubbled in a cast iron pot fit for a wagon train and baby beef ribs sputtered on the grill beside a dozen ears of roasting corn dotted with spices. On a metal folding table he had assembled cole slaw, baked beans and raisin-dotted brown bread in the shape of a coffee can.

"Mother taught her boys to be independent. Perhaps that's why I stayed an old bachelor." He tapped his teeth on the empty pipe, sucking back a smile.

"You could have taken your pick of twenty thousand OSU co-eds with that training," Judith said, refilling her glass from a bottle of Maker's Mark and a container of chipped ice. Tut chased Fred's young male cat around a lilac bush until a swift feline swipe convinced him to take refuge under a chair, licking his injured nose.

"I've been thinking," Fred said. "That area around Paria where you were searching with Hick?"

"Have you been there?" Terry reached for a sprig of rosemary, inhaling the scent like a tonic. For remembrance. For Melanie.

"My practice keeps me too busy for travels. Chris Robbins' family used to own acreage over that way. As a curious boy, he'd have ridden his horse all over the place. Go see him at Robbins Aviation east of town, or give him a call at home. We're pretty casual around here. Nice fellow. He'll help if he can."

Judith poked her niece's arm. "What a coincidence, Terry. Why you and—"

"Meet a hopeless matchmaker, Doctor. Judith knows every song in *Hello, Dolly.*" Pink to rival the hollyhocks climbing a twig arbor nearby washed over her cheeks, and she gave an embarrassed laugh.

Eager for an excuse to reconnect with the man who'd sent her pulse on a Nascar track, she used the portable phone Fred brought from the kitchen along with a directory. Chris answered at home as Judith chatted with Fred, casting an amused eye on her niece.

"You're still here? That's wonderful. I wanted to drop by the trailer, but I've been away this week. Flying job, then stuck in St. George waiting for a set of ignition wires," Chris said with a hopeful timbre in his deep, resonant voice. "How much longer will you be in town?"

"A few days. Until my aunt is mobile." Terry gave a brief

explanation of their perilous hike along Pine Creek. "Trying to climb into an alcove at her age. Can you imagine?" She laughed as Judith shook a mock fist in the air.

"I'm sorry about her accident, but I'm flattered you took a second look. Means I made a good choice. And she found initials in that alcove? I've seen them, too. Everett Ruess, an eccentric roamer, signed himself NEMO."

"Yes, an old prospector told me about him. I hadn't made the connection."

Closing her eyes transported her to a magical narrow ledge overlooking a millennium of stories in stone. No matter how many times she walked those canyons, she'd need to return. The experience was like a drug. Shaking herself back to reality, she began her tale about Hick and his beloved badlands.

Chris cut her off. "This is no way to have a civilized conversation, my lady. I miss those turquoise eyes. What about dinner tomorrow at my ranch?" He paused with a self-deprecating chuckle. "Don't expect the Ponderosa. Everything's a ranch out here, even a trailer."

"All set," she said, explaining as Fred heaped their plates. "I hope he's as good a chef as he is a pilot. Do all men cook out West?"

"Ancient frontier custom. Beats starving." Fred placed a gravy bowl of dark brown barbecue sauce on the table. "Tell me now what you think of the recipe. Bourbon's the secret."

Judith finished her second julep, giving a thumbs-up. "Why aren't I surprised?"

Late the next afternoon, Terry plucked the last bottle of wine from their supply. After that nightmarish experience following Nick's hefty cabernet, she had avoided reds. The vintage was a shy pinot blanc from Mirassou on California's central coast. Chris had hinted that they might be having fish. She pondered the practical but uninspiring clothes in the mini-closet, choosing a cream pair of retro pedal pushers and a loose blue shirt with rolled sleeves over a raspberry tanktop. Even though she hadn't brought any, jewelry seemed alien to the landscape.

Following his directions, she drove east, then wound north on Route 12. Over the perilous Hogback near Calf Creek, she held her breath again as she neared the death-defying thousand-foot drop-offs on each side. *Go with the flow. Don't fight it,* she told herself, turning up the CD. As Enya's ceremonial drums and chants rose and fell, came to a climax, then diminished, as if scripted by the same invisible wand, the land tamed itself, settling into lush green pastures with metal irrigation wheels linked by pipes. A few miles and turns later, she arrived.

Chris had been duly modest. The prefab bungalow was simple and compact, designed for one or a very close two. She hadn't asked his status, saw no ring, but a married man wouldn't have invited her home . . . unless his wife was away. Mental bells tinkled advice about women getting into trouble from hasty assumptions. Still, he hadn't pursued her after their hike. Had he really been that busy, presumed she'd moved on, or worst of all, dismissed her as a casual encounter? Through his business, he must meet eligible women primed for Western charm every other day. She set her jaw against the idea that he romanced a chorus line. No mistaking the interest in his voice when she'd called. The dating game had such psychological pitfalls that maybe arranged marriages had distinct advantages.

The house was surrounded by red hardpan dirt interspersed with grass clumps along a gravel drive where the Navigator was parked. A large propane tank sat to the side. Underground natural gas delivery wasn't a rural option. No garage, scarcely necessary in the mild climate, but an aluminum shed for tools and storage. A small RV covered by a tarp sat in one corner of the large, wire-fenced property. Black-eyed Susans and daisies straggled by the door in a cement block flower bed long neglected. The house was vinyl-sided, the uninspiring but practical variety she wished for Judith's home instead of intensive-care wood demanding a paint job every five years. She smiled at a vintage cast iron bootscraper on the porch.

Chris opened the door without a knock. "Saw you pull in. Enter at your own risk. Be warned that I'm no fan of cleaning." Terry followed him into a tidy living room with a chintz-covered sofa, duct-taped leather recliner and portable television. "My old friend Maria Gonzales comes over every two weeks to suck up the larger chunks."

" 'Kept a sparkling house' isn't what I want on my gravestone." She presented her wine.

Rotating the bottle with an approving *hmmmm,* Chris took it through swinging, louvred doors into the kitchen, calling over his shoulder, "Get comfortable. Back in a flash."

While sounds of culinary business occupied him, Terry noticed evidences of a long family history documented on the walls and bookshelves flanking a gas fireplace. Grandparents posed in sharp black and white while parents bleached into pastels. Some photos sat curling or in piles, as if he liked to sift their memories. In one gold-framed 8 × 11, Chris straddled a sturdy pony, lariat in hand, a gap-toothed grin on his face peeking out from under a five-gallon hat. No sign of another sibling . . . or girlfriend.

Aside from a shelf of biology, botany, and zoology texts husbanded from university days, the books echoed parental selections, mostly 60's and 70's *Reader's Digest* fiction condensations, except for a battered blue Peterson's bird field guide and a prominent positioning of *Riders of the Purple Sage.* Recalling his kinship with the novel, Terry picked it up as if meeting a mutual friend. "To my son the cowboy. Long may he ride" was inscribed inside, pages loose from decades of reading. Terry blinked in witness of the sense of belonging as she replaced it carefully. How fortunate to have grown up with a loving family. Then she swallowed back self-pity. Judith had done double duty.

Sporting a "Cook Rules" apron over his wheat slacks and checked shirt, Chris brought two glasses of wine. "I've been admiring your family pictures," she said. "Do your parents live in town?"

"Passed on ten years ago. Mom had a tough time getting pregnant before those wonder drugs. When I came along, almost like a grandchild, they'd been married nearly twenty years. Poured their youth into the ranch until I arrived to help out. A stroke for Dad. Quick and merciful." Chris ran a hand through his lustrous black hair, and a delicate citrus aftershave wafted her way, a sharp, clean scent, unlike Jeff's cloying Brut. "Mom couldn't coax her heart to go on without him."

"My parents died in an auto accident when I was eleven." Terry frowned. She hadn't meant to make this sound like a contest.

"I'm sorry for your loss." He lowered his head in respect. "So your aunt raised you?"

"When I wasn't raising Cain." She inspected the landscapes behind the people, framing lives with daily demands as they enriched spirits. "And these pictures were from the old place near Paria? Doctor Fred said that your family's ranch was out that way."

"Couple miles east of Church Wells. Three generations. Granddad left Kansas City and bought out a Jack Mormon during the Depression." At her confused expression, he explained. "That's what they call a rebel who can't cut the religious rigor."

"Sounds like winter Shakers back east. They came in the fall after the harvest and left before work starts in the spring. And after all those years, you had to sell? That must have been a hard decision . . ." With an empathetic smile, she pointed to the boy with the lariat. "For a cowboy."

"It takes a large family to work a ranch. Mom and Dad managed only me. Expensive machines solve some logistics, but it's more than a full-time job. And the droughts are brutal." Clearing his throat, he touched a finger to the picture. "Now I fly my ponies."

Sensing his pain, Terry switched directions, noting the straw-yellow color as she swirled the pinot blanc. "How's the wine?"

"Great choice. Light and dry. A whiff of pineapple and lemon. I had a white Bordeaux, but it might have been too heavy."

"At home, I alternate between jugs of Gallo white or red. Vacations spoil me."

"You deserve to be spoiled."

She turned to hide a blush, gesturing toward the swinging doors. "So what's on the menu?"

He slapped his broad forehead. "Whoa. I knew there was something I forgot." He led her into the compact kitchen where head lettuce, tomatoes, and yellow cubanelle peppers sat next to a hunk of Monterey jack cheese and a deep fat fryer of vegetable oil. Two baking potatoes needed washing, and a crusty homemade loaf seemed the sole progress toward a banquet.

"Maria brought the bread," he said as he checked his watch with a groan. "She promised her famous chiles rellenos, but time got short. Grandson's birthday."

"They're delicious. I've looked at some recipes in a local cookbook. Give me a tour of your cupboards and light the coals," Terry said, pulling off his apron while he raised his hands in mock helplessness. "And I need a beer for the batter."

He headed for the fridge. "Shiner Bock from Texas. Save a sip for yourself."

Within twenty minutes, she had the oil heating, the peppers

stuffed with cheese, waiting for the yeasty coating. A quick salad waited in a bowl. After slicing the potatoes, she added butter, salt and pepper, and nestled them in foil. “These need a head start,” she said as he returned.

With a flourish, he pulled a pan from the fridge and watched her expression. “German brown trout. I flew a dot.com whiz to Fish Lake and brought these little guys back in dry ice.”

Time for the cave woman to admire the kill. “Corn meal and spices. Perfect. They won’t have died in vain,” she said.

He refilled their glasses. “I’ve lived here all my life, but my dream is to raise vintage grapes in California.”

Another side to this complex man. “Seventh heaven. You might have a chance to compete if you stayed small and exclusive.” Despite the humble home, Robbins Aviation must be doing well. Starting a winery would cost a fortune.

Finally they assembled the meal on the rear patio at a rustic table covered with a blue cloth. Colourful Mexican dinnerware had been arranged with the cutlery. “The kitchen’s too small. Maria thought this would serve.”

“Biggest dining room in the world. The western sky’s a blockbuster movie. I should have grabbed more pictures, but what can do it justice? Besides, the rolls I took are crowding the fridge.” As Terry relaxed in the shade of the cottonwoods, a zree of a bird made her turn.

“Mom put feeders all over the yard at the old house. Cedar waxwings, piñon jays, and even a wandering mountain bluebird on a lucky day. Her Peterson’s guide has her master list. Over one hundred species.”

“Did you hear that—”

“Notice the last note?” he asked, touching her arm. “It’s a warbling vireo. Like the purple finch, but with a telltale ending note that rises in pitch.”

“The bold magpies hopping over the campgrounds make me

laugh. We should get a field guide for the West."

Chris picked up a serving spoon. "Don't scorch yourself on the rellenos. The inside is molten lava," he warned.

The fish was pink and flaky, the potatoes tender. Lathered in sweet butter, Maria's bread vanished as quickly as the tossed salad. They took turns complimenting each other like newlyweds.

After dessert, a Sara Lee chocolate cheesecake, Chris brought coffee. He spread out his long legs and made a comic motion to expand his belt. "We've been talking about everything but your adventures. If you don't want to spend the night," he gave a theatrical wink, "better start talking."

She'd nearly forgotten why she had come. Terry assessed him with a fanciful grin. Wouldn't that be a poser for Judith, trading sex for information? "It sounds foolish, but I might be onto something about Melanie Briggs. I've been track—"

"Mel . . ." Chris's eyebrows rose in a question. "Wasn't that the girl you found in the caves? I don't understand."

Half an hour passed as Terry explained the complex puzzle. Across the table, Chris's sensitive face reflected her horror and exasperation at the slight but tempting evidence.

"After the sheriff read me the riot act about meddling, I've been debating about showing him this," she said, placing the charm onto the table. It had replaced the shard as her amulet. It belonged in the present, unlike the shard. She was beginning to wonder if she had a right to keep it.

He picked it up with a sad expression. "So she lost it in the Chinle badlands, then ended up dead in the Batty Caves. Senseless. Sure I know that area," he said, leaning forward with his hands folded in the darkness, the candles wavering as a freshening wind moved the still air. "Very rough going. It's a day's ride from our ranch. Had to camp out when I explored as a kid."

"And Hick Jacet?"

"He's a Utah institution. Doesn't stray far from his patch. As for the old place, a couple from Boston owns it now. Writers." His laugh had a bitter edge. "Guess the scenery inspires them. Hard work motivated my folks, for all it got them. A working ranch is a live thing. These people bought a museum."

"Hick sent Melanie searching for relics back into the flats. What she found, I haven't a clue. The situation with the bar falling into place on the door looked suspicious." She'd used those words so often that they were becoming fact. A reporter's fatal temptation to turn chimera into reality.

He leveled sober blue eyes at her, and she noticed how they changed with each meeting, like the Western skies. "I admire your analysis. You've covered every possibility. Accident, practical joke gone wrong. But murder? Are you considering Tocho, because how could he—"

"At first I suspected him, but he's been cleared." She frowned. "Something odd, though. Fred said Tocho's allergic to alcohol. Didn't you say—"

"God, really? Could be that brother of his I was thinking about. Did some time for break and enter."

Welcoming the chance to summarize her data for the keen mind of a disinterested party, Terry drummed her fingers as her list of suspects dwindled. "A rather nasty girl at the dig disliked her. They both had a crush on the handsome professor in charge. With Melanie gone, apparently she's first in line for a hefty scholarship to graduate school."

"Cui bono? Sounds like a motive."

She recalled Amy's strong arms and belligerent attitude. "Women don't kill women . . . according to statistics."

He reached across the table and tapped her hand. Even in the faded light, she could see the brightness of his teeth. "But they are the deadlier of the species. And catching up fast. Ever watch CourtTV?"

"Aunt Judith is a pistol, as my mother used to say. Maybe I'll mature into the role," she said. "Reporters have to be tough. It's my first real story. Normally I'm a bug on the society page. What's also pushing me on is that I have a feeling someone doesn't want me to probe any further. A shadow man. Eminence grise, my aunt would say when she exercises her vocabulary." She felt lines of worry cross her forehead. "It could be Dove."

Chris's mouth made a silent "what." "Dove Randolph? What business would he have with that girl?"

"This is another matter. He's running a pension scam." Terry filled in the details about their experience at the ranch and their contacts with Dick.

"Three dead women? But he couldn't have—"

"I'm sure they died of natural causes, and perhaps he'll stop now that suspicions have been aroused. I don't imagine he has long to live anyway."

"Yes, I heard about his illness."

As the breeze freshened and the candles guttered out, she rubbed her arms. What had begun as a gala evening was turning into a post-mortem.

Chris stood up and motioned toward the house. "You look cold. Want to go in?"

The sun had surrendered in a ball of flame, simmering dull orange behind the dark chocolate hills. The temperature had dropped a few degrees. "At home we're inside six months of the year. Sunsets aren't on the menu unless you live in a high rise. Could you bring me a sweater?"

"Time for a Café Diablo." He flashed an OK sign.

Hearing the soft hoot of a night owl echo through the shadows, she willed herself soaring with Chris down a canyon, free as an eagle. She'd have to store these memories against the long Cleveland winter, yet watching a video of *Riders of the Purple Sage* might move her to tears.

Cardigan over his arm, Chris returned with two mugs on a tray. He nestled the sweater over her shoulders and sat down. "Let's think this out. Fill in the blanks. Make a timeline. If Dove fiddled the pensions, it was in collusion, since your aunt was in contact with her friend well after the shift in banks. Then you arrived and upset his plans, had him wondering if you'd take the information anywhere."

"What about the other women? Didn't they have friends or relatives?" The spicy cinnamon concoction laced with brandy was an ideal chill-chaser, its steam a potent promise.

"I guess not. That's why he's gotten away with this. But moving the bodies? He's a sick man. Everyone in town can see that."

"Got some help from the staff on the ranch. This scheme isn't a one-man job. All it would take is a truck or a wagon."

With the warmth of the spiked coffee restoring her, Terry thought of Judith's lecture on Bismarckian politics. The art of the possible. "I wanted to like him. He's in desperate need of money, begging for credit at the grocery, yet he keeps gathering indigents like stray puppies."

"Several seniors I know live there. So Dove's a modern Robin Hood. Everyone hates the government out here." He traced a finger along the lip of his mug. "Let's return to something you said earlier about a person in the shadows. This worries me. Have you been threatened?"

Terry sighed, wondering if Chris would take her seriously. "Let me tell you about the propane."

As he listened intently, nodding at each detail, his face creased between the eyebrows, and he blew out a slow breath. "You, your aunt, the dog. It would have taken a lot of nerve and a steady hand. I suppose those layouts are common."

"Not much variety when space is tight. Where's the stove in

your RV?" She pointed to the tarped vehicle at the end of the yard.

"Never been in it. Belongs to one of my mechanics. He stores it here since he lives in a small apartment over a store. Takes it to Fish Lake every August." He swirled the coffee in concentration. "You've been here awhile. Did anyone else go into your trailer? Someone from the park?"

"No, I . . ." She paused, remembering Nick's visit. He had used the washroom. "Not really."

"Not really often means yes." His expression was quizzical but he didn't pursue her ambiguous answer. "If you're sure about the lock, I'd say you've been either brave or foolhardy to stay, though I'm glad you did."

"The lock's like Melanie's death. Always the one percent possibility that it was an accident. So why not find the last unturned stone about her travels? You agree about the time factor, don't you?"

"Paria is a long way." He thought for a moment. "Her Jeep ended up at the caves. Doesn't compute."

"I'll say. Have you been there?"

"Those two Lichtenhahn brothers who blasted the caves were a local legend long before my time. I've passed by on the main road. Nothing up there I want to see."

The wind swirled a tiny tumbleweed across the patio stones. "We're leaving in a few days. Can you give me a tour of the area past Dead Fox Hill? I don't expect you to fly for free. Whatever you—"

He placed a fingertip on her mouth in a gentle motion. "In minutes we can cover her options. Technology has given us the tools. I'm at your disposal."

Chapter Twenty-Five

"Lift-off at nine," Terry said, taking a coffee to her aunt, who was fumbling at the curtain. The evening before, humming "If Ever I Would Leave You," Judith had wakened her with the shower noise and dissolved into giggles when reminded that it was nearly midnight. "Did you ask Fred about Adrienne and Blanche?"

Judith gulped at the mug, decorating her pajamas as Tut dashed past. "Give me a minute to warm up the engine. I'm not as young as you used to be."

After taking the dog out, Terry returned to the breakfast table, picking up Walter's Fremont book, which had captivated her aunt. Published by the University of Utah, it was an oversized paperback with seventy pages, full of illustrations of artifacts and scenes of Fremont life.

Emerging from the bathroom, yawning a bit deliciously, Judith sat down and snapped a salute. "Reporting for duty. Tricky to keep our investigation a secret, but get a man talking about himself and good night, nurse. Fred does pro bono work for the elderly. Blanche and Adrienne had pneumonia last winter and were slow recovering, so he was surprised to hear that they'd relocated in Provo."

Terry gave some thought to the friendly doctor as she muddled a spoon around a bowl of Rice Chex. "I hope you didn't make him too suspicious. It's clear that you like Fred, and he seems nice, but—"

"But me no buts. Get to the point." Judith propped her leg onto Terry's bed. The foot was yellowed, but the swelling was nearly gone. She'd been walking slowly with less pain.

"He's the only doctor in fifty miles. He had to have known about the fraud at Sunset Years."

Judith's pound to the table made Terry's bowl jump and set Tut's ears at an angle. "Absolutely not. He's a saint."

"Too many saints in Utah, or haven't you noticed?"

"Case closed on my doctor. You should have more faith in anyone graduating from the Higher State, as we called it. And I hope Chris is picking you up." Judith poured milk over her Grape Nuts. "Because I need to return Walter's wonderful book. They should be back at the dig now, so I'll want the truck. Too bad you were too busy to read it." She turned to one page and pointed to a pictograph from the Ashley-Dry Fork Valley. It showed abstract anthromorphs with high headdresses, wearing decorative triangled pectorals, the pattern mirrored below the waist in symmetry. The eyes were slits, the hair braided. With a teacherly annoyance in her voice, she said, "This is what I was *trying* to tell you about before you pranced off to Paria to see your prospector."

Clearly her aunt was miffed about missing the adventures. A quiet exit would be best. With an eye on the time, Terry focused on her plans with Chris. Could she hope to trace another step in Melanie's travels? Whatever happened, the trip would be another new experience, perhaps the last, judging from the nagging calendar. She got up to place water bottles in her daypack. "What did you say?"

"Snap out of your romance and learn something new. The last signal feature of the Fremonts." She turned another page. "This magnificent clay figurine, the prehistoric equivalent of a Faberge enameled egg."

Out of politeness, Terry joined her, captured in an instant by the geometrical design in three dimensions, a linear concept made solid. She wondered if the Fremont dressed like this or accorded the costumes to their gods. "Exactly like the pictographs. Space age figures. Maybe Von Daniken was right. How large are they?"

"Seven to eight inches. One side was flat. This is their totem, perhaps designed for a fertility ritual. Only a shaman had the power to possess them. Unbaked clay. Very fragile, which explains why the only ones found were buried. A set of ten was unearthed in a cave in 1950 by Clarence Pilling. A museum in the Price-Wellington area farther north has them on display. They're insured for three million dollars. I'd love to see them. Maybe next time."

Terry gave a low whistle. "That makes the prices for those Tularosa pots Nick mentioned look like bargain basement specials. As Walter would say, 'Unbeeeelievable.' "

Judith traced a finger along the margin. "Walter must have been impressed. He's made notes to do more research, even drawn a smiley face. I thought he was more serious."

"Poor guy. Now that I recall, he was trying to tell me about them at the dig."

Chris's Navigator pulled up, and Terry snatched up the pack, nudging her aunt in payback she couldn't resist. "Don't wait up."

Chris held the truck door as Terry skipped down the steps. "All set," he said as he raised her hand to his lips and planted a mock kiss. "This time you're getting the $9.99 tour."

At Robbins Aviation, the parking lot was empty. "Sunday's not a work day," he said. "Lip service to the Mormons, I guess, because now and then my mechanic comes in for maintenance."

Terry felt chagrined about keeping him from more important matters, not to mention the costly flight time, but she promised herself that they wouldn't stay out more than an hour. Time enough to fan out from Dead Fox Hill.

Shortly after Chris's thorough safety check, they climbed into the Enstrom 280 FX and belted up. He helped her adjust a pair of earphones. "Believe me, you can't hear yourself think without these."

Then they lifted off, the rotor blades spinning dust around the helicopter, the engine roar a muffle in her ears. In the huge bubble, Terry was amazed at the immediacy with the craft, a lightness of being, like being reborn a dragonfly.

As they flew, Chris explained their route. Coal Bed Canyon, then straight toward Canaan Peak. Crossing massive prows of the Kaiparowits Plateau, they headed southwest to Headquarter Valley and a place Chris called the Gut. "There's Grosvenor Arch," he said. A few Tonka toy cars sat in a parking lot, and miniature doll people walked up to the spectacular double arch formed in Dakota sandstone.

"One hundred and fifty-two feet high," Chris said. "This isn't the most direct way, but it'll give you enough appetizers to know what you'd like to see . . . next visit."

Chris continued over Round Valley, then over to the parking areas, camping sites, and wandering paths of Kodachrome. He pointed at the fabled "pipes," ancient volcanic stems of glass formed when geysers and mineral springs filled with debris, later exposed by erosion.

Then the land grew raw and foreboding as they turned south, canyons and gorges relieved by the occasional bench. Impossible to drive. Improbable to trek. Only science fiction would give access to this planet on a planet, and all the better for that limitation, she thought.

Terry blinked at the power, riding a personal high, sitting back to still the pulse at her temples, suddenly aware that her face ached from the constant smile of amazement.

Chris gave sidelong glances as he monitored the controls.

"Want to try?" he offered, tapping the stick with a grin that challenged her.

"And kill us both in a ball of flames?" Surely he was joking.

"Don't be afraid. I'm right beside you, and I have fast hands," he said with a twinkle in his eye. With infinite patience, he explained the use of the collective, the helicopter's primary altitude and power control. The cyclic governed the bank and pitch, the primary airspeed control. He would work the anti-torque pedals to compensate for her moves. "Use smooth, slight pressures, nothing abrupt. Changing one control requires corresponding movements of the others. Think of a gyroscope."

She held the craft steady, trying a gentle lift and fall, then easy turns as they danced in the air. "Soft but sure. Like a more intimate activity," he said, laughing, then snatching the stick as a downdraft sent them careening.

Terry wheezed out an asthmatic breath, one step from panic but enjoying the thrill. "This is barbaric. Why doesn't it have a steering wheel?"

"No mystique." They both laughed in a connection growing with each encounter.

"How long does it take to qualify on a helicopter?" she asked, massaging her leg, which shook spastically from an adrenaline rush. "Do you have to be a . . . regular pilot first?"

"You need to pass all ground school courses. Then a hundred and fifty hours in the air, fifty as pilot-in-control. And a commercial license requires another more rigorous round of certification."

"That must cost a mint," she said, then regretted her crass observation.

He passed a hand over his brow, one black curl falling forward like the face of a Greek statue. "It nearly broke me, but I knew that the training would pay off. Ten thousand for the pilot's license, and nearly triple for the commercial designation. I was tempted to sign on with a corporation, but that work wouldn't suit me. Too independent."

"I hear you. My editor's a bear about deadlines." As the ground rushed by, she tensed in another thrill. She could get used to this. Flying was addictive.

The higher they rose, the more benign and diminutive the land appeared, belying the dangers, like playing a video game. The cab was comfortable, the sun flashing a thousand spotlights. Protected gods, they were seconds from charred flesh below. She shivered from pleasure, hoping Chris wouldn't interpret it as fear. Something unfair and unnatural about dismissing this bony realm so easily instead of humping along like Hick with his mule Buster, reaching for a canteen and searching for a cool rock overhang like a wise reptile.

Twenty minutes later, Chris pointed at an adobe ranch house with a barn and corrals. A broken windmill leaned over an empty stock tank. Red, yellow, and blue patches clustered around the house in decorative beds. "That's our family homestead," he said, shaking his head. "All they grow now are flowers. And check out the dogs." Three dachshunds, better suited to concrete city paths, scuttled under the porch.

Like a ribbon in the distance, Route 89 appeared, then the road to Paria. As they swept over Hick's house, Gerry ran barking, snapping at the air. She'd miss the old man, sorry that Judith had lost the opportunity to meet a character in search of an author. Maybe she could find an Indian motorcycle calendar at a Borders bookstore and mail it to Kanab general delivery.

"This the way?" Chris asked. "Kitchen Corral Wash?"

"Right." She gave herself a shot upside the head. "I mean correct. Then through the switchbacks and across the plateau."

"We used to run our horses to the mesa for fresh grass after the rains." His voice reflected a nostalgia for a time out of joint, a bittersweet memory.

She noticed three mule deer sprinting below, spooked by the noise. "They look larger than the standard Bambi."

"Tasty, too. Though venison's a bit lean. Mom larded it with bacon for her Sunday roast."

Terry tried to imagine the centuries of paths below, natives impressing moccasins upon the landscape and pecking footholds up slick rock to the sheltering alcoves, their days starting and ending with the journey of the sun. Grandmothers by thirty-five, ghosts at forty. Where had they gone? Why so few traces? Then she began to understand. These people rejoined the land without ceremony or trapping and became part of it. They hadn't the egos of those who built pyramids in 3000 BC. How would they have comprehended Forest Lawn?

The land rose and fell, carving out canyons like a serrated knife through butter. "The Paria drainage system is massive," Chris said. "Some cliffs reach a thousand feet. A walk down Wall Street except that there's no escape to catch a quick cappuccino."

Squinting on this magical carpet ride, Terry located the parking spot where she had found the charm, pointing out Dead Fox Hill. "Hick said she would have gone on foot not far from here."

As they passed the rockslide and the track opened up, Terry watched massive sandstone structures swell up on the plain. The shadows made assessment difficult, yet below one varnished bluff she glimpsed a tempting darkness. "See that, Chris?"

"Sure. Caves are all over the place. I called that one Robber's Roost. Guess it's tempting to play God and name your landmarks."

"I did the same thing as a kid, I'm ashamed to say. Would you believe we smashed bottles in a vacant lot where a business dumped excess cement? Christening, we called it. Urban outlaws. Can you take us down?"

"No problem. But the girl wouldn't have found any relics. It's empty. I rode all over this area by the time I was twelve."

They settled into a landing spot. Terry reached for the door, but Chris grasped her arm. "Hold your horses, Lone Ranger. Wait until the blades stop. You'll be pummelled by the downdraft or get those pretty eyes blinded by the dust."

Willing her tapping heart to slow, Terry marveled at how easily they had arrived. Unless strict access rules were established in the Monument, soon this most desolate territory would be vulnerable to anyone with enough cash and connections.

The peach sandstone alcove sat twenty feet up a gentle incline with no need for steep climbing. Already the cave was under siege from nature's forces, a rock structure fallen from the roof. As they walked into the amphitheater, their bootsteps echoed. While Chris sipped from a water bottle and watched her, Terry walked the perimeter, which sloped toward the back. She stepped around a crumbling wall, the remains of brickwork with a tiny shelf set into the corner. Gently she explored its precision, imagining sleeping on a woven mat, her belly full of rabbit stew. Space for a medicine bag? A painted cup? The gaming pieces Nick had shown her?

As she returned toward the sun-drenched opening, she stopped in wonder at a smooth wall, mesmerized at the gradual illumination of a panel of a wispy, triangle-chested figure flanked by five hands, red-ochred onto the smooth surface in a message as personal as fingerprints. With Chris standing behind her, she waited in amazement as another half inch emerged. Every morning, the people who had fashioned this art could watch the show, like the ancient Brits had used Stonehenge as an astronomical calendar. "I feel like I'm intruding into someone's living room," she said in a hushed voice that echoed in the vastness.

"Perhaps the spirits are lonely and appreciate visitors. Used to be another hand on the right, but it eroded." He surveyed the site, the size of two tennis courts. "A couple of families. No more than a dozen people. They moved on when the droughts hit or the deer and rabbit populations fell." Then he paused with a serious expression that snapped her back to reality. "There's something I want to show you. I never told anyone, except Dad."

Terry brushed sand from her hands. Nick and now Chris. Why were men always confessing to her? Was it an effort to put her off guard or a genuine impulse? More to the point, was Chris a reformed pothunter?

With a sigh, he explained that he had found an arrowhead here, a birdpoint, and had taken it home to show his father. "He made me bring it back. I wonder if it's still . . ." As his voice trailed off, he walked to a deep cleft in the wall, a natural hiding place. Slowly he pulled a large rock from the hole and reached in, his face breaking into a mischievous grin.

Into her hands he placed a thumbnail-sized red jasper projectile point. It had been chipped perfectly, almost machine-tooled. "See the blood groove?" he asked. "Makes the kill fast and merciful. It's very fine work. I've often wondered if it might be Navajo and not Fremont or Anasazi. I'm no expert, and I didn't want to arouse suspicions about looting by asking someone who would know."

"How could you give it up?" She asked the question from her own guilt, her shard wrapped in a Baggie in her personals pack.

"It's always waiting for me, or will be until the roof falls. That's the natural order of things, isn't it? Nothing lasts forever."

Did she mistake a touch of sorrow in his voice for something between them soon to be lost? Yet his story had taught her a lesson. If Chris could be that ethical, so could she. Judith would have to learn the truth to explain why they would have to revisit the Dittert site. Still, she had the urge to protect it. She'd find a niche in a rock formation, tuck it carefully away.

As they reached the helicopter, Terry turned a glowing smile to Chris, her eyes meeting his as if answering a call. "What a lovely and sacred place. Thanks for trusting me with your secret. You did right in returning it to its home." Now she knew what Judith had felt in that Pine Creek alcove, the call of another world. She didn't believe in reincarnation, but surely her DNA paths had crossed the Fremonts' in that massive surge out of Africa.

He paused, eyes crinkling as he watched a Cooper's hawk swoop past the alcove with a reproving *kek-kek-kek,* then soar into the distance. "I've been thinking about what you said about Dove and that vanishing graveyard."

Terry bit back a laugh. "Anywhere in the Monument, Judith says. 1.7 million square miles."

"We have an advantage the sheriff never used, cheap bastard."

"What advantage? More manpower?"

"Flypower. From the air, patterns emerge that aren't evident below. Ancient roads and paths. It's possible that the logistics of moving bodies would leave traces. Let's roam over Sunset Years, take that trail to the . . . the . . ." He looked to her, rotating his hands in a gesture for memory.

"The Poodle." Dear Thelma and her *idée fixe.* Was she, too, on Dove's list of donors?

They returned to Escalante, traveling back of the ranch on the same route as the women had ridden, guided by the creek, the chuckwagon, and the final turn before the gravesite. In minutes, they had reached the spot. At the Poodle, they saw no graves, only the dark remnants of the so-called barbecue area. "Looks like he's an expert in camouflage," Chris said. "We'll be scientific. Do concentric circles."

Half an hour later, Chris's stolid expression signified that he was ready to give up. Terry twisted her fingers in frustration, guilty about the waste of expensive aviation gas. Then suddenly he made a sharp turn and craned his head. "Look over there, by the cholla patch."

She saw the faint trail of the occasional sage and blackbrush flattened by tires. It tapered into the distance, a faint and stuttering track. They followed as it appeared and disappeared, shadowed by rocky outcrops and often invisible in the sandy soil. Terry said, "There's nothing out here. He doesn't run cattle. Why come unless he needed to conceal something?"

Chris pressed his lips together as his voice softened. "We'll find the place. Dove's a tender-hearted man. He wouldn't have left loved ones buried without care."

Five miles and the same in minutes later, they passed over an open space hidden inside a high, irregular enclosure of huge rocks. Tiny crosses were erected and pebble mounds defined the graves. "You were right," Terry said, leaning toward Chris and placing a hand on his knee for balance. Briefly he covered it with his own, giving her a squeeze.

They set down in a clear area nearby and waited for the blades to stop. Then they walked over, climbing up the rock and then down into an opening hidden at ground level, like a room with no ceiling. From a cleft in one corner, a clump of mauve daisies struggled for life, husbanding in deep roots the moisture that fell as a brief blessing.

Chris bent to examine the three graves, wiping sweat from his face. "To be honest, your theory sounded farfetched. Forgive me for doubting you. Yet I almost hate to bring the man to justice, whatever that means. It sounds pompous and doesn't consider the situational ethics. He's cheating the government, but helping those who can't help themselves. Medicaid doesn't pay for room and board, and what about those under sixty-five who are disabled but don't qualify for a pension?"

"I feel sorry for him, too. But he has to answer for the fraud."

After the climb, Terry was short of breath, scorching her lungs with each footstep. She was beginning to gauge the temperatures with some accuracy. At 110 degrees, even breathing was painful. Thank God they had the helicopter. "So what's our plan now? Back to the sheriff?"

"I'll contact the Highway Patrol. I don't trust Reg in this sorry business. He's married to Dove's sister."

"Why aren't I surprised? I suppose he'll call me in. I'd love to toss this in his face, but kicking people when they're down gives me no pleasure. At least this case is closed." She didn't describe her disappointment in losing Melanie's trail. Chris had done more than enough.

Back at Robbins Aviation, he refused payment for the trip. Terry frowned, spreading her hands in embarrassment. "How can I thank you?"

He pointed at a poster tacked to a bulletin board. "Come with me to Frontier Day tomorrow."

"What's Frontier Day?" She studied his eyes, yet another blue, cerulean this time.

A corner of his mouth rose in amusement, and he chucked her under the chin. "You'll find out at dawn, Miss Ohio. Unless you wear ear plugs."

Chapter Twenty-Six

The night was black velvet when Terry sat bolt upright, peering out the window, then at the glowing microwave clock. Five-thirty. Explosions echoed through the still town. What was happening? Had a group of rogue militiamen taken over?

Judith chuckled from the queen bed, and a low growl expressed Tut's uneasiness. "Fred told me what to expect. Thought you'd get a kick out of it."

"Sounds louder than gunshots."

"Dynamite, my dear. A modern homage to their forebears who blasted a path down to the Colorado. Can you imagine this on Clifton Boulevard?" She rose and put the coffee water on. "Do you suppose Dove's in jail? Will he get bail?"

"Chris said that everything would be handled at the county courthouse in Panguitch. Given his need for money, he'll have to use the public defender, and you know what they're like. Good luck getting a decent defense."

At nine Fred arrived with folding chairs in the back of his Jeep. "We won't be at the supper," he said as Judith put on her shoes. "We're going to Kodachrome, and after that we'll hit Grandma Tina's in Panguitch for a buffet. Tut can come."

Terry went to the fridge and retrieved a plastic bag for Judith. "Can you take my film rolls in case they have a quick-service place? Any longer and they'll grow mold."

Soon after they left, Chris arrived at the door with a small package carefully wrapped in gold foil paper. Where had he bought that out here? “For a special lady,” he said, as she tugged at the red bow to find a copy of Peterson’s *Field Guide to the Birds,* Western version. In crisp jeans, a dark blue embroidered cowboy shirt, and a huge Stetson, he had a Texas grin.

Terry placed a hand on her chest, embarrassed and touched. “This was your mother’s. I can’t—”

“Sure you can. But it’s a selfish gesture. Maybe this will bring you back to start your own list.”

The celebrations began with a Main Street parade. Every wheeled vehicle in one hundred miles rolled by to display civic pride along with marching veterans, children waving flags, strutting horses in shining silver-studded saddles and rosetted bridles, the high school band, scouts, local politicians shaking hands, and endless floats with country singers. Behind the horses, an efficient team of road-apple collectors dressed as clowns hustled shovels and buckets. Terry watched a dozen duded-up motorcycles roar by, hoping in vain to see Hick. Eager children with handy bags rushed forward to gather candy tossed from the floats, Halloween in July. A huge flatbed with a cabin featured women in gay calico dresses and bearded men in dark suits. “One Hundred Thirty-Two Years of the Prophets,” the banner read, complete with dour, interchangeable portraits of the bearded patriarchs.

“I don’t agree with polygamy,” Terry said, her arms folded.

Chris waggled a finger. “Don’t be so judgemental. Many women settlers who lost their husbands would have been destitute. Remarrying gave them security, and an extra hand in the kitchen or at the cradle was always welcome.”

“Oh really? Men need to help with chores rather than rationalize a harem.” She barely suppressed a smile.

The parade was concluded by a fire truck shooting water cannons into the air, creating sparkling rainbows and a welcome shower in the high noon heat. After collecting hot dogs and ice cream cones from a vendor, she and Chris joined a crowd in front of the post office. A noisy argument between two dance-hall floozies in red taffeta frocks had degenerated into a hair-pulling contest. As the play unfolded, a black-garbed desperado with an off-center Pancho Villa moustache and bandolier faced off against a hero in white in the middle of the wide street. Blanks were fired, and everyone cheered as the villain spun around theatrically and fell, twitching on the dusty asphalt before managing a convincing death gurgle.

Aggie and the kids from Second Chance Ranch gathered across the street. When the two boys she'd met at the trailer park waved at her, Terry remembered the alien lights in the desert. Chris said something, but it didn't register.

"OK?" he asked, placing a gentle hand on her shoulder. "Are you a million miles away?"

The last thing she wanted was for her reporter's nose to spoil this lovely day. "Just filing away a few more images for my memory bank."

Visiting the nearby Mormon cabin staffed by the DUP, Daughters of Utah Pioneers, Terry was impressed by the simple piety and friendliness of the elderly volunteer in a black dress and bonnet who offered her succulent ripe apricots from a majolica bowl on the desk, one of several period antiques carefully trundled across the wild prairies. A display about plants interested Chris. "This is interesting. Boxelder sap was used to make a low-grade syrup. 'Boxed' meant tapped. It's a member of the maple family."

"My aunt loves details like that. She'll have to see this place."

After she scanned a brochure on Joseph Smith, Terry's questions about women's roles in the church triggered the recruitment spirit. "If you're interested in learning more about our commitment, a witness can call at your home," the woman said as Terry deposited her fruit pit in a wastebasket, declining with courtesy. How had this faith, with its cornerstone resting on the mumbo jumbo of magic spectacles and golden tablets, spread across the globe? Other religions had their miracles, but one or two thousand years gave them more credibility. Was she a short-sighted bigot? She and Judith attended church only at Christmas, enjoying the pageantry and music.

A scenic drive through the Red Canyon and then down the heartstopping Waterpocket Fold switchback on the edge of Capital Reef whiled away the rest of the afternoon. They returned to Escalante to the high school for the brisket supper. Men doffed their hats, well-behaved, tow-headed children chatted, and women with plastic garbage bags collected paper plates as fast as they emptied. So many blondes. A German heritage, she'd read. Despite or perhaps because of the patriarchy, was this the most innocent place in America? Encouraged to take all they wished, they stacked their plates with the fork-tender meat, potato, macaroni, and multicolored jello salads, finishing with mile-high chocolate cake and cherry pie. "Gotta have water with dessert," one man said, refilling their glasses.

Chris toasted him with his Styrofoam cup and winked at Terry, whispering, "They're not all teetotallers. Liquor runs to Colorado every weekend."

The evening's rodeo was held at the fairgrounds behind the RV camp. Walking off their calories, Chris and Terry arrived early for a prime view. Slowly the stands filled. Latecomers crowded the fences, pop cans and water bottles in hand. Not a cigarette or a police officer in sight.

As a bugle sounded, a panoply of five riders on handsome golden palominos trotted their flags around the inner circle and saluted the audience as all stood for "The Star Spangled Banner" on the loudspeaker. People sang loudly in unashamed patriotism, hands over their hearts, their expressions earnest and proud. The first event was the sheep riding. One by one, over thirty children, half female Terry was happy to note, lurched from a pen atop bewildered sheep, fingers gripping the thick wool for dear life. Some beasts were uncooperative, frozen in confusion or sinking to their knees. Riders with frisky mounts waved hats in the air and tightened their legholds. Whatever the result, the crowd cheered each youngster wobbling toward the gate. The fallen, with dusty, tear-streaked faces, were snatched up and consoled by solicitous parents hovering by the fences.

Later came calf roping, barrel running, and a game of musical horses. As darkness pooled and the events ended, the crowd gradually dispersed. Terry bathed herself in the friendly atmosphere of an old-fashioned small town. In a week or two, she'd be home putting up storm windows, getting her sweaters out of mothballs, and writing about damask dresses and bouquets. Time was running out for Melanie. Had the death been a bizarre accident after all?

As they were leaving, Chris excused himself to visit the bathroom under the stands. Terry leaned against a light pole as a woman in pearl-buttoned western shirt and jeans walked by. "How's the pup?" she asked. "All systems go?"

Terry blinked, then recognized the vet, Rita Kinsolving. "You did a great job. He was walking easily within a few days. We watch him more closely now."

"Did you enjoy the—" As Chris came around the corner, she stepped back.

He cleared his throat. "Rita." He looked from one to the other. "I guess you've met."

The vet's soft eyes turned glacial. With a quick goodbye, she walked off.

"Did I cause a problem?" Terry smiled nervously.

He shuffled his feet, his face saddened in the twilight. "Rita and I divorced a few years ago. Just a clash of personalities. Our dreams headed in different directions. Maybe people should fill out a questionnaire before marrying."

So that was Chris's history. Terry greeted the information with mild relief, remembering her high school tenth reunion. Who wasn't divorced these days? Was serial monogamy more ethical than polygamy? Only wedding photographers, florists and lawyers were getting rich on bad choices. She'd never even lived with a man. Caution or cowardice? As they stood in awkward silence, she said, "People meeting online are doing that already. Maybe it'll start a trend." Happily, her quip drew a reluctant smile.

She invited Chris back to the trailer, darkened and empty. As he took a seat on the sofa, Terry poured glasses of Wolf Blass chardonnay, having discovered a limited but decent liquor source at the Outfitters Store on Main Street.

"Your aunt's not here? I hope that ankle—"

"She's having a great time with Fred Muldoon. They both went to OSU." She explained their budding friendship.

"No kidding. Fred's been our family doctor for twenty years. He's a great guy. Escalante's lucky to have him." Then one eyebrow rose. "Do you mean that your aunt might choose to—"

"A month ago I would have said that Judith was last in line for a whirlwind romance. But the West has a way of changing perspectives." She stopped short of kissing his cheek, which had lost its fresh-shaven blush and now wore a slight shadow. How serious was she about this man?

The early supper had left her hungry. Getting up to pull a package of mesquite-flavored chips from the cupboard, she noticed a package on the counter. A note on top read: *Back late. Don't wait up.*

"My pictures!"

After adding a container of the roasted chipotle salsa to the chips, she sat down beside him on the sofa bed, and they began leafing through the images, making a game to see if Chris recognized the places.

"The Kaiparowits. Devil's Garden. And Dance Hall Rock. What's your aunt doing?"

"A polka. Strictly Cleveland." With apprehension about her skills, Terry nodded as he pointed out other familiar spots. "Those are the pictographs from our hike at Pine Creek."

"I'm just getting into photography." She was embarrassed at the obvious flaws. "I should be more patient. Ansel Adams said that one good picture a month was his standard. You know what Geminis are like. Doing ten things at once."

"Gemini? Same as Mom. I'm an Aries. Ram-headed. And I love Adams' work. Those Yosemite photos. Wish I could afford to put him on my wall." Chris stopped to rotate one picture. "Ah, a descanso. You don't find them in Ohio, I suppose."

Terry nestled in. "Melanie Briggs's friend Danny built that tribute. Isn't it touching? I snapped it from several angles so that my aunt could get the idea. And I was thinking of writing an article about the custom."

"Was this taken at the caves?" He turned on the clip-on bed-lamp to better examine it.

She spread out the series on the kitchen table, noticing a sun flare in the corners. Not professional enough for publication, but a start. Next year she'd have more time and a better focus. Chris's strong thigh was warm against hers. "Up a pretty little draw around the corner. I can see why Danny didn't locate it anywhere near the doors. Too gruesome." She shivered. "Looking at it takes me back to the death scene."

Chris picked up another. "This one with the paperback is a real winner. Good composition and sharpness. If you're serious, why not consider writing a book? Descansos of the Southwest. Some photographers can't write, and some writers can't photograph. You have the perfect combination of talent. And it would give you a reason to return."

"Please take it, Chris. You've been so generous." Terry basked in the praise, unable to respond with more than a juvenile shrug. Come back? All the armies in the world couldn't stop her.

As she replaced the rest of the pictures in the crowded corner cabinet, a green cloth biker hat with goggle-eyed aliens fell onto the table. "Another wild and crazy Gemini fashion concept?" he said with a teasing nudge.

Terry put it on and mugged for a moment. "It's a joke gift for a friend. I saw it at a New Mexico truck stop and couldn't resist. I hear you have aliens around here, too."

He leaned forward as a hearty laugh escaped from his lips. "Aliens?"

Terry told him about the boy from Second Chance Ranch who saw the strange lights in the desert hills on Hole-in-the-Rock Road during his escape from a camping trip. "I forgot all about it until I saw the boys at the parade." Then she paused in thought, for the first time remembering the significance of the date the boy had mentioned. "That must have happened about the same time that Melanie disappeared."

"Weird. Sounds like St. Elmo's fire. An eerie condition occasionally seen on ship's rigging, lights dancing about. Something to do with a plasmic energy field."

"Even in the desert?"

Chris leaned back, stretching his long legs in the tiny nook. "Believe it or not, that phenomenon once struck a herd of cattle on a trail ride. Ran around their horns. Nearly drove them berserk. Several animals died in the stampede."

Terry's eyes widened, and she tucked the hat back onto the shelf. "Poor beasts. Sounds like a bad acid trip." Chris coughed at a swallow of wine. "Not that I was into that stuff," she added.

"Big city problems. One more advantage of life in the wilderness, though I'm sure the occasional pot plant grows in secluded spots."

She saw their circled calendar on the table and cradled her chin in her hands. Why hadn't she been born out here? She recalled Nick's quote, "Tell me the landscape in which you live, and I will tell you who you are." What did that make her? A frog paddling in a Rocky River creek?

"I'd offer you a penny, but the dollar's falling," Chris said.

"We have to leave this week. I wish I could get a job and stay." She tried not to meet his gaze, yet something drew her toward the familiar planes of his face, someone she'd known all her life, confounding the facts.

"And I wish I could hire you." His eyes glistened, the color of her favorite cobalt blue crayon in the September school pack of sixty-four, and he took her hand. "Maybe granting a more practical wish would help. What one last thing would you like to do? Name it."

Terry looked out the window to a pinpoint in the coal black sky. Venus. The evening star. Her earlier fears were diminished by her trust of Chris and his knowledge. "A slot canyon, I guess."

He turned to her, his strong, sensual mouth broadening into a smile. "I've been planning that ever since you mentioned it on our hike." As his voice picked up speed like a sprinter, she imagined preparations running through his quick mind. "Do you know that we might have the longest slot canyon in the world? Buckskin Gulch. The narrows run for an uninterrupted fifteen miles, about half the whole trip."

"Is it far?"

"You've already been over by the Paria River tributaries. The road to the north trailhead's just past Kanab."

"But thirty miles? Surely we can't—"

He put an arm around her. Through his chest wall she could hear his heart beating strongly. "Relax, city girl. I know a shortcut entry point that will give us a walk in the park. Might be muddy in spots, and there's a new rule about packing out all waste, if you get my meaning."

"Ziploc is my middle name."

He stood reluctantly, picked up the photo and placed it carefully in his breast pocket. Then he kissed her on the cheek. She felt the slight sandpaper rasp of the stubble, wished for more, yet who knew when Judith would return? "Give me a day or two to arrange things at the office. And we'll have to watch the weather, of course."

When Judith returned at eleven, not long after Chris had left, Terry told her of the upcoming trip. "I'm envious of your adventures, but I've had more than my share. He'll be the perfect guide. All this time together lately. I wonder if . . ." One of her frizzy eyebrows spoke louder than words.

"Marriage isn't my career goal." Terry's brusque tones lacked conviction. "How could I earn a living out here? And don't start singing 'Love is a Many-Splendored Thing.' "

Her aunt rubbed Vaseline Intensive Care lotion over her face and hands as she struggled against a yawn. "Remember that you're talking to America's Number One Feminist. But if you're that fond of him . . . and I understand how you love this place. My dear, take the risk."

Terry softened at Judith's empathy, recounting Chris's dreams of owning a vineyard. "Do you suppose he has that much money? The planes and helicopter aren't new, but they're not like cars, traded in every few years."

"Perhaps with the park opening up, he plans to sell out. The business might be a gold mine." She sat down with a bittersweet expression. "Fred took me over to the dig, and I said goodbye to everyone. Nick invited me back next year."

"That's great." Terry thought for a moment. Months fluttering by like the pages of a calendar in an old movie would give her time to think things out.

"Want to come along? If not, I can take the Buick and stay at a lovely B and B behind the Serenidad Gallery that Nick suggested. He's the sweetest man."

So he was, especially to a mother figure, Terry thought. Attractive, friendly, knowledgeable. Their first meetings had piqued her interest as they parried about artifacts. But somehow the electricity shorted out. Was it his fussy hand-wringing about that student years ago? The embarrassing details in Melanie's diary? If he'd been innocent, he should have fought it like a man. "I'll miss Walter. He was a character."

"We had another long jaw about the figurines. Next time out we have to visit the museum at Price-Wellington." She snapped the cap on and pursed her lips. "Apparently Melanie read that book, too. Those were her notations next to the Pilling illustrations."

Terry rolled her eyes at her mental lapse. "That smiley face in her diary. I wonder if it meant anything." Tocho's words drifted through her memory like elusive smoke. "What had she learned?"

Chapter Twenty-Seven

A few days later, primed with a huge pancake breakfast, Terry and Judith were ladies in waiting. Chris had called the night before to set up their hike. On his morning constitutional, which brought him to the RV park on a regular basis, Fred strolled over with a local paper and fresh chives as the women were sipping coffee at the picnic table. "Was this why you were grilling me about Blanche and Adrienne, sly one?" he asked Judith, who smiled enigmatically and patted the seat.

"It's a very long story, Fred. After we get back from Zion Park, we may be up until midnight again." She winked at her niece.

"Triple Murder in Escalante?" the headline read, as Fred summarized the details. Dove was in jail in Panguitch, a bond hearing pending on the charges. Other workers at the ranch were suspected of complicity, but despite his growing frailness, he had insisted that he acted alone. His statement indicated that the women had made diversionary out-of-town banking arrangements with him well before they died of natural causes. Knowing that Sunset Years teetered on the edge of bankruptcy, the childless women had wanted to provide their less fortunate friends at the ranch with a means to live more comfortably. Dove admitted to the fraud, but stood firm about their wishes to be buried in the land they loved.

Fred set his jaw in disbelief, nearly snapping his pipe stem. "Pure bullshooting about murder charges. Interfering with the bodies is all they can pin on him, if he lives long enough. I know the woman from Salt Lake who'll do the autopsies," he said, tossing the paper onto the ground. "Nothing's going to emerge other than heart failure and a half-dozen tired old organs. I'll wager my practice that there's not a hair out of place."

Terry wriggled at the literal translation. Fred was a "what you see is what you get" man, the perfect combination of passion and principle, like Chris.

"No toxic substances then?" Judith asked, sniffing the bag of chives in delight. "And thanks to your herb garden, how about a platter of ham and eggs? I'll bet you left the house with only coffee."

After the pair went inside, Terry found herself drawing frowny faces and ruminating about Melanie's interest in the figurines as the Navigator pulled in. She waved off Chris's help and tossed her daypack into the rear. A few disjointed words stuttered across the crackling radio as he switched it off. "Danger of" was all she heard.

"What's that about?" As he drove off, she adjusted her belts and leaned back in leather-lapped comfort, always happy to let someone else drive. Soon enough she'd be hauling that Prowler uphill heading east.

"Pardon?" They both winced as a thirty-five-foot rig made the sharp turn into the campground, kissing the mailbox with its rear bumper.

"The radio was saying—"

"Oh, that. Train derailment near Green River. They're worried about ammonia leaking from a tank car. I saw the paper on the ground, so I assume you heard about Dove. And I'm afraid the sheriff wants to see you for a corroboration. Try not to be too hard on him. He's old and tired. Two months away from retirement."

She pressed the lumbar supports and lowered the height of the seat, then turned to him with a salute. "You'd make a great lawman. And think of that handsome uniform."

"I'd die of boredom. Escalante's such a quiet place. Or it was until you came," he said with a laugh.

"At least that's settled, but Melanie's story will never be written. That gives me a percentage of fifty," she said.

"The Diamondbacks would love you in a two-out, two-on, bases loaded situation. Even Woodward and Bernstein couldn't have done a better job. The important thing is that you followed the investigation to its conclusion, so you're the real lawman . . . woman . . . person. But be warned," he said with mock seriousness.

"What do you mean?" Terry noticed a loose bootlace and tied it securely.

"Not to disparage your job, but from what you've told me about your assignments, you won't be satisfied there after this experience."

"True enough. Indulge me some more about Melanie's travels." She pulled out her deconstructing map and opened it against the dash. "Hick told me about a back way to Escalante behind the Kaiparowits."

"Smoky Mountain Road. Looks like a shortcut but it's triple the time against the usual way on Routes 89 and 12. Brutal terrain."

Terry traced the route. "By way of Collet Top, it connects with Hole-in-the-Rock, where the kids saw the lights. Could Melanie have driven there in the Jeep after dark?"

"This is getting weirder. I might see her taking Smoky Mountain if she had no idea how rough it was, but why the detour instead of back to town? It's pure hell down Collet Top in the light of day under the best of circumstances. That would make a bad situation worse."

"She wouldn't have finished up in Hick's area until late afternoon. Every logical explanation should have sent her back on Route 89." Terry shrugged her shoulders. "But Tocho said something that got me thinking, the idea that she could have learned information dangerous to someone."

Chris's surprised expression formed two lines between his brows. "You saw him again? He had the nerve to come to the park?" Pulling over at a viewpoint, he looked into her eyes with concern. "He didn't cause any trouble, did he? Maybe I should—"

"No, it's fine." Terry filled him in. "After hearing his story, I changed my mind. Kaya would never stay with a dangerous man. And here's something more intriguing." She told him about Walter's book. "Melanie was very interested in these figurines."

"I know pictographs and petroglyphs, but that's a new one. What are they?"

Terry described the artifacts. "Very rare and very valuable. A wise old press room boss always told me to follow the money. Easy to say, hard to do, not that I get hot news assignments. Weddings are murder. I ought to write a book about that."

"Works for me. Never even had a honeymoon. Vets are ruthless." They laughed together, and Chris rubbed his chin, baby smooth, with a scent of lime aftershave that lingered in the cab like a caress. "But three million dollars. That's a chunk of change."

As they drove, he explained that the usual route involved leaving a vehicle at the White House Trailhead to the south, coming back by road and starting at Wire Pass. "That's a two-day hike. With my plan, we'll avoid the early part, which is nothing to boast about, but still see the petroglyph panels. We'll go down the Paria to the confluence, a lovely camping spot." Log jams on the other route would have meant delays and tricky rope navigations between unstable rocks and driftwood.

"Any water that's drinkable?" Having noted the cloudy sky and cooler temperatures, Terry had brought only two litres and trusted that Chris carried his own supply.

"The Paria is often dry, but Buckskin's good for a clear trickle at the confluence. Maybe the pioneers had cast iron stomachs. I wouldn't trust it. You can get giardia, a microbial gastrointestinal upset from animal dung in the water. Serious stuff. I was dog sick for three weeks after a scout trip near Moab. Lost ten pounds."

"Beaver fever we call it up north."

"Believe it or not, we have beavers in Utah. Adaptable little guys. And pretty though the upper part of the canyon is, it has lots of standing water, some stagnant. The Cesspool is one place you don't want to linger."

"The Cesspool?" She made a Mr. Yuck face. "I was hoping for a plunge pool."

"You never know. Nature writes the scenario. Did you bring a bathing suit? No matter. Skinny dipping's the rule around here." His cobalt blue eyes sparkled under his dark lashes.

"You mentioned a campsite. Does the canyon get that wide?" She was beginning to regard Pine Creek as a Disneyland version of a slot canyon. As in the helicopter, she felt tremors of anticipation, secure with Chris's expertise.

His arm moved across the seat to touch her shoulder. "Pure postcard country. Got your camera, I hope?"

"Sure do." She pointed to the rear toward her pack.

"There's a large grove of maple and box elders on the benches of dry sand above the canyon floor. Eight hundred feet straight up."

"People camp in a slot canyon? Isn't that dangerous?"

He shrugged. "A calculated risk. Anyone with a brain monitors the weather reports."

As Terry looked at the unsettled sky, her ears pricked, and she shifted in her seat. Was that distant thunder? "I missed the forecast today. Doesn't it look like rain?"

"I get the National Weather Service bulletins. Just overcast, a lucky break from the heat. We'll be fine." Hearing her sigh, he turned to her, brows creased in concern. "I'm not being very considerate, am I? If you're really worried, we could drive to Capital Reef. Fruita's a lovely old Mormon town with—"

"I shouldn't have mentioned it. Silly of me. Lead on, captain." Terry stuck out her chin. When would she have this opportunity again? All of Chris's planning, and she was acting like a timid mouse. He opened the storage box that separated their seats and passed Terry a jewelcase. "Like Three Dog Night, or is it too much of a moldie oldie group for you?"

"Judith gave me one of their CDs. Whenever I clean the apartment, I use the energy for inspiration." She eased it into the slot. Soon the raucous sounds of "Mama Told Me Not to Come" filled the cab.

Two hours later, after stopping in Hatch for coffee, they passed Kanab and drove once more along the Shinarump Cliffs and across Telegraph Flat. The names were becoming part of Terry's home territory, and she mouthed them silently as old friends. She tried to imagine life as an unending series of breathtaking discoveries. Not alone, though. Her confidence didn't extend that far. Even experts fell victim to a rattler bite, a broken ankle, bad water. Hick was right to resist the temptation of taking the land for granted, like a beautiful, amoral woman who could show someone the time of his life and snatch it as payment. Ruess had learned that, as had Melanie.

As they made a right turn down an unmarked, rutted road, Chris swore under his breath. "What's wrong?" Terry asked.

He pointed to a pile of smashed beer bottles littering the way. "Disgusting, isn't it? New Mexico's the broken glass capital of the universe, and Utah's catching up fast. I don't want that in my tires." He got out, picked up the cardboard carton, and began collecting the shards.

Feeling cramped after the long drive, Terry got out to stretch. While Chris had his back turned, she saw Tocho's unmistakable blue truck approach on the highway and gave an energetic wave. He slowed in response, then saluted before his vehicle disappeared around a curve.

Chris stared at his finger as ruby drops fell onto the sand. "You cut yourself," Terry said, coming to his side. "How bad is it?"

"Won't kill me anytime soon. Just messy," he said, ever the stalwart cowboy. "Can you bring the first aid kit from the back? Open a couple of large Band-Aids."

In the wheel well in the rear, as she rummaged for the kit, Terry saw a handgun tucked under a towel. From her limited experience, it looked like a revolver. Did they call that a six-gun? She shrugged, supposing that different rules applied out here. Lakewood probably had as many of these as fingers on a hand.

After Chris had cleaned up, his injury tamer than a slice Terry had given herself carving a recalcitrant pumpkin one Halloween, they continued on. About a mile in, he braked abruptly to avoid a roadrunner, shoving his arm in front of her in protection. "Sorry," he said. "Reflex reaction. Mom must have done that to me a thousand times."

At last Chris steered into a parking spot overlooking the Paria River, flowing far below in shallow, rainbowed ribbons across sand and pebbles, its banks wide and dappled with green bushes and riparian grasses. Chris pulled up to the rim, so close that she gritted her teeth. Leaving the truck, Terry scanned the abyss while he busied himself in the rear of the Navigator. Was there a set of steps, a switchback path, some gentler access?

"Uh, are we going down there?" she asked, struggling to keep her voice cool. Though she had gained confidence in the last few weeks, she didn't want to reveal her remaining insecurities.

He hauled a long rope ladder from the SUV, returning for a set of webbed nylon straps. "I have a harness for you from my search and rescue equipment, but it's only a hundred feet, not close to a thousand, like some of the canyon. Going back up will be a piece of cake."

How many feet? Terry couldn't imagine the relativity of heights from ant perspective. The West was too massive for human comprehension, a stage for giants slightly appreciated from distances and mind-boggling close-up. In sheltered Ohio, she found universes in grains of sand. Now she had become a grain of sand herself, a humbling experience.

"I brought lots of film." From her daypack, she retrieved the Minolta and uncapped the lens. "And lunch for three."

He gave a thumbs-up. "I have plenty of sandwiches, too. We'll work up an appetite." Chris rigged the ropes in the same leisurely but methodical fashion he'd used to check the helicopter, pulling, tying, eyeballing the equipment at each step.

"You've thought of everything. Sorry I'm such a wimp," she said, moving an inch toward the edge where a yellow flower clung to life amid the rocks, its familiar face reconstructed to the environment, the foliage slender and efficient in the heat. A dandelion in the desert. Terry snapped a few grab shots. If plants could adapt, perhaps she could, too.

"Standard procedure for sane people. Rock climbers die every year in Utah. Not my choice of sports, hanging upside down like a bat and wearing those silly shoes."

Terry nodded in agreement, talking out of nervousness. "Every fall I put on my aunt's storm windows. Even an eight-foot drop can be fatal." Watching Chris's forehead crease in concentration over a tricky connection, she chastened her gabbling mouth, realizing that she sounded like what Judith would call "an old woman," a generic term for both sexes.

While he worked, the sun climbed into mid-morning orbit. In the distance she glimpsed side canyons etched like savage wounds into the Paria watershed. Across the void, a bird circled, rocking and tilting. An eagle? She took out the binoculars, watched it feather down to join another large black, redheaded comrade on the plateau, ripping and tearing. Turkey vultures sampling another entree in nature's smorgasbord. Despite the heat, she shivered at the gory scene, her imagination filling in the blanks.

Chris had secured the rope ladder and harness onto hooks beneath the front bumper. He straightened the lines and helped her arrange her pack. Then he buckled her into the nylon webbing. The harness pulled at her crotch, making her glad that she had chosen cotton cargo pants instead of shorts. "All set? I'll steady you."

"Feels like a parachute," she said. "In fact, I could use one."

On her knees like a penitent at nature's shrine, Terry stared with rising regret into the depths. The descent wasn't straight down, but steep enough that ascending would be impossible on the slick rock for anyone but an expert with pitons. Chris reached out to guide her as her hands trembled. His calm eyes found hers, and she blinked, managing a crooked smile.

"Mistake One for rookies. Once you're secure, never, but never, look down," he said.

Terry gulped, turning her back to the canyon, facing the Navigator's front tire, smelling hot rubber in the still air, and memorizing her last sight on earth. Chris knelt, one brow raised as if wondering when she'd find the nerve to take the first step. Being a good sport was important. He wasn't the type to enjoy mewling, helpless women. At least he wasn't laughing at her obvious cowardice.

"Just remembering where I left my will." She took a long breath, held it, then exhaled, hoping that the tension would ease, knowing it wouldn't. "I'm ready. Scout's honor."

She braced herself, grabbing the ladder with sweat-greased hands, one bulky hiking boot groping for the slack rung, finding it, testing the feel, then placing the other foot. The equipment was new, no frays or breaks, telling witness of Chris's cautious preparations, a pro in every sense.

His voice kissed her ear as her heart pumped. "You're doing great. Easy as she goes. Take as long as you want. We're not out to set a speed record. Stop to smell the flowers. See that one by your hand?"

With toothed leaves and dense clusters of yellow-orange flowers, it bore a resemblance to field mustard. "What is it?"

"You're looking at the most versatile plant in the Monument, in all Utah, in fact. A wallflower. Grows from two thousand feet all the way past twelve thousand. Isn't that amazing?"

He was trying to relax her with his conversation, take her mind off the descent. All she had to do was move her feet and arms. It was impossible to fall. Terry imagined the tempting rock art and heart-stopping discoveries ahead. She was prepared to get muddy. Maybe they'd find a delicious plunge pool after all. After that night at his home where she'd stopped his advances like a . . . wallflower, she was prepared to follow romance with a stronger resolve. After all, she was hardly a virgin. What better place to make love than the cool paradise of a slot canyon, a personal bower? As Chris had said when he blessed them with gentle hands, her scars were survivor's medals.

She took a hesitant step, focused forward at the angled truck wheel as her sight left the canyon rim. Something odd about the tire tread, a lightning pattern with a cross-cut irregularity where a stone had damaged it. Where had she—

"Anything wrong?" Chris touched her hand. "You came to a sudden stop. Feel OK?"

"I'm on my way. You were right about not looking down. I need to act, not think."

Wisps of grass woven into the rock crevices tickled her arms as she descended, counting mindlessly to dampen her queasiness. This was a finite task, a given number of inches and feet. She passed the abandoned clay nest of a canyon wren, in the bottom a broken shell. Had the fledgling winged off safely, or had a raptor pillaged it from its cozy bed? Why hadn't she stayed in hers? This was crazy.

After thirty feet, the angle of the sun left her side of the canyon in shade. Despite the cool embrace of the rock, salty beads trickled down her face, stinging her eyes. Gulping air, close to hyperventilation, her lungs ached as if she were running a marathon underwater. And once at the bottom, wherever it was, a long drink was going to be her first indulgence. The fragile pink petals of the rockcress plants attracted her attention. Delicacy amid strength. Then one foot slipped, and her leg passed through to the thigh in the ropy squares.

"Waaaa!" The ladder swayed, scraping her knees on the cliff face. She felt humiliated to scream like a child, but sheer terror was calling the shots.

Chris's calm and even tones echoed from above as he tightened the line. "Don't panic. I've done that too. Thought I'd taken myself out of the gene pool by strangling the family jewels. I can come to free you, but you're safer disentangling yourself. Get a firm grip and stand slowly. Use the belay as leverage."

"I'm stuck!" She was off balance, one leg caught, the other helpless. Her arms and shoulders would have to rescue her.

Trussed like a Christmas turkey, wheezing, she shut her eyes against dizziness born of panic. A temporal rush of blood stopped her ears, and her heart pounded as she said the Lord's prayer. She hadn't been to church since leaving high school. Ascension Episcopal on Detroit Avenue. Ascension. Now there was a concept she'd rather pursue. As Chris coaxed her, she eased up agonizingly with her right foot and slowly pulled the left leg onto the sagging rung, thigh muscles shrieking against the punishment. "OK," she called, her face red with effort.

"Good girl." A few pebbles fell over the edge, and she ducked. Bad idea to look up or down. Focus on the task.

Finally, taking no step for granted, she reached the bottom, kneeling to kiss the sand, then hooting a relieved yell of triumph that bounced around the canyon. As she shrugged out of the gear, she muttered, "All's well that ends well. Judith had better give me a medal or a chest to pin it on." She chuckled at the old family joke.

With her heart rate returning to normal, she retrieved her binoculars and looked up to notice Chris's figure bending over the edge. Why hadn't he started down? Was something wrong? He hadn't given her any directives for this stage. Should she steady the ladder, or was he going to rappel to the bottom? She swallowed with difficulty, her throat dry and dusty, then reached into the pack for a drink, gulping it so fast that she nearly choked, closing her eyes to quell the gag reflex. An image came into view. The tire tread. No wonder it had held the attention of her subconscious mind. She had snapped a picture of that same damaged lightning pattern, imprinted into the dried mud beneath Danny's descanso. Chris had said that he had never visited the Batty Pass Caves, and that no one else ever drove his precious truck. Hearing a clatter, she turned to watch in horror as the harness and ladder rose beyond her reach, bumping up the wall. In the distance, thunder moaned like a woman in pain.

"I'm sorry," he called as he yanked the apparatus hand over hand like a fisherman collecting his net.

"Sorry? What are you—"

"If only you hadn't mentioned the figurines. No turning back after that." His voice was distorted in the echo chamber.

"Come down! You're scaring me."

"Ever since we met, I hoped that you'd drive back to Ohio and forget this place. But you're too good a reporter. You were always adding new pieces. That charm. The lights the boy saw when I towed the Jeep. Your innocent eyes can't lie. Only a matter of time before you connected me with the girl's death."

"Why, Chris?" And how, she wondered, but the possibilities were flying like a shower of golden coins. How charming he'd been. Weren't they all? Scott Peterson had wept crocodile tears not long after he dropped his dead wife into the San Francisco Bay, weights tied to her limbs and her eight-month fetus Conner suffocated in her womb.

"I had four figurines from two corners of Robber's Roost, but I knew there were more. A perfect symmetry. A buyer in Frankfort offered me a million for the set. It took weeks. I had to plot the directions and unearth them so carefully, go back time and again. They were buried deep, and I couldn't take a chance on breakage. The day I found the fifth, she saw my vehicle parked by the rockfall. The Jeep had broken a fuel line. She couldn't believe her luck to find someone. She came up so quietly. One look said it all. Even as a student, she knew their value."

"So that's why—"

"We struggled. She got knocked out falling on a rock. Truly, I thought she was dead. I towed the Jeep back to 89 and over to Smoky Mountain Road, across the Collet Top to Hole-in-the-Rock. I hoped it would make some crazy sense to someone. Damn near broke an axle myself."

"You thought she was dead? You didn't care. Like the propane. You nearly killed us."

"I wanted you gone. Everyone has an alarm. How could I

have known?"

"So I'll hike out. Or are you going to . . . shoot me with that gun in your truck, you coward? How would you explain that? Aiming at a rattler?" From somewhere deep inside flamed a rage for a man who had robbed a young girl of her future for a fortune he didn't need. Even Dove had been helping others.

"You won't go anywhere. A flash flood will come through the canyon in half an hour."

She gazed in alarm at the leaden sky, heard another distant grumble and the muted strike of sheet lightning. "But you said—"

"No one's hiking today. The radio issued a warning, and the trailheads have been closed by the BLM. The storm's dropping the rain fifty miles away, but you remember Antelope. It'll be fast, not like the girl."

"You bastard! Use her name. She was Melanie Briggs, and if there is a God or a shred of justice, you'll pay for her death!" she screamed, only to hear a hollow wail blast back and forth across the walls.

A muffled roar of a truck motor, a plume of dust, and he was gone, sinister silence in his wake. Terry whirled around as if an enemy lurked behind every rock. She stumbled along the sandbar, tripping over driftwood, searching in vain for purchase to climb from this tomb. A ledge caught her eye. Thirty feet straight up and over twice that to the rim. It might as well have been a thousand. Where the rock wasn't slick, it was crumbly. Chris had hiked the area all his life, and he knew the perfect spot. She looked in desperation at her watch. It seemed like hours since she'd left the truck. Ten minutes, fifteen gone? Time more precious than Hick's Queen Silver.

Around the next corner, she reached the shallow Paria with its iridescent ripples, harmless at this frozen point in time. The canyon twisted, the lower end hidden, the upper reaches a maze of massive logs trapped at the narrows in the last flood. Unleashed, the dam would crush her like a salamander. She could imagine it happening in slow motion, her body battered, clothes ripped off in the fatal rush of churning water.

At that point she made her only choice. Go back up the side canyon to escape the worst of the fury as the water chose the straight path. She wheeled and retraced her steps, splashing in the shallows, scanning up for a handhold, an easily reached ledge. She could hear her watch ticking, counting the seconds before the onslaught. Swallowing huge draughts of air to fuel her, she followed its sinuous depths and started to sprint in the firmer sand, her calves aching from the effort, thighs propelling her like a separate beast. Fight or flight, the mechanism that had kept her DNA current from the time man stood on two feet.

Maybe Chris's prediction was wrong, but with the stakes so high, she guessed not. Thunder didn't lie. How fast did water travel? Fifty miles an hour? Seventy? She measured the daunting cliffs thirty feet apart. If they narrowed enough, perhaps she could leverage herself between them, climb away from the killing path of the deluge and wait. As hope lifted her spirits, her ears listened for a distant rush.

Chapter Twenty-Eight

The side canyon was dead quiet, except for the forlorn twitter of an invisible bird. Along the ruthless rockface, Terry searched for footholds. Three times she climbed, only to fall back, her knees and elbows skinned raw in the attempt as her clothes shredded. She felt no pain, ignoring the trickles of blood, remembering with gritted teeth how she had played nurse to Chris's pathetic cut. Had he gone back to town to summon "help," or was he waiting somewhere to witness the flood washing away any evidence of his guilt?

On she walked through the muted light of the wandering canyon as it slowly narrowed, sucking her belly, undulating in the embrace of a cool lover with sand-rasped cheeks, dipping, arching, standing again as it widened, a dance with steps sculpted by millions of years of erosion. Sometimes she crawled, the shaft closing overhead, darkening her path. The way turned muddy, coating her boots, oozing gray silt across her legs, stinging her abrasions. She'd been wrong about gradual shrinkage—it opened as quickly as it closed.

Scrambling over a chokestone that blocked the way, she heard a hiss as a faded midget rattler coiled in the spot where she had intended to place her hand. She jumped back with an involuntary screech, and the snake slithered into a sheltering cleft. Charged with fear, she could have pelted it with rocks, but what would have been the point? The poor creature was as instinctive as she in its reactions, unaware of the approaching destiny they shared.

Then the canyon widened to a few yards as she glimpsed the battleship gray sky. Still no rain, but that gave her little comfort. Small bushes nurtured in a daily kiss of sun clipped at her skin while the brief perfume of a rock rose went unnoticed. And still she heard nothing. For a deluded moment she told herself that Chris had been wrong. Then he would have to find her and dispatch her another way. Her footprints waited as witness to even a blind tracker.

Adrenaline surged through her body, willing her to do whatever it would take to survive, then smear his name across headlines from Maine to California. Capital punishment had never been her cause, but lethal Texan injections seemed kinder than this slow torture. Catching her breath and letting her leg cramps ease, she hunched on a ledge that might soon be underwater, fighting the temptation to collapse in a heap and sob into her arms like a soap opera starlet.

What would Chris say? That they'd been separated when he saw the water rush? That he'd been lowering himself down the wall to join her and watched in horror as her body was carried off, tumbling in the vortex? Only after heroic attempts to fling rope or clutch her weakening hand, no doubt. As for penalties, the surviving guide hadn't been charged for negligence after the Antelope Canyon disaster. He could claim that they planned to descend only for a few snapshots and hadn't heard the forecasts. Stupid but hardly criminal.

A few wagging fingers about taking chances would be replaced by consoling pats on the back, and once he'd concluded the bitter bargain of the figurines and sold the business, he'd be heading for Napa. Or was that, too, a fabrication?

Primitive instincts pushed her to her feet again. Looking ahead, stumbling a dice-roll of fallen rocks, she turned another corner of the endless maze as the canyon reopened. Forty feet up, ambient light cast a glint on the smooth stone, revealing a glyph of several sheep, connected with a rope around their necks, heading cooperatively to the slaughter like her. A few days from a safe exit from Escalante and what did she do? Feed Chris so much information that he had no choice other than to silence her growing suspicions. Then she shook her head in disgust at thinking like a self-serving murderer, providing excuses for his monstrosity. Wiping her hand on her jacket, she felt the tiny charm in her shirt pocket. Melanie's struggle, the torment of slow starvation and dehydration. Next to that, drowning would be easy.

A warning pounded at her temples. Why try and sentence Chris when her imminent death would write a different scenario? Anger and revenge were wasting time. Be here now, she remembered from a college study skills course. Survival skills would have been more useful. Suddenly an idea flashed across her mind. What about the glyphs? If the natives had been foraging in the canyon . . .

Her frantic eyes noticed a series of pecked footholds beckoning up the rockface, a Moki stairway to heaven. The higher she got, the better her chances. One vertical foot, inches even, could spell the difference between life and death. Taking off her boots and socks, tying the laces with trembling hands and dangling them around her neck Indiana Jones style, she urged herself up, grabbing a sturdy manzanita plant, pulling, testing, praying that it wouldn't rip free. The grainy sandstone was tacky on her bare feet, almost prehensile in their gripping ability. Hadn't Judith boasted that Terry had picked up pencils with her baby toes in an amusing trick? Up and up she scrambled, ten, twenty, then nearly forty feet, too fast to assure safe contact. She slipped and nearly overbalanced, her pack heavy with water bottles pulling her backward. She flattened herself against the rock, gazing up in panic to glimpse an overhanging ledge. Her bruised hands were weakening, her muscles pierced by a thousand daggers. Seconds from her collapse, an ungodly roar issued from the canyon like a freight train at full speed. Maddened water splashed her pants as she pulled herself over the brink into a small alcove and screamed to an audience of one.

She peered over the side at a living horror. A milk chocolate-y mass surged forward, boiling with branches and driftwood. Panting with exhaustion, cold and drenched from the spray, she took off her pack and sat in amazement. The land was transformed as the water sluiced out everything in its path. She leaned back and closed her eyes. Would the churning cauldron sweep her from her perch?

Judith would be frantic, insisting on leading the search with Dr. Fred at her side. Protecting himself by reporting a fake scenario, Chris would never bring anyone to the place where they had descended. To her wonderment, suddenly the sky cleared as if scripted by Moses, and the sun made a short appearance, already slanting out of sight, its rays barely warming her shelter. Tonight would be cold, but there would be a tonight. Ravenous from her exertions and jubilant at her survival, Terry groped for the lunch, growling at the irony of having prepared it so carefully for a romantic rendezvous. What a trusting fool she'd been. She unwrapped a sandwich and crammed it into her mouth, greedy for life. Swiss cheese and tomato, they'd keep until tomorrow. She needed to ration supplies. With an ironic smile, she considered the bag of pork rinds, a favorite snack. Tempting but too salty.

Two water bottles wouldn't last long. When the water receded and she climbed down, she'd have to risk drinking the muddy Paria. Giardia be damned. Fred could give her medication. Her mind forged on. Which trailhead was closer, which path easier? Surely the dam at the narrows had burst. Hadn't Chris said that ropes were needed farther up? Downstream it should be, a one-day trip. Terry sighed as her thoughts outstripped logic. How could she be sure that this even was Buckskin Gulch? Their relationship had been one glorious lie.

While she waited, marking the levels on rocks across the narrow canyon, she noticed that the water had crested, spent its worst force. How long before the flood would recede? Hours? A day or two? What did it matter? She had food and water, and eventually she could hike down to the trailhead.

Chilled from the splashing, she shivered, appreciated the bosom of the rock as she scuttled back into the shallow cave. A honeymoon suite or a refuge for a hunting party. Her wandering hand brushed a packrat's nest. Dragging away the foul-smelling mess with a twig, she found a few desiccated piñon nuts. Probably rife with bubonic plague. The wind began to rise, coaxing the soft rustle of bushes. The alcove roof was fire-blackened. Gently she touched the charcoal traces of a life that bridged the millennium. She crawled to the edge and looked to the sides. Once the sandstone might have supported a circuitous upper exit to the rim, but the rock had eroded, leaving a sheer cliff above. Forty feet separated her from salvation. Below, she noted with sheer joy that the water had receded another foot.

Aside from the lunch, a tissue pack, and her useless wallet, she carried nothing. This had been a day expedition, not a wilderness exploration. Keep calm and think. Panic killed more people than bad luck. Making a mental map, she calculated their parking spot a mile away, probably less, taking into account the serpentine route. If only someone . . . She closed her eyes as purple shadows escorted the evening. The Paria watershed wasn't Bryce Canyon. Hikers didn't pass by every half hour, chatting about scenery and discussing restaurant choices. Chris's comment about the closed trailheads rang true—even liars told the truth when it suited. She pillowed her face on her bleeding hands in a supplicant's posture. Exhausted by fatigue and stress, she welcomed the dark, comforting hand of sleep.

Some uncounted hours later, a bright light flashed against her eyelids. Terry awoke with a start, bumping her head on the low ceiling sloping to the back. Where the hell was she? In a living nightmare? She shook her sore head and blinked at the full moon that had summoned her, its faithful light creeping into the alcove like a shy bridesmaid. Crawling to the edge, she watched mercurial clouds slash the luminous pocked face. The same moon that rose each night over the quiet and peaceful Ohio street where she lived in another dimension. The wind began to howl, and she was glad that she had worn her light jacket and long pants.

Terry stretched, and dozed, and dreamed. When she'd been a toddler, a tornado had hit on July 4, felling two-hundred-year-old trees in Lakewood Park, killing one young girl. Fireworks were canceled as people rushed home in panic, Clifton Boulevard filling with churning water pushing storm drains past capacity. Then she was sitting with Judith at Symphony Hall watching *Aida,* breaking into tears at the final dungeon scenes. It was all so similar. Why hadn't she seen the connections? Melanie's tomb, now her own. With every hour she felt a renewed kinship with the ambitious student whose crime had been a passion for truth that took her to dangerous places.

As a gray dawn broke, Terry awoke confused and shivering, groping for the plush blanket and touching a cold rock shelf. She choked back a sob, then with parched lips sucked at a water bottle. She looked down at the receding waters beginning to reveal the sand. A light rain was falling, making descent too slippery to risk. At the distant *whomp-whoop* of a helicopter, she tensed in hope, leaning as far out of the opening as she could, yelling her lungs sore, seeing nothing. As quickly as it had come, it departed. Chris would lead the search team everywhere else but here. How well had he slept?

She shook her fist in impotence, energy fueled by rage. "You fucking bastard." Judith would have more creative names for the man. Then she ate the third sandwich. One bottle of water left. At least rain would keep the heat down. Everything was a trade-off.

The monsoons poured at intervals, stopping only as darkness fell again. In an attempt to relieve herself, she nearly pitched over the edge. And even in the cave, she wasn't safe. A black scorpion brandishing its toxic tail had crawled toward her. Holding her breath, with steely self-control and a twig, she'd brushed it to a lower ledge, telling herself that if she let it live, its spirit would strengthen hers.

That second night she slept fitfully, nightmares of Chris haunting her dreams. His handsome face had morphed into Mr. Hyde's, huge orbital taurus shelfing a hairy brow, with a jaw of squared teeth in a rictus laugh, and a greenish tinge to his skin. Memories returned from a book report she'd done on Stevenson in English Lit Survey.

In the cool morning, a brilliant sun woke her. No food or water remained, even the salty pork rinds. Her empty stomach growled, triggering a persistent nausea. She was restive from enforced idleness, the inability to move, fighting a fury that had no outlet except for murderous thoughts. Everyone was capable of killing. She knew that now.

She hunched forward and peered over the rim. With the water gone by circuitous paths to ancient aquifers, the quiet canyon looked nearly the same as before. The stubborn desert plants that had withstood the deluge clung to their clefts. Her parched throat ached as she eyed the small pools below, and she knew she had to leave now while she had strength. Tying her sock-stuffed boots together and tossing them downward, she found the set of steps and started along the sheer cliff, too eager, too careless. She missed her grip and tumbled, hitting her head on a half-buried log and thudding onto the soft sand. Her last memory was a cool seep of water into her clothes . . .

At last she opened her eyes to a pounding headache and a whiff of vertigo, then closed them. If she felt pain, she was alive. What did a few more minutes matter? As she returned slowly to consciousness, she rolled over, removed her pack and took a deep breath. How long had she been out? Her faithful Timex, its crystal scratched, read seven-thirty. Half an hour had passed. Sitting up, Terry rubbed a tender goose egg on the back of her head, her fingers painted with a bloody smear. A concussion? Carefully she wiped sand from her brow, protecting her eyes. Blinking, she focused on a plastic Coke bottle that had floated into a pile of debris caught in a bush. The label was clear and sharp. No double images. Slowly she rose to her feet, wobbled, and reached out a hand to brace herself on a boulder. She sat down again, submitting to her body's demands, willing the throbbing in her temples to subside, hoping her mind would clear. As she groped in her pack for a drink, she recalled that her water was gone.

When the dizziness had fled, she put on her socks and laced her boots. Then she stood, eyes narrowed with purpose, and took the first step down canyon. Soon after, from a small, clear pool in the rocks she drank deeply, then filled her bottles. Rainwater was safe, wasn't it? Cool and refreshing with a piney aftertaste. Slowly, gauging her bearings as the headache fogged her thinking, she began to retrace the route to the Paria. Under ordinary circumstances, her body well fed and rested, it would have been an easy and interesting hike, but after her ordeal, its sinuous slots and chokestones presented a challenge. She wondered about the snake. By some small miracle had it survived?

The wet sand sucked at her boots, making each step a labor. In the wider spots, the sun's high beams made her faint. Her hat had probably crossed the Arizona border by now. Everett Ruess's story was rewriting itself. Stooping, her knees aching, she drank from the bottle. Trickles of blood ran down her ear, and she swiped at it. Scalp wounds always bled profusely, she recalled from watching CourtTV. At least her headache was easing.

Hours later, her legs buckling like a spavined cow, she reached the Paria, scene of a veritable bomb blast. Huge logs lay balanced precariously like pick-up sticks. The jam at the narrows had broken. Perhaps that had bought her precious seconds.

Looking up to where she had descended in her rocking cradle from the rimrock eternities ago, she traced the small features that had charmed her. The broken nest. The delicate flowers. "Piece of cake" to go back, Chris had said. But she had no rope ladder. With weary shoulders, she turned to follow the river downstream to the White House trailhead. How many miles? Five? Ten? Or was that as much a fabrication as his life?

Then a noise came from far above, causing her to step back and shield her eyes. With a sweetness like a chocolate soda at a long-vanished fountain at the corner of Clifton and 117th Street, she looked up and saw movement at the canyon edge, a splash of robin's-egg blue. Tocho's pickup was parked where Chris's truck had sat, and she heard a door slam. From her extreme perspective, she could see only a bobbing Stetson.

"Down here!" she screamed, her voice emerging as a croak. He didn't seem to hear.

She grabbed a rock and with her last unspent force, hurled it upward in an arc that broached the top. Summer softball and a season in left field had served her well. Its clink brought Tocho to the edge, and he peered down at her, waving his good arm.

"I see you. Wait for me. I have to go back," he yelled. He said a few more words, but the wind blew them away.

"Go back? No, please! What do you . . ." Her voice trailed off as his truck started up. Was he in league with Chris? How far would paranoia lead her? Maybe she should forge downstream as planned. She thought of their meeting in the dark of the trailer park. From that moment, she'd trusted him. But she'd trusted Chris, too.

She'd give him half an hour, no more. Part of her wondered whether she was sealing her fate by remaining, a convenient target. If only she knew what lay down canyon. Rescue might be around the corner. Finally, half-rising to leave, a sob in her throat, she caught something in her peripheral vision. A thick rope snaked its way down the slick rockface. A disembodied voice reached her. "I went to Rusty's for the gear. Tie this around you strong and tight, under your arms, then through your legs. Do you know anything about knots?"

Terry laughed for the first time in days. "I was no Girl Scout. Granny knots are my limit."

"You're tying them for your life, so do a good job. I have a winch on my truck. Shout when you're ready."

Ascending was fast, but a downdraft pushed her toward the wall. Her only task was to keep her legs and arms free of the entangling brush. Tocho called out at intervals, monitoring the winch speed as he watched her progress. Finally, he lugged her over the edge, and she lay panting, more from relief than exertion. She rolled over and kissed the warm, smooth rock like a lover.

"That's a bad wound," he said, touching her forehead with a gentle hand.

She fingered the bloody crusts, feeling the satisfying pain of survival. Would she need stitches, another scar for her collection, welcome now and not a fearsome reminder? "Dr. Fred will handle it. I'm sure he expected to do a post-mortem."

Shivering from shock, despite the heat, Terry climbed into the truck while Tocho found a towel from behind the seat to warm her. She grinned in surprise as he handed it over. "My old lion towel," she said. "I forgot that I left it with Kaya."

"Must be fate. Tocho means mountain lion. That was my third name." He opened a water bottle and passed it to her.

"Third?" She drank greedily. Wouldn't a beer be heavenly?

"Hopis have four names. One at birth, one at six, one at adulthood, and a final secret one whispered just before dying."

Terry couldn't imagine the bureaucratic red tape, but decided not to comment. This man had saved her life. "What brought you here?"

"You must be hungry. Sorry that this is all I have." He broke open a package of jerky with his teeth and offered her some. "I was coming back from visiting my mother at Page when I passed you and Robbins at the turn. Didn't think much about it until the next day when I heard you were missing."

"Missing and presumed dead, I suppose." She munched with renewed saliva, feeling like an honorary Fremont.

"You got it. Robbins organized search parties all over Buckskin except here. Said you started a few miles from White House trailhead and went up the canyon. He had second thoughts about the weather and tried to get you to a climbout when the flood hit. You weren't anywhere near there when I saw you. It didn't make sense."

"I thought he'd try that." She relaxed with a sigh, making a pillow of the towel, sweating from the heat pouring from the vent and wiping her brow.

Tocho caught her gesture and turned off the knob. She noticed how handily he managed the controls, using his prosthetic for leverage.

"My aunt must be going crazy with worry."

He threw back his head in a hearty laugh. "Tough old girl,

that one is. 'No' is not part of her vocabulary. Got into the first helicopter like a general. Your disappearance has taken over the news for the last forty-eight hours."

They drove directly to the sheriff's office, where Gail had set up a command post to direct volunteers. Tocho held the door as Terry walked in.

"Lookie who's come back from the dead," Gail said, getting up to embrace her as if they had been schoolmates. While Terry gave a brief explanation of events, she placed her in a chair and brought fresh coffee, laced with sugar.

Terry sipped and grimaced. "I take it black."

"Good for shock. Don't argue." Gail chuckled. "More like you might admire some of Reg's personal stock." She reached into a drawer and pulled out an unopened bottle of Jack Daniel's, ripped off the plastic, and added a generous portion.

"Reg ought to be back soon, since it's lunchtime," she added. "He's been at both trailheads dropping off kids from that dig. You sure have plenty of friends." She narrowed her eyes and looked at Tocho. "Chris Robbins. Jesus wept. I remember when he got divorced from Rita. Thought about going after him myself. Never did have a lick of sense in men."

"I know what you mean." Her romantic musings about a new life in the West had evaporated faster than the flood. One thing she knew. Jeff was still out of the picture. She could do better.

Half an hour later, fortified with a generous take-out meal of spaghetti and meatballs, salad, and milk from Cowboy Blues, Terry smiled tiredly to see the sheriff coming up the path, Judith at his heels.

"I know, ma'am, but we already—" he was saying as she shoved past him.

"I demand that the FBI be called in," Judith said, but as she pushed into the office, she stopped as if a mallet had hit her, lines of worry smoothing as she put out her arms.

Both women embraced without words. Gail was dabbing at her face, and Reg was eyeballing his bottle, down by several inches. He spoke briefly with Tocho, then sent him home. After taking Terry's statement, he added, "Get a good night's rest and return to check the details tomorrow. I'll have her typed up," he said.

"Where's Chris now?" Terry stood, hands on her hips, strong as a lioness.

"Scouring the Paria again, inch by inch. Probably hoping to find your body caught in a tree like buzzard bait. He's been up for the last two nights straight. Told him it wasn't safe anymore for him to keep flying."

"No doubt he's been sleeping like a baby," Terry said.

He sipped at the bottle. "Soon as he hits the tarmac, we'll be waiting with a set of pretty bracelets. Get us a warrant to search for them figurines. You say there's a picture of them in a book somewheres?"

Epilogue

Thanks to Nick's generous offer of the refurbished Jeep, Terry and Judith had navigated the wicked final five miles of Hole-in-the-Rock Road. Perched in the rear of the small vehicle with its stiff suspension, Terry appreciated the comfort of the GMC.

"Did you hear that Dove died in custody?" Nick asked.

Both women sat silent until Terry said, "So he wasn't far from his own Promised Land. Putting on a brave show, I suppose. What's going to happen to the seniors at the ranch?" She braced herself as the vehicle lurched over a rockface at a thirty-degree angle.

"Relocated to a place in Salina, over by the Fishlake National Forest. Scenic spot. Not too hot in summer. Good medical care, being close to Salt Lake. Woman who runs it heard about the disaster and stepped in, so the sheriff said."

After they parked, Terry scissored herself out of the rear and followed Judith and Nick to the edge of the historic Mormon road. An official metal plaque commended the pioneers who made the "perilous descent" to ferry twenty-six wagons across the river.

Nick stood with arms folded as the women surveyed the fearful set of crumbling switchbacks that led to the Colorado. Far across, traces of the route to Bluff chronicled the brave journey of the faithful. The unnatural blue of the Colorado contrasted with the red rock. Two-thirds of the American flag.

"It's worse than I thought," Terry said. "Totally impassable."

Nick added, "One small victory for nature. But man will return."

"So he has." Judith shook her head. "Lake Powell has backed up the Colorado, destroying thousands of rock art sites. Here it's covered part of the old road at the bottom near Register Rocks. Debris has fallen in. Uncle Ben's dugway doesn't exist anymore. Yet this is the place, to paraphrase Brigham. And it wasn't a one trick pony. The road was used for a few years, out of sheer stubbornness."

"For what purpose?" Terry asked. "It's like trying to settle the moon."

"Exactly. Why did astronauts go to Northern Ontario to train when they had a perfect substitute here?" Judith made a few notes on her pad.

They walked back to the Jeep and drank deeply from their water bottles. "You'll be back for the trial, then? It'll probably take over a year to get underway."

"Unless he plea bargains." Terry dreaded revisiting her memories from the flash flood. "Does Utah have the death penalty?"

He gave a broad laugh. "I should say so. Lethal injection or firing squad. Remember the Lori Hacking case? Husband killed his wife and made it look like an abduction," Nick said.

"Utah's got a high proportion of high-profile cases," Judith said. "Let's not forget Elizabeth Smart. Hidden in plain sight for nearly a year."

"Lakewood was nothing like this," Terry said. "But I never looked under any rocks."

Judith gave a light laugh. "I forgot the best news. Remember that comic book I picked up at the Batty Caves? I don't think it qualifies as a relic. Those men are long dead."

"That *Mad* magazine?"

"Walter's a collector. He says it's worth five thousand dollars.

Modern archaeology pays off."

Terry laughed. "Are you sure that you threw out all my Captain Marvels?"

Bluff, Utah Summer, 1880

. . . the days are so hot here that I don't know how we will stand it. I never suffered so with the heat in my life. I cant eat a thing but I think I could if I had some vegetables. We did not get any garden in till late and it will be a good while before we get any thing green. Ide give anything for an onion or a radish. I have just weaned Genie, I did not eat as much at a meal as he did for I had to wean him. He is the best baby I ever saw. I have been takeing bitters for a week but Ive been telling Em that I guess it is the effects of liveing out in the cold all winter, now liveing out in the heat through the summer and its just thawing the frozen bread out that we eat last winter and no wonder we feel a fool . . . I am going to have a house this week and then it will take four yoke of oxen to ever get me out of it again. Write soon.

—Lizzie Decker

LIST OF WORKS CONSULTED

Benson, Joe. 1996. *Scenic Driving UTAH.* Helena, MT: Falcon Publishing.

Bureau of Land Management, Utah, and Southwest Natural and Cultural Organization. 1997. *Grand Staircase Escalante National Monument* (annotated map). Houston, TX: Western Lithograph.

Fagan, Damian. 1998. *Canyon Country Wildflowers.* Helena and Billings, MT: Falcon Publishing.

Madsen, David B. 1989. *Exploring the Fremont.* Salt Lake City: University of Utah Press.

Miller, David E. 1966. *Hole-in-the-Rock.* Salt Lake City: University of Utah Press.

Patterson, Alex. 1992. *A Field Guide to Rock Art Symbols of the Greater Southwest.* Boulder, CO: Johnson Books.

Rusho, W. L. 1983. *Everett Ruess: A Vagabond for Beauty.* Salt Lake City: Gibbs M. Smith.

Slifer, Dennis. 2000. *Guide to Rock Art of the Utah Region: Sites with Public Access.* Santa Fe, NM: Ancient City Press.

Turner II, Christy G., and Jacqueline A. Turner. 2002. *Man Corn: Cannibalism and Violence in the Prehistoric American Southwest.* Salt Lake City: University of Utah Press.

Urmann, David. 1989. *Trail Guide to Grand Staircase Escalante National Monument.* Salt Lake City: Gibbs M. Smith.

Vigil, Arnold (Ed.). 1995. *The Allure of Turquoise.* Santa Fe: *New Mexico Magazine.*

ABOUT THE AUTHOR

A dual citizen of the United States and Canada, **Lou Allin** is the author of the Belle Palmer series, starting with *Northern Winters are Murder* and ending with *Memories are Murder.* The novels take place in Sudbury, Ontario, the Nickel Capital of the World. She also wrote *A Little Learning is a Murderous Thing,* an academic mystery. Now retired from teaching and living on Vancouver Island with her border collie Shogun and her mini-poodle Friday, she is working on a new series where the rain forest meets the sea. *On the Surface Die* features RCMP Corporal Holly Martin, in charge of a small detachment on the picturesque south coast of British Columbia. Lou's website is (and she may be reached at) louallin@shaw.ca.